DANGER ON THE TWILIGHT RIVER
When all twelve moonchunks showed clearly visible, Sam began to regard Reardon intently. Reardon's head lolled against his left shoulder; he might have been sleeping.

The first thing Sam noticed was the fur. Great gray clumps of it began to sprout on Reardon's face. Reardon's mouth formed a narrow crease filled with sharp fangs. His nose was a flat black snout. Deep in his throat, he began to growl.

Then he lunged. . . .

TERY IN TROUBLE
Jon found the door in the rock wall . . . just as water rippled behind him in the pool. He turned and spotted something floating on . . . no, rising *from* the pool. He could not make out the shape and did not care to. Whatever it was, it did not wish him well.

He tapped out the access code on the door's studs, then grabbed for the notch. The door stayed firm. He tried the code again and still no result. A glance over his shoulder showed him that something monstrously large had risen from the pool and was looming over him. . . .

BINARY STAR NO. 2

THE TWILIGHT RIVER

Gordon Eklund

THE TERY

F. Paul Wilson

A DELL BOOK

Published by
Dell Publishing Co., Inc.
1 Dag Hammarskjold Plaza
New York, New York 10017

Dell ® TM 681510, Dell Publishing Co., Inc.

ISBN: 0-440-11090-4

Printed in the United States of America
First printing—February 1979

THE TWILIGHT RIVER

by GORDON EKLUND

WARLOCK'S DAUGHTER

Hunkered behind a blood-red bush, Dreadful Sam, the music man, peered through the twilight mists blanketing the edge of the Long River and grinned at what he saw. "Now will you just look at that," he said in a cautious whisper. Cazie, a six-foot cobra with bright patterned skin, lay coiled around his broad neck. "Isn't that the prettiest thing you've ever seen?"

He meant the girl. Naked, she stood knee-deep in the river and, bending down with cupped palms, splashed water on her lean, lovely body. Sam breathed heavily. As a musician, he was entranced by beauty wherever he found it. Cazie stirred in response to his emotion. Sam rubbed her belly just below the lower jaw, a dark patch of skin covered with crisscrossing lines and violent swirls. "Easy, girl. Let's not frighten her away."

With the approach of night, Sam had slipped away from his burrow in the hills to scout the land in search of food worth stealing. The presence of the girl had caught him totally by surprise. He guessed she must be the one of whom he'd heard ribald tales upriver, Trina, the only daughter of Kaspar, the local warlock. An unpleasant, selfish old man from what Sam had heard, a typical sort for the Rangels to choose for warlockhood. Long ago, Sam knew, the warlocks had served a real purpose. Survivors from the priesthood of the old religion, they were wise men designated to protect their communities from the malevolent supernatural beings who supposedly prowled the river late at

night, but the passage of time, the absence of evil
spooks, and the lessening sway of religion had turned
most of them into nothing more than Rangel toadies,
whose involvement with the spiritual world was limited to casting empty spells and mixing brackish po-
tions. Most, too, like Kaspar, had set themselves up as
guardians and regulators of local moral behavior. The
warlocks would be the worst enemies of vagrants like
Sam, if it weren't for the fortunate fact that nearly all
of them were so damned stupid. Kaspar, it was said,
kept his young daughter, Trina, a stunning beauty
with corn-yellow hair, sky-blue eyes, and sun-pink
freckles, under lock and key in a back room of the
chapel. Despite these precautions, there had been certain episodes (or so Sam understood); the girl was
quite experienced, he gathered. Sam studied the
bather with special intensity: yellow hair, ivory skin,
too dark to see eyes or freckles. The dim outline of a
chapel stood a few hundred yards deeper into the hills.
Sam nodded: this had to be Kaspar's daughter all
right. If the old warlock could only know what my
vagrant eyes have glimpsed, thought Sam, he'd probably bust a gut.

In the river, Trina knelt down, her backside as bony
as a boy's. The poor thing, thought Sam, with pity.
Next to Cazie and his harp, Sam loved food best of all
the things in the world. To see another deprived of
this pleasure hurt worse than the slash of a knife.
Trina needed someone to care for her. If given the
chance, Sam would gladly have fed her tomatoes, ap-
ples, carrots, lettuce, peaches, and beets. He would
hunt wild game and roast the meat above a roaring
fire.

Distracted by these reveries, Sam failed to keep close
watch on the river. When his thoughts cleared, he noticed that Trina was no longer alone. On soft, silent
feet, the Rangel approached from behind. Trina also
failed to note the alien's presence.

The Rangel was an ordinary member of his breed.

Totally bald, he stood ten feet off the ground, as thin as a stick, with big red eyes, tendrils instead of ears, and saggy yellow-brown skin. Sam's anger rose when he spotted a glass eye fixed to the belt around the Rangel's waist. Sam knew about these eyes; they worked like real ones. Anything that passed in front of the eye could be seen immediately in the watchtower high above the river where the Rangels made their home, and right now what the eye was seeing was the warlock's daughter.

The Rangel stopped a yard behind Trina and spoke in a booming voice. "Go up—go home." The Rangel gestured toward the chapel. "There is possible danger."

Sam guessed that the Rangel meant him. The presence of a vagrant in the area would not go long undetected.

Trina's reaction was immediate. Spinning in the water, she tried to hide her body every place at once. Sam was puzzled. What was the problem? It wasn't as if she was a virgin or, like Sam, an outlaw sought by the Rangels a thousand miles up and down the Long River. It wasn't as if she was in any danger.

Apparently, Trina failed to recognize this. Her hands flew to her mouth and she screamed. Sam hugged his ears, and poor Cazie, disturbed beyond hope of continued slumber, dropped to the earth and slipped into the underbrush.

Trina tried to run. Crazily, she headed straight into the river, no wise place to go wading at any time. The Rangel, protective of his charge, chased after her. Catching her arm, he whirled her gently around and pulled her toward his chest.

Still screaming, Trina pounded the Rangel with clenched fists. Amazed by her ferocious attack, the Rangel staggered back, caught a foot on a protruding branch, and started to fall. Instinctively, he threw out his arms, and as he did, Trina spilled from his grasp. She hit on her rump in the mud and let out a howl.

Sam jumped to his feet. Trina had her hands around the fallen Rangel's neck and she seemed to be squeezing. What was she trying to do? Sam had never witnessed such madness in his life.

Letting go of the Rangel's neck with one hand, Trina slid her fingers slowly down his side. It took Sam a moment to realize what she intended. On his belt, beside the glass eye, the Rangel carried a heatgun. While Sam watched in amazement, Trina jerked the weapon from its holster and shoved the barrel against the Rangel's chest.

Sam acted from impulse, not logic. Charging forward, he waved his arms. "No! Don't! He won't—!"

The heatgun hummed. Sam, stunned, stopped in his tracks. The odor of cooked flesh wafted past.

Trina rolled away from the dead Rangel. She pointed the heatgun at Sam. "What the hell do you want?"

"I—I—" The words wouldn't come. Instead, Sam pointed. "You murdered him."

"Sure, I did." She jerked the gun. "You want to be next?"

Sam couldn't believe his ears. Was this the same girl whom only moments before he had proclaimed an earthly personification of heavenly beauty? "Put that stupid gun down."

She met his glare. "Are you going to make me?"

"No—no, I'm not. Stay where you are—don't move." Cautiously, Sam came forward. He bent over the Rangel's body. Holding his breath against the stench, he removed the alien's belt and brought his foot down hard upon the glass eye. All the while, he'd taken care to keep clear of the line of sight.

Trina stared curiously at him. "Why did you do that?"

"Don't you know?"

"I always wondered what those shiny things were."

"It's an eye. With it, the Rangels in the tower can `everything it sees."

She laughed. "That's silly."

"I'm afraid it isn't."

"But that would mean they know what I've done."

"If they don't, they will soon enough."

For the first time, she looked genuinely worried. "They'll be angry, won't they?"

"Trina," said Sam, in a patient voice, "they'll kill you."

"My father is Kaspar, the warlock."

Sam grunted, unimpressed. "He won't be able to protect you from this. Even if he wanted to. Which I rather doubt."

"My father worships me," she said smugly.

"Then he's different from any warlock I've known. The only thing they worship is their own skin." He pointed to the pile of clothing on a flat rock. "Get dressed. They're apt to be down on us any minute."

Recalling her nakedness, Trina put on a pouting face. "You ought to feel damned lucky. No man has ever seen me like this before."

"That's not what I heard."

"Who said that?"

"Never mind. You've got more important things to worry about than your bare butt. Like murder, for instance."

"But the Rangels aren't really—"

Sam lost his patience. He reached out, grabbing her, but as soon as his hands touched her sleek wet skin, he dropped them. It had been ages since he'd last touched a real woman. Since Ellen O'Denver. He bit his lip. That wasn't something he wanted to start remembering—not now. "Get dressed," he said.

Suddenly obedient, Trina went over and picked up her gown. She started to dress, then sprang in the air and screamed.

Sam hurried over. Coiled in the folds of one of her undergarments lay Cazie. "She's mine," Sam said, putting the cobra around his neck. "Her name's Cazie."

"But that's a poisonous snake. If it bites, it can kill you."

"Cazie only bites people I don't like."

Spurred by the implied threat, Trina dressed quickly. Done, she announced that she was ready to go. "How about this?" She showed him her hand. Until now, Sam had forgotten the heatgun.

"Give me that," he said.

Out of deference to Cazie, Trina complied.

Sam hurled the heatgun far out across the dark river. It made a distant, muted splash.

"We might have used that," Trina said. "What if, on the way to the chapel, we meet another Rangel?"

"We're not going to the chapel. Haven't you figured that out yet?"

She shook her head, standing firm. "Oh, no, you don't. If we're not going to see my father, I'm not going anywhere. He's the only one who can help us now."

Sam shook his head. She couldn't really be as dumb as she seemed. "Let me explain one more time. Your father is a servant of the Rangels. They made him a warlock and can unmake him whenever they please. I've got a burrow up in the hills, a safe hiding place for now. Go home to your father if you want. I'm getting out of here."

Turning, Sam plunged into the underbrush. He began to climb away from the river.

He hadn't gone far when he heard Trina. "I decided it would be more fun to keep you company," she said, catching up.

"Shut up," Sam said, "and walk quietly."

"You don't have to be nasty."

"I am nasty."

Whenever the river brought Sam to a new locale, the first thing he did, after concealing his raft, was find a secure burrow. Chances were usually good that he'd stumble on something. Here he'd found a cold, damp cave in the side of a hill overlooking the river.

Sam kept his ears cocked for any evidence of Rangel pursuit. He knew the familiar whistling of their airships as well as his own heartbeat. It was a quiet night. He heard the cry of a prowling cat. A plump mosquito buzzed past his ear. In the sky, four moonchunks beamed, while two more climbed patiently toward a midnight zenith.

By the time they reached Sam's burrow, Trina was breathing heavily from the climb. Cautiously, Sam pushed aside the thicket of leaves and branches concealing the cave entrance.

In the moonlight, he saw Trina frown. "In there?" she asked, with evident distate.

"It's either this or risk dying."

Trina seemed uncertain. "Can't we just wait out here? It's a warm night and we—"

The sound was loud enough so that even Trina heard: a shrill rising whistle.

Sam grabbed Trina and shoved. "Get in!" He dived after her, landing smack on his belly, and twisted like a snake. Reaching outside the cave, he grabbed the thicket and drew it back into place.

Sam and Trina lay huddled together in total darkness. Outside, the whistling grew louder. "It's wet in here," she said.

"Be quiet."

"Well, it is."

"Hush, damn it."

Gradually, the whistling faded, then ceased. Sam let out his breath. "They must have landed by the river."

"Then you were telling the truth. About that eye."

"Of course I was. Why should I lie?"

"It sounded too much like magic to me. My father says there's no such thing. It's just a trick to impress the villagers."

"The Rangels have their own tricks," Sam said, "but theirs work."

"So what are we going to do?" Sam felt her shiver. "I'm freezing."

"Come with me." Sam led her a dozen yards down the tunnel to where the cave floor sloped away and the ceiling climbed higher. They stood upright. Feeling with his hands, Sam found the lantern he had left and turned the switch. The light revealed a broad chamber. Sam waved his arms expansively. "Here's home."

She made a sour face. "What's that thing on your arm?"

Sam looked at the red-and-green dragon on his bicep. "It's a tattoo."

"Well, it's ugly." Trina looked around the cave. "I guess it's not so terrible I can't stand it for an hour or two."

Sam didn't have the heart to explain that she would either learn to bear this cave—and a hundred more like it—or else die.

She would find that out on her own soon enough.

LAIR OF THE FREE MEN

As the night slowly passed, Sam and Trina waited in the faint lantern light in the burrow in the hillside above the river for the advent of dawn. Trina complained loud and often of unendurable hunger until Sam visited his stores at the back of the cave and brought her two handfuls of nuts and berries.

Trina frowned. "I can't eat this. Don't you have any real food?"

"I picked these on your father's land."

"Well, it's not for us. We feed that junk to our laborers. It's not fit food for a warlock's daughter."

"It's either this or nothing," Sam said. He went on to explain that it was now impossible for him to accomplish his usual nighttime foraging. The Rangels would be shaking every bush and tree within a five-mile radius and, if they somehow managed to avoid finding the burrow, that would be a combination of his brains and her luck. "Whatever made you do such a stupid thing?" he finally asked. "I don't care how your father kept you sheltered, you still ought to know better than to kill a Rangel. And don't tell me it was because he saw you without your clothes. I saw you naked"—he smiled at the memory—"and I'm not dead."

"You will be if my father catches you."

"Did he catch all the others?"

She glared bitterly. "That's not fair. It's not as though I'm a whore or something. I just get bored sometimes. Being a warlock's daughter isn't the easiest

thing in the world, you know. People gossip at the slightest provocation. Besides, my father doesn't know about the others."

"Then he's even dumber than I thought. But I don't care about him. I want to know about you. If we're going to stick together, I have a right to know why you did what you did."

She seemed to consider whether confession was really appropriate. Finally, when she spoke, her voice carried a new sincerity of tone. "I did it because I hate them—the Rangels. I always have—since I was a little girl—because of the way they treat my father. The people in the village, they all hate him. Not because of who he is or what he is—because of the Rangels. They treat him like a slave—or worse. It's wrong. He's the warlock and them—they aren't even human."

"But they are the strongest. We can't fight them. We have to do what they say."

"Do you?" she asked bluntly.

"No," he admitted, "but I'm not a warlock, either. I'm a vagrant and an outlaw. I don't have a warm chapel to call home. I have to grab my food catch-as-catch-can."

She giggled, pointing at Sam's broad belly. "You seem to make some awfully good catches."

"I've had practice." Cazie slept beside him. Sam stroked her hard, flat skull. "I may have a lot of freedom but I don't have any comfort. With your father, it's the opposite: plenty of comfort and no freedom."

"But what good are they? The Rangels, I mean. Why do we even need them?"

Sam shrugged. "Why do they need us? Who can say? All I really know is that the Rangels came to Earth from another world. They weren't born here."

"Another world, like the moonchunks?"

"One much father away than that, so far that we can't even see it."

"But that's impossible. Or magic. How would they ever get from there to here?"

"They have airships. Some are a hundred times bigger than the ones we see. It's not magic. They're just smarter than we are."

She laughed nervously. "The one I killed didn't seem very smart."

Sam decided to be blunt. "I don't think that's funny, Trina. Killing is wrong, even killing a Rangel. If you're going to stay with me—"

"What makes you think I'm going to do that?"

Sam sighed. He realized it was going to be necessary to force her to comprehend her true plight. He tried to be as gentle as possible. "If you don't want to stick with me, you don't have to, but I think you ought to know what your options are. I'm a vagrant. I've got a raft and I'm headed downriver. You're more than welcome to come with me. That's one option. Another is for you to go off alone and build your own life. But that's tough. The chances are the Rangels will grab you inside of a couple days."

"And a third option," she said, "is for me to wait for all this excitement to die down and then go back to my father, which is just what I intend to do."

Sam shook his head in sorrow. "The excitement isn't going to die down, Trina."

"The Rangels can't hold one silly mistake against me forever."

"They can and they will."

"No, you . . . you're lying."

"Trina, you killed one of them. Consider what that means. Their power is based on absolute obedience. They can't let you get away with that. Look at me. I've never harmed a Rangel. Even when they were this close to nabbing me and I knew it might mean my own life, I didn't do it."

Some of what he was saying appeared to reach her. "But I don't want to be a vagrant," she said.

"I know. But that's not an option. When you pulled the trigger on the heatgun, you decided."

"I was angry—frightened. I just didn't think. I wish I was dead."

Sam didn't want to believe that. He wished he could bring out his harp and play her some music. Past experience had shown him that music was a most marvelous soothing device. "Let me explain some things about being a vagrant," he said, "and maybe it won't seem so bad to you. Remember, you said yourself you liked the idea of freedom."

She nodded, her cheeks damp. Sam confirmed some earlier impressions: her eyes were as blue as the morning sky, her face lovingly riddled with rusty freckles.

Sam said, "It began for me when I was just thirteen. Before that, I lived with a woman—with my mother—aboard a ship. So I've known the river my—"

"But why did you leave?" she asked pointedly. "Didn't you love your mother?"

Sam hadn't intended to get into that subject. He suppressed a frown of irritation. "She wasn't a good person. She was . . . very bad . . . evil. I met someone—a friend who was a vagrant. We went away together."

"A girl?"

"A woman, yes."

"Oh." Now it was Trina who seemed uncomfortable. "And what about your father? Where was he all this time?"

Sam shook his head. This was all very peculiar. He had told few people any of this before—and never on such short acquaintance. "He left the ship when I was still a child. I never really knew him."

"Did he leave because of your mother?"

"Yes," said Sam. "I guess he did. I heard that was what it was."

"Then he wasn't evil?"

"Oh, no, not at all. They say he was a very good man. But he loved my mother. That was what hurt. As evil as she was, he loved her."

Trina shook her head sympathetically. "In a way,

it's a lot like me. My mother died having me, so I never knew her, either."

"I'm sorry."

Trina shrugged. "I wasn't. I mean, I was just glad to be me."

Sam smiled slightly. He thought that made good sense. "But, look, this isn't what I wanted to tell you. I wanted to talk about the good things of being a vagrant. I wanted to talk about how I built the raft and threw it on the river and started drifting. That was five years ago and I've been doing the same thing ever since. It's not a bad life, Trina, it really isn't. I usually stay in one locale a few days at a time, then move on. The Rangels know all about me, but they usually leave us vagrants alone. I've met maybe a hundred people just like me in my wanderings, and they're the most interesting people in the world. I think you'll like meeting them, too."

"I hope so." She smiled suddenly. "I do like you, Sam."

"Why, thank you," he said, glowing with almost visible delight.

"But there is one thing I don't understand. In all this traveling, you never seem to get much of anywhere. Is there a point? Do you have a destination in mind?"

Sam hesitated before replying. This was something else he seldom told anyone. Still, wasn't Trina his partner now? Didn't she have a certain right to know?

"Well, there is one thing," he admitted at last. "It's a place that I'm not even sure really exists. The Lair of the Free Men. Maybe you've heard of it."

She shook her head, strands of blonde hair brushing her forehead.

"Well, it's supposed to be the one place on Earth where the Rangels won't go. It's a place where everything exists in total harmony, where the food sprouts right out of the ground and nobody has to tend it. The Lair is a lot like what some warlocks call heaven, except that you don't have to die before you can go there."

"Do you know where it is?"

"That's part of the problem. I've got a map, but it's only part of a map, and I'm not even sure it's accurate. For five years I've been trying to follow it, but look at me now. I'm not there yet. I'm not even close."

"Where did you get the map?"

"Well . . ." He hesitated again but decided to go on. "My mother had it. I took it from her."

"Then where did she get it?"

"From my father. When he lived with her, he took half and gave her the other half. It was a sort of bargain between them. He was the one who'd actually been there. He'd visited the Lair and made up the map from his travels. That's part of the reason why I want to get there. I have a feeling he may already be there, waiting for me."

"And that's why you haven't given up looking?"

He nodded and got a faraway look in his eyes. "I don't suppose I'll ever do that."

She looked straight at him, and for a moment he feared that she was on the verge of mocking him, but in the end she said, "Then I guess I'll go looking for it, too."

From that moment on, no matter what might happen subsequently, Dreadful Sam loved Trina, the warlock's daughter.

Sam's hesitant nature cautioned him not to risk straying from the burrow even with the coming of dawn,
which reached him and Trina dimly through the sheltered mouth of the cave. Trina felt differently. Once
the afternoon heat became oppressive, she insisted. It
was crazy to stay cooped up here when only a few
yards away a fresh wind was blowing. Sam continued
to say no. Trina said he was a coward. Sam said he'd
rather be frightened than dead. Trina said by the time
they finally moved she'd be too sick to leave. Sam offered her a handful of nuts and berries. Trina said
she'd rather die. Sam said the heat of the cave was pre-
ferable to the heat of a gun blast.

"All right, then. You asked for it."

Sam glanced up. "Asked for what?"

"For this." In a brisk motion, Trina removed her
gown. She shed her undergarments, kicked off her
shoes, and stood naked before him.

Sam looked uncomfortably away. "I don't think you
should do that."

"Why not? It didn't bother you back at the river."

"This is different." Sam switched off the lantern.
He could see only the high, pale tones of her slender
frame. "What if they—the Rangels—what if they found
us now?"

"I didn't know they could see in the dark."

"You killed one of them for it before."

"And you said I was wrong. All right, now I agree."

Sam heaved a sigh, recognizing the futility of further argument. Nonetheless, he remained adamant, refusing to budge as the long day dwindled toward night.

Finally, as he and Trina sat silently in the dark cave, he nodded to himself. "You can put on your clothes, Trina. It's night."

"How can you tell?" It was the first time she had spoken to him in hours.

"You pick up a sense of time being a vagrant. Most of us don't carry clocks."

"Are you positive it's safe?" Now that the moment she had been awaiting had finally arrived, Trina acted hesitant.

Sam saw no reason not to be frank. "I'm not the least bit sure."

"They may be out there—waiting?"

"It's conceivable. That's what I've been telling you all day."

"Oh," she said, in a muted tone. Sam understood what she was feeling. For the first time in her life, Trina had received an intimation of her own mortality. "What should we do?" she asked.

"We haven't much choice. If they're close and we spot them, we'll try to duck back here."

"And if they see us before we see them?"

Sam fingered his large floppy ears. "Then I'll hear them. These have saved me before." He stood, stretching. "Ready?"

"Just let me get these on." She meant her clothes.

"Don't bother with anything except the gown and shoes. Where we're going, you won't need any underpants."

While Trina dressed, Sam placed Cazie around his neck and slung his harp over a shoulder. He felt confident the raft was secure where he had hidden it at the edge of a muddy pool covered with thick briers. The raft was his lifeline, his one sure means of escape. He guarded it with a care seldom extended to his own life.

When Trina said she was ready, Sam moved for-

ward, crouching down, till he reached the mouth of
the cave. Cautiously, he pushed aside the concealing
thicket and let the cool air of early evening wash over
him. He stuck out his head and cocked his ears.
Above, two large moonchunks cast their light. Sam let
his senses flow with the world. He sought a single
wrongful note, anything that failed to fit with the
symmetry of nature.

"All right," he said finally. "Let's go."

Their bodies close to the ground, they crept down
the hillside. Sam knew she meant well, but Trina
made enough noise to rouse a watchtower full of Rangels. She stepped on loose twigs. Her breath huffed
and rasped. When she passed a bush, the branches slid
noisily against her body. Sam put a finger to his lips.
"Hush."

"I haven't said a word."

"I'm not talking about your mouth."

He remembered another woman he had known, a
vagrant; Ellen O'Denver was her name. Ellen hadn't
merely survived in the open, she had prospered. It was
she that Sam had started to tell Trina about, the
woman who had seduced him into becoming a vagrant. Ellen was the only person he had ever known
capable of stealing the Rangels' own stores. She glided
through the night like a gray shadow. They spent six
months as partners before his mother on her ship
caught up with them. Ellen had taught him everything
he knew. She was thirty years old when they met, his
first love.

"Get down," said Sam, in a hoarse whisper. They
had reached the flat marshland at the foot of the hill.
"Hurry." He pulled her toward him. Confused, Trina
fought back, squirming in his grasp. Sam tried to hold
on. The faint whistling noise he had detected grew
louder. Hearing at last, Trina lay supine. Sam felt a
scream building in her throat. He put his fingers inside her mouth. She bit him. Sam struggled to stifle
his pain. The golden lights of the Rangel airship

burned overhead. Sam knew there was no way they could avoid being seen. He lowered his mouth and pressed his lips against Trina's. He put his arms around her back and pretended to moan passionately. Trina punched his chest and tried to knee him. Her sleep disturbed, Cazie slipped away into the brush.

The airship hovered for only a moment, then drifted slowly downriver. Sam didn't move until he was sure they were safe. Releasing Trina, he gripped his injured hand. "I'm bleeding," he said, in a hurt voice.

"Bastard," said Trina, springing to her feet. "What did you think you were doing?"

"Hey, take it easy." Sam pulled her down. "I wanted them to think we were lovers. Their ships have glass eyes, too. They could see every move we made down here. They don't know about me. They were looking for you alone. I thought, what better excuse could there be for sneaking out at night?"

"You bastard," she said, but some of the anger had left her voice. "I knew that's what you wanted all along. All right." She held out her arms. "Take me. I'm defenseless. Go ahead. Have your way. I just hope my father catches you. If he finds out what you've done, he'll murder you with his bare hands."

Sam stared at her. "Trina, sit down and shut up. I'm not going to do anything. We've got to get moving."

She dropped beside him, her entire demeanor changed. "How far is the raft?" she asked quietly.

"Not far. Now be quiet. Let's go."

Sam had done his work well: the raft remained where he had hidden it. Sam uncovered the raft as quickly as possible and pointed the bow toward the open river. Cazie slid aboard. Sam reached out for Trina.

She drew back. "Are you sure that thing's safe?"

"It wasn't built for two people." The raft measured no more than twelve feet by eight. "But it's all we've got."

"Well, remember that I can swim." Trina placed a tentative foot on the raft and flexed her leg. "Here goes," she said, but just then, on the hillside above, a lantern glowed. From the height of the light, Sam guessed that it was held by a human hand. He thought he saw a faint figure, too.

Trina also saw something. Springing away from the raft, she waved her arms. "Father!" she cried. "It's me—Trina! I'm down here!"

Before Sam could stop her, Trina turned up the sloping bank. He made a hopeless lunge for her feet and, missing, sprawled on his face.

"Father, here I am!"

Sam never hesitated. Sensibly, what he ought to have done was leap aboard the raft and get out of there. Instead, he went after Trina. With his short, squat legs, he couldn't hope to match her hurtling pace. Ahead, on a path, he saw the figure of a man dressed in the heavy robes of a warlock. Sam tried to pump his knees faster. Trina had almost reached her father, who seemed frozen in place, unable to move.

Then Warlock Kaspar was running, too. He raced along the path away from Trina, the lantern bobbing crazily in his hand. "Father, stop!" she cried, dashing in pursuit. "Father, please!"

Trina won the three-way chase. Throwing her arms around her father, she brought him to a stop. "Father, I knew you'd come for me," she cried.

Warlock Kaspar spun like a top. "Monster," he said in a shrill, angry voice. "How dare you approach me?" There was the sound of a slap. Sam slowed his pace. Moving silently, he edged toward the figures on the path ahead.

"Father, don't you know me?" said Trina.

"Oh, I know you all right. Bitch! Whore! Murderess! Have you no shame! Have you no—?"

Reaching the scene at last, Sam cut off Warlock Kaspar in mid-sentence. He let his right hand fly. Kaspar tumbled backward. The lantern slipped free of his hand. Quickly, Sam snuffed out the light.

"One word out of you," he told the figure on the ground, "and I'll stamp in your face."

Turning, Sam took Trina gently by the arm. "Are you all right?"

"I—yes. Sam . . . Sam, he hit me."

"I know. I heard. I—"

In spite of Sam's warning, Kaspar refused to keep silent. "You've destroyed me, you young bitch. I saw the pictures they took. Like a slut, a whore, you took off your clothes to tempt them. You've done it before. Don't think I didn't know. A hundred times. A thousand times. You've defiled my name."

"But I was only taking a bath," Trina said.

"Hush," said Sam, holding her loosely. "Don't listen to him. You and I know what really happened."

"But he hates me."

"I hate all whores," Kaspar said.

Sam kicked him. It was unusual for him to pick on a defenseless man, but for Kaspar, he made an exception. The warlock sagged in the folds of his black robe.

Trina struggled not to cry.

"Come on," said Sam. "We've got a long way to go."

Trina let Sam lead her down the slope. "He didn't care about me. He only cared for himself."

Sam wasn't about to brag that he'd already told her that. What she was learning had to be learned through experience.

He helped Trina aboard the raft and pushed away from the bank. In the shallow water, he paddled briskly with the long board. At last, gripped by a gentle current, the raft moved without assistance. Cazie, curled up near the bow, was again fast asleep.

Sam knew there was little he could do for Trina. She wept soundlessly. Taking the rudder, Sam steered the raft toward midriver. Eventually, when the current grew stronger, he lay on his back and looked at the sky. Trina's breathing had grown soft. Her tears stilled, she had fallen asleep. His hands behind his head, Sam stared at the familiar, intimate pattern of the stars. He took his harp and began to play. In her sleep, Trina stirred.

IV

A TOOTHFISH STORY

The instant the morning sun broke through the thin mist overhanging the granite cliffs on the eastern shore, Dreadful Sam stirred and opened his eyes, the scent of damp wood keen in his nostrils. Turning his face toward the brightening sky, he took several deep gulps of morning air and cautiously flexed his muscles, chasing away the stiffness of the night. Beside him, Trina slept soundly, oblivious to the dawn, her gown bunched around slim pale thighs. Reaching over, Sam drew the hem to her knees, then stood up. Moving silently, he headed for the stern.

He was hungry. There had been no chance in the night of bringing any of the food stored in the burrow. Kneeling down, he picked up a long whittled stick and gave it a tentative shake. This was one thing he always kept right on the raft: his fishing pole. Digging through his pants pockets, Sam found a tangled ball of yarn. Unraveling a strand, he attached the end to the tip of the pole. In another pocket, he found the bent piece of wire he used for a hook. Snapping the yarn at a proper length, he fastened the hook to the broken end. Now he would need something for bait. In a shirt pocket, he found a few berries. He fastened three to the hook. Standing, throwing back his arm, he cast the line into the water. Then he sat, the pole balanced in his lap. He watched the line floating in the wake of the raft.

In time, Sam caught a foot-long batfish and then a second. He ate the first immediately, taking care not

to swallow a bone. He had seen a man choke to death in just that way. As he brought the second batfish aboard, Trina turned over. Her eyes were open, and she was watching him.

Sam smiled uncomfortably. A half-dozen times, his mouth jerked open, but he never made a sound.

Finally, Trina spoke first. "I remember you. You're Dreadful Sam."

He nodded, tucking the butt end of the fishing pole under a heel. "Did you have a good sleep?"

"Not especially." She pulled something out from beneath her head. "What's this thing? It stinks."

Sam felt flush with embarrassment. "Oh, that's mine—my jacket. I thought you might want a . . . a pillow."

"How sweet of you." She tossed the jacket toward a far corner and slid to his side in a graceful crouch. "What's that you're doing? What's the stick for?"

"It's a fishing pole. I'm trying to catch dinner."

"I'd say it was breakfast time."

"Well, whatever you want to call it." He pointed toward the batfish at his feet. "This one's yours."

She made a face. "That thing stinks."

"Well, it is dead."

"You expect me to eat that? It's not even cooked."

"I ate one. I can't light a fire out here."

"And I can't eat that thing." She waddled away from him, sitting several feet away. "I don't know what you're so worried about. There's a village less than a day's ride from where I used to live. We can go ashore there and find all the real food we can eat."

"If that's the village we passed in the night, it's a long way behind us now."

"What? How could you be so stupid? I wanted to get off there."

Sam turned, his anger getting the best of any unease he had earlier felt. "Look here, Trina, I'm getting sick and tired of your insults. Can't you understand the simplest thing? The Rangels are watching for us. If we put in this close to where it happened, they'd have us in their hands in ten minutes. We've got to move farther downriver where they won't be expecting us to show up. They don't know about the raft. I'm sure your father didn't spot it. As long as they think we're on foot, we've got an advantage."

"Then you think my father told them about you?"

"I think he told them every damn thing he could."

"I see." She nodded softly, and Sam realized he had hurt her. Trina was a funny person: as tough as a clam on one side, as tender as a worm on the other.

Ashamed of himself, Sam concentrated on fishing. He could hear the sound of her fingers drumming against the smoothed logs of the deck. "How am I supposed to do this?" she asked.

He turned in surprise and saw her with the batfish in her hands. Her eyes were squeezed nearly shut, as if afraid to look. "Give it to me."

She handed the batfish to him.

"Well, for one thing, don't eat these." He stripped the wings and head. "Now bite from the side. Peel the skin with your teeth until the pink shows. Chew carefully. There might be bones."

Trina took the fish and followed Sam's instructions. She took a nibble into her mouth and ground her teeth slowly.

"Perfect," he said. "Now swallow."

"I don't know if I can." Her eyes were shut again. "Try."

Her throat bobbed once, twice. "Salty," she said, with a crooked frown. "It doesn't taste like the fish I've had."

"That's because it's real. Cooking robs a lot of the taste. Try again."

She nodded and raised the fish toward her mouth. This time, swallowing, her throat bobbed only once. "Better," she said.

He pointed to his pole. "Want me to catch another?"

She shook her head quickly. "I'm . . . I've always been a light eater."

He looked at her bony frame. Too light for her own good, he thought. "I'll just catch another couple for me."

It was a clear, cloudless day. As he fished, Sam kept watch for any indications of aerial Rangel activity. When he found none, he had to assume that the raft had already passed safely beyond the range of immediate pursuit. On both sides of the river, sheer cliffs vaulted high into the air; they couldn't have landed here even if Sam was ready. Trina could tell him little of the local geography. She thought there might be at least one large town farther downriver, because she remembered her father going away once to receive a special ordination. Sam tended to avoid towns. Most had their own police, which made foraging a delicate operation. Sam was about to explain all this to Trina, when a sudden loud splash erupted in front of the raft and a wall of water cascaded down on top of them. Sam grabbed Trina and held her tight against the deck as the raft bounced like a feather in a high wind.

"What—what is it?" Trina cried, when the river had calmed somewhat.

Sam looked at the water ahead. A few yards in front of the bow was the center of a series of concentric circles. The point marked the spot where the beast had briefly surfaced before diving below again. Sam grabbed the rudder and twisted it toward shore. "Hold this," he told Trina. "I'm going to paddle."

"But what is it?" she said, responding immediately. She took the rudder from his grasp. "Is something wrong?"

"Toothfish. If it comes up again, we don't want to be sitting on top of it."

Sam, crouching at the starboard side, paddled furiously. The current was strong and difficult to fight.

"How do you know it won't come up over there?" said Trina, indicating the way they were headed.

"The water's too shallow close to shore. It's the only safe place when a toothfish is around." They were making better progress; he thought they might well reach safety.

"They don't really eat people, do they?"

"It's been known to happen."

She shivered dramatically. "I've never seen one."

"You don't want to." The biggest toothfish Sam had ever seen must have measured fifty feet from snout to tail. He had heard stories of some twice that length. A toothfish wasn't a real fish—they breathed air. The ones Sam had seen reminded him most strongly of enormous white-skinned slugs, with bright red eyes and broad flat tails. This toothfish did not immediately reappear. Sam paddled through the murky water close to shore. Trina kept glancing anxiously toward the middle of the river. Sam understood her problem. Most shore dwellers regarded the Long River as a serene place; another of Trina's preconceptions had been shattered. Sam wanted to cheer her up. He decided to tell a story.

"I knew a man once who was swallowed alive by a toothfish."

She looked at him curiously, her wet hair stuck to her scalp, her face covered with a thin sheen. "A dead man, I assume."

"No, and that's what makes it an interesting story. He only told me about it after it happened."

Trina managed a flicker of a smile. "All right—I'll bite. Tell me how it happened."

"Well, he was a vagrant like me and he had his own raft." As he spoke, Sam continued to paddle. It was possible that the toothfish might still be tracking them, farther out. "One hot day he decided to go for a swim. Just as he hit the water, a fifty-foot toothfish surfaced and swallowed him up in a single gulp. That was how he avoided being torn apart by the teeth. He was never bitten. It was a real miracle."

"You can't swallow something alive," Trina said. "If nothing else, the stomach grinds everything up."

"I know," said Sam. "My friend knew that, too, which just goes to show how lucky he was. Because, as he was sliding down the throat, he reached out desperately and caught hold of something and stuck fast. Only later did he figure out that it must have been a bone lodged in the soft membrane of the throat. Whatever it was, my friend held on for dear life, while down below he could hear the big belly digesting the rest of its meal."

"So what happened? He can't still be dangling there."

"Oh, no. I told you he was a lucky man. He wore a feather cap. Removing the cap from his head with his free hand, he extracted the feather from the cloth with his teeth."

Trina looked suddenly suspicious. "This friend of yours went swimming with a cap on?"

"Oh, didn't I tell you? He was bald—bald as a beet. He wanted to avoid sunburn."

"You did forget to tell me that."

Sam grinned. "Stupid of me. Well, anyway, guess what he did with that feather?"

"I'd hate to have to guess."

"He rubbed it against the throat—that's what he did. Now, if you've ever been tickled on the outside you have some idea what it's like. On the inside, especially for a toothfish, it's a thousand times worse. The fish shivered and shook, coughed and gagged, snorted and spit. My friend kept on tickling. Finally, it got to be just too much for the poor fish to endure. It sneezed, a mighty sneeze, quite likely the grandest in history. My friend was blown clear up out of the throat, past the teeth, into the water, up past the surface, and into the air. He finally landed on the bank in the soft branches of a fir tree. He was a lucky man, and he was saved."

Trina gaped at Sam, shaking her head. "You're crazy," she said, with admiration.

Sam grinned. "Not me—my friend."

"I think you're both crazy."

Sam pointed to his fishing pole. "Another fish?"

She considered for a moment, then nodded. "All right—a fish."

Sam smiled with real pleasure. For the first time he truly believed that Trina had the makings of a first-class vagrant.

V

THE BLACK SHIP

Several days later, the granite cliffs along both sides of the river finally receded, and a thick green forestland spread outward instead. Shortly before sunset, the raft slipped around a broad bend in the river and discovered ahead, nestled in a cove, a fair-sized town. Sam hastily drove the raft toward shore and let it beach against a muddy ridge. "As soon as it's late enough," he said, "we'll sneak past while everyone's asleep."

Trina frowned, pushing aside a clump of matted hair and showing angry eyes. "No, you don't. I'm tired and I'm filthy and I'm sick. I never want to see another batfish as long as I live. We're stopping here."

"We can't."

"Why not?"

"Because . . . well, it's still too risky. What if the Rangels—?"

"Oh, screw the Rangels." She slipped deftly past him and grabbed the fishing pole. Backing protectively away, she gripped the pole in both hands. "Either promise me or I'll break it."

"Trina, don't be stupid."

"Who's stupid? I'm hungry."

Cazie, roused by the disturbance, lifted her head and glared sternly around.

"Give me the pole," said Sam, holding out a hand. "If you break it, I'll just go into the woods and cut another."

"If you can find a pole, why can't you find me some food?"

"Because the Rangels don't care about tree branches."

"What Rangels?" She pointed over her shoulder toward the town. "I don't see a watchtower. Do you?"

Sam had to admit that she was right. The absence of a tower was something he should have noticed before. "That could be even worse. The Rangels must trust the townspeople."

"Oh, Sam, don't you understand? I just don't care. You can't expect me to be miserable forever. I'm not asking for much—just some food."

He saw how close to tears she was. As the sky grew darker, the lights of the town winked on. The presence of electricity was a good sign. Privileged towns tended to be complacent towns, unaccustomed to the baser aspects of existence. Finally, Sam could no longer resist her sad eyes. "All right, I'll go."

"Oh, Sam, will you?" Letting the pole drop, she rushed to him and kissed his cheek. "While you're gone, I'll take a bath. When you get back, I won't stink anymore."

He gave her a wary look. "Well, be careful who sees you."

"I can take care of myself," she said blithely.

Sam recognized the sound of approaching horse steps. He put a finger to his lips and jerked his head toward the woods. "There must be a road up there," he whispered.

Trina gave him a gentle push. "Then go catch a ride into town. You can get back faster that way."

Sam hesitated. "A lot of people don't like strangers."

"Then give them a good story. Tell them about your friend who was swallowed by a toothfish. Go on—go. I'll be all right."

Urged on by Trina, Sam jumped ashore. The beat of hooves still echoed clearly. He headed for the woods.

"Sam, wait a minute," Trina called, in a harsh whisper.

He paused, turning back. "What is it now?"

"Sam, do be careful. I wouldn't know what to do if I lost you now."

He shook his head in bewilderment. Was she deliberately trying to confuse him, or was this just her way?

Once in the woods, Sam moved easily and swiftly, his awkwardness transformed into an unmistakable grace in familiar surroundings. The fused scent of sap, tree bark, needles, and pine cones played on his nostrils like soothing music. Estimating the distance to the road and the velocity of the horse, Sam moved at an angle to the river. Breaking through a spiny hedge, he reached the dirt road. Twenty feet distant, a two-wheeled cart approached. Sam waved his arms. The cart stopped beside him.

The driver was a thin-faced man, well dressed in a long black coat. He eyed Sam curiously. "I don't believe I recall you," he said, in a slow soft drawl.

"I'm a stranger here." Sam had prepared what he hoped was an acceptable story. "I live a ways upriver and I've come to visit my brother."

"Would I be apt to know him?" The cart was empty, a fact that Sam regretted. If it had contained food, he might have been on his way back to Trina inside of ten minutes.

Sam shook his head. "I doubt it. He's new in town himself."

The driver stroked his thin gray moustache. "A slim fellow with a hooked nose? Thick eyebrows that grow together? A quick but kind of sad way of talking?"

Sam didn't think this could be a trap. "That sounds like him, yes."

"Then I believe I know him. He arrived in town last week." The driver made room on the seat beside him. "Hop aboard. I'm Snick. You?"

"Sam," said Sam, situating his broad bottom on the narrow plank that served as a seat. Snick jerked the reins, rousing the old horse. The cart swayed and pitched on the rutty road.

"I'm a merchant," said Snick. "Clothing, to be specific. I'd be pleased to offer you something, but as you can see, I sold the lot on my latest trip."

"You must travel the river a lot."

"Just alongside of it. Fifty miles this way, fifty miles the other way. Anybody lives farther can come to town and visit my store."

"During your travels, have you ever seen a black ship on the river—a black ship made wholly of iron?"

Snick shook his head. "Can't say that I have. Ships are pretty scarce items, you know. In fact, the only one I can remember seeing was when I was just a boy. It was a paddlewheeler and a magician was running it. He stopped at the town and put on a show."

Sam nodded politely, volunteering nothing additional now that he had achieved his primary aim. As risky as it was, he'd felt that he'd had to ask about the black ship and was reassured now that he'd learned it was not nearby.

Snick drove his horse in silence. In a matter of a few minutes, the cart reached the first log houses of the town. "We call it Lomata," Snick said. "It's the biggest and most progressive community within a five hundred mile range along the river. No watchtower, either, as you may have noticed. Twenty years ago, we convinced the Rangels to pull out."

"That must have taken some convincing," Sam said.

"Not especially. The Rangels finally figured out we could handle any vagrants or thieves well enough on our own. A decent town has no use for riffraff."

"I quite agree. It makes me sick just seeing them. People who think they can live without working. It's disgusting."

"You can say that again," said Snick.

The town wasn't quite as large as Snick boasted. Most of the houses were one-story log cabins. Electric lamps illuminated the main thoroughfare, and Sam made out a number of stores, their doors locked now, specializing in various forms of food. There were few people about. The citizens of Lomata, like most men on Earth, preferred to steer clear of the shadows of the night.

"You can drop me anywhere around here. I should be able to find my brother easily enough." They had just passed a large, padlocked general store. Sam guessed he could find anything he desired in there.

"If you want, I'll take you right to him," said Snick. He clucked his tongue at the horse, urging further haste. "I happen to know where he's staying."

"I wouldn't want to put you to any trouble."

"No trouble. It's on my way."

Sam shrugged. He couldn't argue without arousing suspicion. If he came face to face with his supposed brother, he could always say it was just a mistake.

Snick turned down a darker street. The houses were bigger along here. Hearth fires burned brightly through clear glass windows. A group of laughing children frolicked in a grassy yard. At times like these, Sam felt a stab of pain. Freedom had its benefits, sure, but so did security. He missed the comfort of a warm home, good friends, a stable life. Maybe Trina could help end his terrible loneliness. It had been a long time since he'd last had a friend—since Ellen O'Denver. Maybe that was why he picked up Trina when he did. He wanted a friend. Maybe.

The cart halted in front of a squat adobe building. Snick slid off the driver's seat and offered Sam a hand. "I'll take you in. I imagine your brother will be pleased to see you."

Sam saw no way to avoid going inside. In the dark sky, the stars slowly unfurled their glorious light. In the east, a pair of moonchunks floated, though more would later be revealed.

Snick knocked on the door. "Toma, Kelp. I've brought someone to see your guest."

The door opened slowly on its hinges. A hog-nosed, thick-jawed face peered out. "What are you talking about, Snick?"

"I met this fellow on the road to town. He says he's Reardon's brother."

"He does, does he?" The face grinned broadly. "Toma will want to meet him for sure."

"I'm Sam," said Sam, stepping uncertainly forward. "I'm a stranger here but—"

"Do come in." Snick stepped aside, letting Sam enter first.

As soon as he passed the threshhold, Sam realized he'd made a mistake. There was a second man inside the single room. The man pointed a Rangel heatgun at Sam's chest. "Put them up," he said.

Sam raised his hands, edging into the room. Behind, he heard Snick giggle. "That's Sheriff Toma," said Snick. "Sheriff, this here is Reardon's brother."

"How about that?" said Toma, a plump man with a whiskery face. "It certainly was nice of him to drop by and say hello."

"There must be some mistake," Sam said. "My brother isn't—"

"I think you'd better come with me." Toma stood heavily and pointed toward a door in the back wall.

Sam went through the door. Beyond it lay a row of iron-barred cells, only one of which, the farthest from the door, was presently occupied. The man in the cell was tall, angularly thin, with hollow blue eyes, a broad hooked nose, and black eyebrows that joined together in the middle of his forehead.

"Hey, Reardon," Sheriff Toma said, "here's someone who says he's your brother."

The man in the cell looked up without interest. "I don't have a brother."

"See?" said Sam. "What did I tell you? It's just a mistake."

"And you could both be lying. Kelp," Toma said, calling the man who had first let Sam into the jail, "open this up. We'll let these two straighten out their own ancestry."

The cell door clanged shut behind Sam. The prisoner, Reardon, leaned against the back wall, hands in his pockets.

"The way I figure it," Toma said, speaking through the iron bars, "is you've got three nights till the last moonchunk rises. After that, if you're clean, I'll consider letting you out."

"Three nights!" cried Sam. "I can't stay in here three nights!"

Toma shrugged. "It's the only way I can tell who's lying."

Sam slowly began to understand. The rise of the last moonchunk could prove only one thing. "You don't think I'm—"

A hand fell on his shoulder. It was Reardon. "I'm afraid that's exactly what they do think, brother. They think we're werewolves."

"But there's no such thing as a werewolf," Sam said automatically.

Toma shook his head warily. "That's what we intend to find out."

VI

WOLF MAN

As soon as they were alone, Reardon waved a thin hand at the bunk hanging from the wall by a pair of chains. "Take that if you want, brother. It gratifies the sheriff when he finds me staying awake all night."

Sam looked at the tiny cell. Except for the bunk, there was no furniture, not even a pail for washing. A hole in the floor served as a toilet, and the barred window in the back wall showed nothing but a blank wall next door.

Sam was too angry to sleep. "How can people be so stupid? Werewolves are nothing but crazy fantasies cooked up by the warlocks to scare people and keep them inside at night. How can any intelligent man believe in such a thing?"

Reardon smiled crookedly. "Are you sure you're not neglecting one factor, brother?"

"Stop calling me brother. We're not related, damn it. Call me Sam—that's my name."

"I'm sorry, Sam, but there is another point. The sheriff isn't quite as dumb as he looks. You see, I am a werewolf."

Sam stared at Reardon, waiting for him to relax and laugh, but he never did. "You can't expect me to believe that."

Reardon shrugged. He sat on the edge of the bunk, his legs bent sharply at the knees. "Believe what you want, but the fact is in three days I'm going to undergo a transformation right here in this cell, after which I imagine you'll be set free and I'll receive a

silver bullet through the heart. That part of the myth
is valid, by the way. Werewolves are impervious to
most mortal ailments, but silver will do us in every
time."

Sam continued to stare. "They wouldn't really kill
you?"

"Sure. Why not? Wouldn't you? Confronted by a
raging beast in the shape of a man?"

"You can't be serious."

"Ah, but I am. When you're my age—I'm somewhere
past a hundred and fifty—you'll be serious most of the
time, too. I didn't even find it funny when you
showed up here claiming to be my brother. I should
have, though. What made you come up with a crazy
idea like that?"

Sam didn't feel like explaining. Thinking of it only
made him remember Trina. She would have finished
her bath by now. Then what would she do? How long
before her nerve snapped and she did something stupid?

"Are you really a hundred and fifty years old?" Sam
asked.

"I am, and it's peculiar. That's what always seems to
astonish people the most. The werewolf who bit me,
the one who made me what I am today, claimed to be
more than a thousand. He said he could remember
what the world was like before the Rangels came."

Sam saw no harm in talking. If nothing else, it made
the time appear to pass faster. "I've always wondered
what it must have been like back then."

"Oh, different from now—entirely different. Better?
For a werewolf, maybe. Few people believed in such
things back then. For the average man, I'd say no. It
was a terrible time, with billions of people spread
across the globe and barely enough food to sustain
half that number. Long before, men had gone all the
way to the stars, but the race was old and weary and
dying without knowing it. Maybe it still is. The Rangels have given us a few more centuries."

"How do you know all this?"

"I thought I explained. The man who bit me told me. After he'd done the deed, after he'd made me what I am, he was very apologetic. You couldn't stop him from talking."

"But what about the Rangels? How did they help us? I thought they destroyed everything—the cities and all."

"That's true. It was a terrible war. Millions died. For a time it appeared the Rangels intended to exterminate everyone, but they stopped, relocated the survivors here along the river, built their watchtowers, and just stayed."

"Then the man who bit you must have felt awfully lucky—to have survived, I mean."

"Most werewolves did. It was funny, but the Rangels never bothered us. They still don't. My theory is that they regard us as a distinct species. To them, we aren't really human."

"Then you aren't the only werewolf?"

"Oh, no. I suppose there's a few hundred others up and down the river. I've never made an exact count and we seldom socialize. Ninety-nine times out of a hundred, the victim of a werewolf attack dies right away. When we're in that state, it isn't possible to exercise self-control."

In spite of himself, Sam felt a queasy twinge. If Reardon was telling the truth, what was going to become of him in this tiny cell when the last moonchunk rose?

Reardon stood up. Approaching Sam, he lowered his voice confidentially. "Sam, there's something I want to ask. Have you ever met a vampire? You know, a creature that lives by drinking blood and never dies."

Striving to conceal the shock engendered by Reardon's question, Sam shook his head slowly. "Not that I know of."

"I ask for a particular reason. You see, I knew a

vampire once, a woman, the most beautiful creature who ever lived. She's ten thousand years old and as wise and terrible as she is beautiful. I'm in love with her, Sam. Have you ever loved a woman?"

"I did—once." He turned away, hiding his face from Reardon's prying gaze.

"Well, then perhaps you can understand how I feel. It was just four years ago. I loved her and lost her. She's a monster, Sam, and she would have killed me. I thought I valued my life more than my heart, but I was wrong."

"What's her name?" Sam asked, the question threatening to stick in his throat.

"Nerdya." Reardon looked up quizzically. "You don't know her, do you?"

His face still turned away, Sam shook his head.

"Then I want you to do me a favor. Look for her. Nerdya prowls the river on a black ship made entirely from iron. If you find her, please tell her this: say that Reardon, the werewolf, died with her name on his lips. Tell her and perhaps she'll understand the agony I've endured since I ran away."

"But you aren't dead yet," Sam said, speaking with difficulty.

Reardon did not appear to notice. He seemed to have vanished into a world of his own. "No, but it's only a matter of three nights. It doesn't matter. Except for Nerdya, I welcome death as a familiar friend. I've seen it all, Sam. I've wandered this god-forsaken world from pole to pole. I've seen the Giant Lake and the Great Sea and everything between. I've seen everything except the Lair of the Free Men, and I doubt that that exists, because if it did, I would have seen it. Promise me, Sam. Promise me that you'll find Nerdya and tell her what I've said. Please. I've never asked anything of you before."

Sam nodded. What else could he do? "I promise."

Apparently satisfied, Reardon turned away. The

recollection of Nerdya the vampire had turned him inward. He lay on the cot and laid his face close to the wall.

Sam looked out the cell door. The iron bars cast broad black shadows upon his face.

VII

NERDYA'S SON

During the next two days, Sam forced himself to question Reardon more specifically concerning Nerdya and her present whereabouts, but Reardon claimed general ignorance.

"I haven't set eyes on her since the day I fled her ship like an utter coward. Now and then during the last four years, I've heard rumors of her presence, but whenever I reached the town or village involved, I found no sign of the black ship. That's what originally brought me here, as a matter of fact, but as you can see, it was another false lead."

"Then you have no idea what her course might be? I mean, if you knew where she was going, then you could get there ahead of her."

"I've thought of that, but it just isn't possible. You see, she's trailing somebody else—she was even when I knew her. It's her son."

"Her son?"

"Yes. A year or two before I joined her, he had apparently run away from the ship, taking something very precious of Nerdya's with him. She wants that back, and she's been searching for this son ever since."

"What did he take?"

"I don't know. She'd never tell me. You don't know her, Sam. Nerdya is the most mysterious woman who ever lived."

For Sam, the worst part of being in jail wasn't his own imprisonment, it was Trina. Where was she now? What was she doing? Whenever Sheriff Toma or his

assistant, Kelp, brought food to the cell, Sam tried to question them. Was there trouble in town? Had a new vagrant recently been apprehended? Were there any visitors in the area? He tried to be as subtle as possible, but Reardon at least guessed something was wrong. On the second afternoon, following lunch, he turned to Sam and said, "So you've got a friend outside, have you?"

"Of course I don't." Where Trina was involved, he trusted no one. "All vagrants travel alone—you should know that."

"Is it a woman?"

"I told you there was no one."

"Pretty?"

"No. I mean, yes. I mean, shut up and leave me alone."

Sam was forced to conclude that his only hope lay in waiting out his period of imprisonment. Once the last moonchunk proved he wasn't a werewolf, then he ought to be set free. Unless Reardon tore him apart first.

That second evening, though, Sheriff Toma removed even that hope. Leaning against the cellblock wall, Toma fingered the Rangel heatgun he wore tucked in his belt. "So we've got a Rangel killer among us, do we?" He looked right at Sam as he spoke.

Sam felt an unpleasant sensation deep in his stomach. "You can't possible mean me, sheriff."

"No need to explain." Toma heaved a sigh. There was something almost admiring in his gaze. Sam didn't think that Toma cared much for the Rangels, either, despite his town's reputation for obedience. "I got a call from the watchtower a few minutes ago. They're seeking a man answering your exact description for turning a heatgun on a Rangel guard somewhere upriver. Apparently, there was a girl involved, too."

"It isn't me. There's some mistake."

"Maybe so. That's not really up to you or me to

decide. An airship is on its way to pick you up. It ought to be here in a few hours." Toma pushed away from the wall. "You don't know anything about this girl, do you? She's the one the Rangels seem most interested in catching. They say she's the daughter of a warlock."

"It's just a stupid mistake—that's all."

"Well, have it your own way."

After Toma had gone, Reardon came over to Sam, shaking his head sorrowfully. "What a terrible pity. And here I thought I was going to have you for dinner tomorrow night."

"Shut up and leave me alone," said Sam.

"A killer of Rangels indeed. I must admit that I'm impressed. Even in my most bestial moments, I've never molested one of them. They seem so harmless, in spite of their role here."

"I asked you to shut up."

"Or was it the girl? A warlock's daughter? You know, that's damnably impressive, too."

Sam went for Reardon's throat, ready to squeeze the life right out of him, but something in those hollow, weary eyes made him stop. It was almost as if Reardon wanted Sam to attack, sought an excuse for achieving an easy death.

Dropping his hands, Sam turned away.

"I'm sorry," Reardon said softly. "Sometimes I do get overly obnoxious." He crawled on the bunk, turned his face to the wall, and in a few moments, slept soundly.

It was nearly midnight before anything else happened. Reardon was awake by then. The cellblock door swung open and the shambling figure of Kelp stepped through. He wasn't alone. A hooded warlock dressed in black burlap came with him. All Sam could see of the warlock's face was the smooth tip of a shaven chin.

"You're sure Toma said this was all right," Kelp was

saying. "He left orders for me not to let anyone back here."

"The rite of exorcism must be performed tonight or never," the warlock said, his voice thin but oddly deep. "If you want, you could go ask him. Or Warlock Quill. He can vouch for my integrity."

Kelp sighed. "I suppose I can trust you." Reaching into his belt, he drew out the Rangel heatgun and waved it at the cell. "Both of you, stand against the wall. The warlock here wants to talk with you."

Sam wasn't much in the mood for conversation, but the gun left little room for discussion. With Reardon, he backed against the wall. Kelp unlocked the cell door and motioned the warlock inside. Then he locked the door again and stood in the narrow corridor, gun poised in his hand.

The warlock jerked his head impatiently. "I must be alone to perform the rite. It is written so."

"But I can't just leave," Kelp said. "If I do, who's going to help in case of trouble?"

"Trouble? What trouble? These men are here and you are there. The cell is securely locked."

"I still don't like it." Kelp moved hesitantly toward the door. "If anything happens, I want you to call me. Scream at the top of your lungs and I'll come running and blast these two."

"I appreciate your concern, sheriff."

"Deputy. I'm only a deputy."

Once Kelp had gone, the warlock took hold of his hood and threw the black burlap aside to reveal his face.

Sam stood, completely stunned. "Trina!" he cried. "Trina, what—?"

She placed a warning finger on her lips. "Sam, not so loud."

"But what are you doing here?" he said, in a softer tone.

She grinned crookedly, showing her teeth. "Didn't

you hear me tell Kelp? I've come to perform an exorcism. You are a werewolf, I believe."

"Not me." Sam pointed to Reardon. "It's him."

Reardon bowed stiffly. "Reardon, a werewolf, at your service."

Trina looked uncertain. "You don't look like a werewolf."

"Wait until tomorrow night," Sam said.

"We've got to get you out of here." Trina replaced her hood. "The whole town's after your neck, Sam. Last month, when all the moonchunks were up, a man and a woman were murdered by a large animal.

Sam glanced at Reardon, who pretended not to be listening. "It's worse than that, Trina. They know about the Rangel guard. An airship is on its way to pick me up. You should have gone when you had a chance. They're looking for you the same as me."

She shrugged, feigning unconcern. "If I'd done that, Cazie would have bitten me. She's very fond of you, Sam."

"Where's the raft?"

"On the other side of town. I moved it last night, when I was sure you weren't coming back."

"But where did you get those warlock robes?"

"Where do you think? I stole them. The local warlock is an old man named Quill, who knows my father. I paid him a courtesy visit this afternoon and let my fingers wander. What about it? You two ready to go yet?"

"But how do you plan—?"

"Just watch." Trina cupped her mouth with her hands. "Kelp! Kelp! Kelp, get in here!" Her voice had reverted to a masculine tone.

Kelp crashed through the door in hardly more time than it had taken to call him. Anticipating trouble he held his gun in readiness. Puzzled, he dropped his hand. "What is it, warlock?"

"I am very angry," Trina said. "How can you expect me to proceed under such circumstances?"

"Well, a cell's a cell," Kelp began.

"I quite understand. What I'm talking about isn't that—it's this." She pointed beneath the cot, where the light failed to penetrate. "This is simply unendurable."

Kelp squinted at the shadows. "I don't see anything."

"Then get in here and look for yourself."

Thoroughly confused, Kelp unlocked the cell. As he entered, Trina stepped surreptitiously to one side, and as he passed, swung her arm up, then down. The hard edge of her hand struck Kelp on the back of the neck. Soundlessly, he fell to the concrete floor.

Reardon applauded. "Bravo!" he cried. "Bravo!"

Trina grinned shyly. "My father taught me that. He believed in self-defense."

"We'd better hurry," Sam said, gazing at Trina with new respect. "The Rangels may be here any time."

"I know." Bending down, Trina scooped up the heatgun.

"You're not planning to keep that," Sam said warily.

She shook her head. "I learned my lesson. I'll leave it in the street."

"Good."

Outside, Trina kept her promise, hurling both the heatgun and the jail keys far into the night. The three of them then moved toward the river. Sam kept watch on the sky. If the Rangel airship came, he wanted to see it first. A cold wind blew, stirring pockets of collected dust. Fortunately, because of the lateness of the hour, no one else was about; only a few houses showed dim lights in their front windows. Trina, leading the way, still made far too much noise as she walked, but Sam couldn't find it in his heart to say anything to her.

The familiar scent of the gurgling river reached Sam fondly. Trina turned down a narrow path that led parallel to the shore. After perhaps fifty feet, she parted a tall hedge and motioned them through. The raft floated in the shallow water on the other side. A motionless heap near the bow was Cazie, fast asleep.

Sam heard a shrill whistling noise and glanced at the sky. The golden lights of a Rangel airship floated past, some fifty feet overhead. "They're headed for the town," he said. "It must be my escort."

"Now what do we do?" Trina said. "We can't risk the river, can we?"

"We'll have to," said Sam. "They still don't know about the raft. I tried to give the impression we hitched here overland. As long as we stay close to shore, we ought to be safe."

Reardon cleared his throat. In the excitement of escape, Sam had forgotten him. "I don't mean to be pushy, but am I invited on this cruise or not?"

Sam was tempted to say no. Stepping aboard the raft, he found the paddle and prepared to push off. "This raft isn't very big."

"If they catch me, they'll kill me—the same as you."

"I thought you didn't care about dying."

"Only when there was no reason to live."

Sam glanced at Trina. Her emotions were easy to read. She felt sorry for Reardon—pity for a werewolf. "All right, hop aboard."

"Sam, you are a most kind and gracious human being."

Sam shoved the raft away from shore. Handing the paddle to Trina, he operated the rudder, steering close to the overgrown weeds along the bank. Turning once and glancing quickly past his shoulder, he caught a last look of Lomata. The town was dark, only a faint outline of civilization. Glimpsed once and then never seen again, he thought. Because of the river's steady current, Sam never revisited his own past. His physical journey through life matched the inexorable nature of his temporal existence. A moment once lived vanished forever. He would never see this town again.

VIII

MYLAN, THE MAGICIAN

Sam fully intended to stick to his resolve and put Reardon ashore the moment they reached another human settlement. Unfortunately, it was nearly dark the next day before they passed even a solitary log house, and by the time Sam spotted a tiny hamlet on the eastern shore ahead, he already realized that the only way he was ever going to get rid of Reardon was to pick him up bodily and cast him in the water; Reardon had been given too much time in which to think—he would be staying.

Trina was ready to defend him, too. Sam knew it wasn't her fault; she simply didn't understand the full situation. And Reardon had been playing up to her all day. She was lady this and lady that, the most wondrous and beautiful creature he had ever encountered. No wonder, as the raft rocked in the shallow water a few hundred yards upriver from the village, that she stamped her foot and said, "Sam, I can't believe you can be so cruel. Look at this place. It's in the middle of absolutely nowhere, and there's a watchtower, too. If you make Reardon go ashore, just how long do you think he can last?"

"About as long as he has so far: a hundred and fifty years."

"Sam, that's not fair."

"Neither is having Reardon aboard this raft."

"Then I think you'd better tell me why."

Sam opened his mouth to explain, but the necessary words refused to come. How could they, with Reardon himself seated only a few yards away? No, it was impossible. Sam had plenty of reasons for wanting to be rid of Reardon, but one definitely outweighed the others: Nerdya, the vampire. Reardon had let slip during the day that he believed her black ship could be found not too far downriver; he had heard another rumor in jail. Sam's raft was thus providing him with an easy means of swift transport. How could Sam explain all this to Trina? The only honest way would be for him also to explain exactly why they had to avoid at any cost coming within a hundred miles of Nerdya. And he couldn't talk about that as long as Reardon might overhear.

"Look, last night you and I made a deal," Sam said, turning to Reardon as a last resort. "If you're an honorable man, you'll go voluntarily."

Reardon smiled blithely. "I'm afraid I must throw myself on your mercy, Sam. I find that I like this river life. I like you and I like the lady Trina. I'm willing to stay, if only you'll have me."

Sam knew it wasn't any use. Night was falling, and his own fatigue was enormous. If he wanted to get past this village and find a safe place to rest, he would have to start now. "All right, stay. I guess I can't kick you out now. But I'm telling you, Reardon. As soon as we're far enough from Lomata, as soon as we reach another large town, I'm making you go."

"Of course, Sam. That's only fair, isn't it?" Reardon grinned disarmingly. "You've both been very decent to me."

Grinding his teeth, Sam took hold of the paddle and thrust deep in the water. His arms ached so much that the slighest effort was agony. The raft slid past the unsuspecting village. Later, seeing what appeared to be a sheltered cove, Sam decided to put in for what he hoped would be a full night's sleep. It was already so dark that the shoreline was no more than a hazy, indistinct shadow. Sam picked his way carefully through the mud and stretched out under the cool, low branches of a willow. A dark shape loomed over him. Looking up, Sam saw Reardon.

"What do you want now?"

Reardon pointed to the coil of rope Sam used as a belt. "Do you think you can spare that?"

"If I do, I'll lose my pants."

"I'm not talking about now—I mean later." Reardon bent down, speaking in a voice too soft for Trina, who lay beneath the next tree, to overhear. "Have you forgotten what the night means?"

Sam looked startled. The truth was that he had forgotten. In jail in Lomata, Reardon's werewolf identity had seemed a very real thing, but out here in the swift, sweet air of the river, the entire concept struck Sam as slightly absurd. "You don't mean it's really going to happen?"

Reardon nodded solemnly. "In a very few minutes the urbane, civilized man you now behold will be transformed into a savage beast."

Sam glanced nervously around, as though the shadows of the night had suddenly assumed physical forms. "And where do you intend to undergo this transformation? Do you want me to ferry you across the river?"

"I'm afraid I can still swim, Sam."

"The river's three miles across."

"Less than an inch to me in my werewolf phase. Look, Sam, it's not my own safety that concerns me. It's you and the lady Trina. When I'm a wolf, there's nothing to stop me from murdering you both without a qualm. I won't even know what I've done until morning."

Sam struggled to sit up, his aching muscles resisting all the way. "What do you have in mind?" he asked wearily.

"That's why I asked about the belt. The only practical method is for you to tie me securely to a tree and then wait until morning, praying that I don't break my bonds."

"And if you do?"

"Then you'd better run, Sam—run and be quick."

Sam swore softly. All that interested him at the moment was a full night's sleep. Climbing to his feet, he went over and explained to Trina what he had to do. She offered to go with him but Sam said no. Reardon concurred with that judgment. In the morning, he explained, at least one of them would have to be sufficiently rested to paddle the raft.

A hundred yards deeper into the forest, Reardon stopped before a broad solid oak tree and suggested that Sam try his belt here. Reardon stood with his spine against the trunk of the tree while Sam wrapped his belt around once and tied a firm knot.

"Give it a try," said Sam.

Reardon strained at the rope until the veins in his forehead showed clearly in the dim starlight. "I guess it'll hold," he said, with less confidence than Sam might have hoped for.

"Now what do I do?"

"Just wait."

Sam seated himself on a bed of needles and leaves. "Can I sleep?"

"You can try." Reardon appeared to smile faintly as he spoke.

It was another twenty minutes before anything definite occurred. Sam kept watch on the circle of sky he could glimpse through the thick foliage overhead. When all twelve moonchunks showed clearly visible, he began to regard Reardon more intently. Neither of them had spoken in some time. Reardon's head lolled against his left shoulder; he might have been sleeping.

The first thing Sam noticed was the fur. Great gray clumps of it began to sprout on Reardon's face. Then he noticed the ears—shaped like pointed arrows—and the eyes—a malevolent yellow, not blue. Reardon's mouth formed a narrow crease filled with sharp fangs. His nose was a flat black snout. Deep in his throat, he began to growl.

Then he lunged.

Sam jumped four inches into the air.

Fortunately, the rope belt held. The beast—Reardon—sprang forward again. The oak tree swayed. Big red leaves fluttered to the ground. Sam came to his feet, poised and ready to flee. It was a fantastic thing to observe; Sam had never seen a werewolf before.

All through the night, the beast lunged, the tree swayed, the belt groaned. Sam thought that Reardon was playing a teasing game. As exhausted as he was, Sam never caught a single wink's sleep. Whenever he came close to nodding off, the werewolf sprang again.

By morning, Reardon was himself again, blue eyes shining brightly in a smiling face. "You can let me go now, Sam. It's all over—for today."

That was the first night. The second, twenty miles downriver, proceeded in a similar fashion. Reardon said that the entire phase usually lasted no more than three nights. Sam looked forward to the possibility of renewed sleep like a thirsty man comtemplating a distant blue lake.

As the third night drew close, Sam beached the raft and forced his tired legs to carry him ashore. "You ready?" he said to Reardon. "We may as well get going."

"I'm as ready as you are, Sam," Reardon said brightly.

"And tonight's going to be the last night? You're sure about that?" The question was one he had feared to voice until now.

"Well, usually." Reardon pondered. "Odd things have been known to happen. Where the supernatural is concerned, there's no telling what's what."

Sam nodded. He wouldn't dispute Reardon's opinion. If he insisted on turning into a werewolf for a fourth night, then he could damn well go off and do it alone. Sam's patience had run out; so, too, had his ability to stay awake.

Finding a fair-sized fir tree out of sight of the river,

Sam removed his belt and bound Reardon to the trunk. Sitting down, he watched the sky and counted the moonchunks as they rose. The stars seemed to flicker like tired flames.

That night, for the first time, Sam actually slept even as Reardon raged. He was out for an hour, perhaps two, dreaming crazy dreams, before the touch of a hand on his shoulder shocked him awake.

Sam jumped to his feet, but it was only Trina. Her jaw slack with astonishment, she stared at the thing tied to the tree.

"Is this what you've been enduring every night?"

Sam nodded. "That's Reardon."

"He doesn't even look like a man."

"He's not."

"He doesn't look like a wolf, either—more like a big two-legged cat."

"He'd kill us if he had the chance."

"I know. I just had to come and see."

Sam invited her to sit with him. She had brought Cazie along, and the three of them observed the lunging werewolf for several silent minutes. Finally, Cazie tucked her head between her coils and fell asleep. As a creature of the wild, Cazie had no doubt seen worse things than mere werewolves. Sam guessed it would take something like a twelve-legged toothfish to keep Cazie awake all night.

"Sam, do you think you've really been fair with me?"

Sam turned and looked at her curiously. "What do you mean—fair?"

"You're keeping something from me, aren't you? You haven't told me everything."

He shook his head. "What gives you that idea?"

She looked irritated. "Sam, I'm not totally stupid. Everything about you is a mystery. And there's something Reardon said today, in the afternoon, while you were trying to sleep."

Sam glanced at the werewolf. It was quiet now, pas-

sive, building up energy for another lunge. Reardon insisted he could recall nothing that happened while he
was transformed, but to be on the safe side, Sam deliberately lowered his voice. "What did Reardon say?"

"He told me about the vampire he's in love with."

"Nerdya?"

"Yes."

"And what does that have to do with me?"

"He said she's looking for something very precious
that was stolen from her. He said she'd stop at nothing
to get it back. I got to thinking. Is it possible that
what she's looking for is a map, a map that shows how
to find the Lair of the Free Men?"

"It's only half-a-map," Sam said quickly.

"But you took it from her?"

He nodded. "Does Reardon know?"

"Not for certain, no, and that's why he asked me.
When he was with her, he heard her describe the person she was hunting. There's nobody else who looks
like you, Sam. Reardon couldn't help but be suspicious."

"What did you tell him?"

"I said it couldn't be you. I said all you owned was
the clothes on your back and a beat-up old harp and
none of those were exactly precious. I said you had a
brother who looked a lot like you."

"Did Reardon react to that?"

"Not especially, no."

"Then thanks."

"You're welcome. But I still don't think it's fair.
Reardon's not your partner, but I am. I can see why
you don't want him to know the truth, but what about
me?"

"I don't want to see you hurt. Nerdya would kill
you—or worse than kill—without the least hesitation.
She's evil, Trina—really and truly evil."

"You were her lover, too, weren't you? Just like
Reardon?"

Sam shook his head. "I was more than that. Nerdya is my mother."

"No!" Trina cried, her voice rising in spite of the caution she had previously exercised. "She can't be!"

Now Sam understood why he had never told her before: because he'd known she would react exactly as she had. "You don't have to worry. I'm not a vampire. It doesn't run in the blood."

She looked hurt. "I didn't mean that. I was thinking of how it must have been for you, living with her, knowing what she was and never quite understanding. How did you get away?"

He shrugged. "My father helped me. He sent a woman to rescue me, Ellen O'Denver, the vagrant I told you about. Ellen came to the ship and snuck aboard every day while Nerdya was asleep. Ellen told me about the map, about everything. I had never known a real person before—just once, one friend—only Nerdya and her lovers and her goblins. The goblins are what I called Nerdya's lovers after they were dead and became her servants. Ellen taught me about the real world and made me understand that I had to run away. She was going to take me to my father. That's why we took the map."

"Was she your lover—Ellen O'Denver?"

"My first one—my only one."

"What happened to her?"

"Nerdya killed her."

"Oh."

"She came about six months after we'd run away. I was gone that night—out foraging—learning how to be a vagrant. When I returned in the morning, the first thing I saw was the black ship anchored close to shore. I ran to Ellen, but I was too late. She was dead when I got there. Nerdya had drained every drop of blood from her body. I had to find a sharp stick and drive it through her heart. It was the only way to keep her from becoming a goblin, too."

"That must have been horrible."

"It was."

"Then you never did find your father."

"No. Ellen only told me a little about him. He had a ship and he was waiting for us. She never told me exactly where. I guess she just didn't expect to die."

"Then you've got to find him on your own."

Sam nodded. "But it's not that easy. There's so much that I don't know. Who is he? What does he look like? Is he still alive? Ellen didn't even tell me his name. If he's not waiting in the Lair of the Free Men, then I don't think I ever will find him."

"Maybe he'll find you. He sought you out once. What makes you think he's given up?"

"But he may not know what I look like, either. I was so young when he left, only three or four."

"A father will always know his own son, Sam."

"I hope you're right."

"But if Nerdya caught up with you, why didn't she kill you, too? Why didn't she take the map back?"

"I guess I was too smart for her. I knew her methods too well. I hid every night and ran like hell every day. It was a miracle, but I got away. She hasn't given up. She's still trying to catch me. The next time, I might not be so lucky."

"You can still hide."

"Sure, but there's so many other things to consider. Like Reardon. He'd gladly hand me over to her. I've seen men like him before. Once they've known Nerdya, she owns them body and soul."

Trina stood up. "Then we'll leave him here."

Sam shook his head. "We can't do that."

"Why? Isn't that what you wanted in the first place? You only let him stay because I wanted you to."

"There's more to it than that. No, Trina, I've made up my mind. I've had plenty of time to think the past three nights. I can't keep running all my life. Maybe it's better if Nerdya does catch up with me. I'm sick of hiding and running. I guess that's why I took up with you. I'm tired of being alone."

"But you don't have to make it easier for her."

"Am I?" He shook his head. "Reardon doesn't know where she is. Deep down, he probably isn't all that eager to find out. Reardon may love Nerdya, but he's not crazy. Finding Nerdya would mean his own death. He says that's what he wants, but I don't believe that either."

"Then you want him to stay?"

Sam waved a hand at the growling, lunging werewolf bound to the fir tree. "He needs us."

That third night proved to be the last in which Reardon was transformed. After that, they made much better time downriver. Sam no longer talked about forcing Reardon ashore, and Reardon himself never raised the matter. They stole food, caught batfish, slept ashore, and just drifted. Twice, they saw Rangel airships, but in both instances, there was plenty of time to find cover in the tall weeds along shore.

This relatively idyllic existence ended with unexpected swiftness one afternoon when the raft turned a sharp bend in the river and Sam saw, bearing down on them at an astonishing speed, what at first appeared to be a house floating on the water.

"Look out!" Sam cried, dropping the paddle. He grabbed the rudder out of Trina's hand and jerked it toward shore.

"A houseboat," Reardon was saying, with apparent awe. "Isn't that the most incredible thing you've seen?"

Sam could hear a motor churning. At the rear of the boat, only faintly visible past its bulk, a paddlewheel churned in the water. A whistle blew shrilly. Sam stared at the onrushing boat. High on the top deck, the indistinct figure of a man stood, waving frantic arms.

"I bet I know who that is," Reardon said, with infuriating calm. "That's Mylan, the magician. Nobody else could have a boat like that. I haven't seen Mylan in twenty years."

The boat was too close. Sam glanced at the shore. "Jump! Both of you, jump! We'll never make it—!"

Sam hit the water. A moment later, close above, there was an explosion like the end of the world.

IX

RENEGADE RANGEL

The big paddlewheel chugged to a stop, and the river-boat lay dead in the water amid the scattered debris of the raft. An anchor on a chain rattled down. On the top deck, a faint figure dressed in robes and a blue skull cap peered down at the destruction swirling beneath him. "Hello down there!" he called. "Hang on and I'll throw you a ladder!"

Sam counted the heads bobbing nearby. There were two—just the right number. For a moment, he thought he'd lost Cazie but then realized the meaning of the heavy weight around his neck. He grabbed hold of a broken log with one hand and patted the cobra's head reassuringly with the other. He never did recollect how or when Cazie had found refuge around his throat.

A rope ladder fell from a window in the top deck. Sam paddled to where it floated and waved at Reardon and Trina to come, too. By the time Sam reached the ladder, Reardon already had a foot in the bottom rung.

"It's got to be him, all right," Reardon said excitedly. "If it's Mylan, this is a stroke of good luck."

Sam couldn't quite see that—not with his raft reduced to splinters. "Who's Mylan?"

Reardon looked surprised. "You mean you don't know? I thought Mylan, the magician, was a name known up and down the river. He travels from town to town, giving shows. Surely, you must have run into him some time."

Sam shook his head. Oddly enough, the name did seem vaguely familiar, but he couldn't place it. "I don't think I've ever heard of him."

"Well, you are young and, now that I think of it, I haven't heard much of Mylan lately. It must be twenty years at least. I wonder where he's been all this time."

Sam didn't have an answer to that. Reardon went on up the ladder. Sam waited for Trina to arrive and then boosted her up.

"Sam," she said, "what are we going to do? Who is this man?"

Sam told Trina what Reardon had told him. The two of them ascended the ladder.

Entering through an open window, Sam found himself in a large room packed with more books than he'd seen in a lifetime, as many as a hundred bound volumes. The man in the blue cap sat in a tall chair behind a broad wooden desk. He was an exceedingly old man, with a creased wrinkled face, a long wispy white beard, and a pair of surprisingly bright green eyes. Looking at him, Sam suddenly felt a peculiar chill, a sense of the past recaptured, but he shook away the feeling, knowing that it had to be wrong. He had never seen this man before in his life.

Standing just behind the old man's chair was a second startling figure. This one was a tall naked Rangel.

"Don't worry about my friend here," the old man said quickly. He looked straight at Sam as he spoke. "This is Urban, a renegade. The Rangels think even less of him than you do."

"You're Mylan," Sam said tentatively.

The old man nodded, his eyes not moving. "The magician."

"Sam doesn't believe in magic," Trina said.

"Sam? Is that your name? Sam?" Mylan seemed less surprised than pleased.

"They call me Dreadful Sam."

"Have we ever met?"

"Sam shook his head. "I don't think so." He wondered whether Mylan had experienced the same chill he had.

"No, I suppose we haven't."

All this time, Reardon had been staring at Mylan in apparent bewilderment. Finally taking note of his fixed gaze, the old man turned his chair in that direction. "Don't I know you from somewhere?"

"Mylan? Mylan, is it really you?"

"I don't know who the hell else it could be."

"Up close you don't . . . you've changed."

"Who hasn't?"

"I'm Reardon. Reardon, the werewolf. We knew each other years ago—far upriver. Don't you remember me from then?"

Mylan shook his head. "I remember as little as I possibly can."

"It was only twenty years ago."

"Too damn long for a man in my line of work." Sam got the feeling that much of Mylan's sharpness was an attempt to suppress another, deeper emotion. The old man shifted his gaze. "And how about you? I suppose you're an old friend of mine, too."

Trina shook her head, smiling. "No, I'm just me—Trina."

"Glad to meet you." Mylan leaned back and put his hands behind his head. "I suppose I owe you all an apology for running into your raft. Sorry, but it couldn't be helped. Except for Urban here, I'm alone aboard this boat. My last crew ran out on me several stops back and I haven't been able to recruit a new bunch."

Sam somehow got the impression that Mylan was lying, but he couldn't for the life of him figure out any reason why he should.

"We'd be willing to help," Reardon put in quickly.

Mylan frowned. "Don't you think you should wait till you're asked?"

Reardon spread his hands apologetically. "You said you needed help."

"In that sense, you're a hundred percent accurate—I do. You see, I happen to need a crew for a number of different reasons. I need people not only to help me with the boat but also with the shows I put on at the various towns. They're the only way I can keep this old body from starving to death."

"We could help you with that, too," Reardon said eagerly.

This time, Mylan ignored him. He crooked a thumb past his shoulder. "I'm afraid Urban here is little help in that regard. If I tried to use him in a show, the villagers would likely tear us both apart."

"Most humans hate and fear me," Urban said. It was the first time he had spoken—the usual singsong delivery of a Rangel. "Actually, I am as gentle as a saint."

"But otherwise as unlike one as you or me," Mylan said. "His own people have proscribed Urban because he fell in love with a . . . a . . ." Mylan hesitated. It appeared as though he had said more than he intended.

"With a female human," Urban finished. "A most foolish and unforgivable deed."

Mylan stood up and circled the big desk. A tall man, he moved with more grace and vigor than he had previously shown. "I'm going to ask the three of you to decide here and now. Either join me or don't. If you're not interested, I'll gladly put you ashore."

"I'm with you all the way, Mylan," Reardon said at once. "I wouldn't miss this opportunity for the world."

"You may have to. It's got to be all three of you or none. Sam, what do you say?" Mylan clenched his hands in front of him, revealing a sudden burst of tension. The veins in his neck showed. "Want to join up with me or not?"

"I can't be sure. You're headed upriver. We just came from that way."

"No problem. We're going the same way. We must have passed each other in the night. I came back this way in search of fuel. The forest gives out in a few miles, and I needed wood. When I get it, I'll turn around again."

Sam looked at Trina. She met his gaze, smiling tentatively. Sam had no trouble guessing her preference. The riverboat was roomy and comfortable, a far cry from the harsh existence aboard the raft. By himself, Sam would probably have decided to return to the river. But he wasn't alone anymore. And there was Mylan to consider, too. It seemed to be very important to the old magician that Sam say yes.

"All right, I'll stay," he said at last.

Mylan beamed openly. "And, Trina, what about you?"

"Oh, I'm staying, too," she said.

"Good," said Mylan. "I won't claim that I'm not pleased." Ducking his head, Mylan turned toward the cabin door. "Come along and I'll show you the boat. After that, we'll all pitch in and gather some wood."

"Oh, Mylan, there is one other thing."

Mylan paused, a hand on the doorknob. "What now, Reardon?" When he turned, his face was streaked. Sam thought it almost looked like tears.

"There is something I've been meaning to ask you. In your boat, you can move up and down the river very quickly. I was wondering if you might have run into a certain person."

Sam felt a tightening sensation in his gut. He knew exactly what Reardon was talking about.

Mylan frowned. "I can't say a thing till you tell me who you mean."

"It's a woman," said Reardon. "She has her own ship—a black ship. Nerdya is her name. Nerdya, the vampire."

Mylan started to reply, but before he could manage to utter a word, a weird, wailing, piercing scream cut through the air.

Sam spun on a heel. Urban, the renegade Rangel, stood with his hands clutching his own throat. His head was thrown back and his face distorted in an expression of ultimate dread. Urban looked as though he had been visited by a spirit of the dead.

A moment later, without ever moving another muscle, Urban fell over on his face, striking the desk and rolling to the floor.

Mylan looked down at him. "I'm afraid I didn't quite catch that name," he told Reardon. "Is it anyone I ought to know?"

X

The more Sam saw of the fabulous paddlewheeled riverboat, the more deeply impressed he became. The tour Mylan conducted revealed wonder after wonder after wonder.

More than two dozen rooms lay scattered through a total of three full-sized decks. Each room was plushly decorated with various ornate furnishings—big beds, bright mirrors, and thick carpets. The galley in the lower deck contained two wood stoves, a vast storage compartment, and enough bottled and pickled food to last the five of them a year or more. On the topmost deck, Mylan proudly displayed his library, an entire large room stocked from ceiling to floor, wall to wall, with nothing but old cloth and paper bound books. "Anytime any of you has a spare second and wants to read," Mylan said, "feel free to stop here and borrow any volume that catches your eye."

Sam looked sheepishly at his feet. The fact was that he could barely read his own name. Trina, on the other hand, seemed excited by the offer and, with Mylan's consent, eagerly removed three books from one tall stack and a fourth from another.

As they were making their way back downstairs, one of the books Trina had removed suddenly disintegrated in her hand. "Oh, I'm really very sorry," she said, staring at the shreds of paper that drifted toward the floor. "I shouldn't have—"

"Don't blame yourself." Mylan drew her away from the debris. "It was old—that's all. The art is a forgotten one. Not the printing so much—I suppose we could manage that—it's the writing. Nobody knows how to do it anymore."

"Maybe I should put these back—before the same thing happens."

Mylan shook his head. "What would be the point of that? The books were written to be read, not kept sealed up in a dark room."

Sam couldn't quite understand all this fuss over a few old books. Still, it was possible that Mylan and Trina knew more about the subject than he did. He felt a sudden overwhelming desire to be able to pick up a book and share the thoughts set down by men and women centuries dead. Maybe that was the real charm of books, the secret of their appeal: books were a legitimate means of communicating with the dead.

As the tour progressed one thing continued to bother Sam, the vast amount of time and energy it must have taken to build this boat. Finally unable to stifle his curiosity, Sam asked Mylan how it had happened.

"Oh, that was actually the easy part," Mylan said. "Gathering the necessary material—the wood and the glass and even nails—that was what took time. Putting everything together was no trouble at all. I just used magic."

"Magic?"

"Sure. I just shut my eyes, pictured how I wanted the finished boat to look, opened them, and there it was on the river before me."

At the end of the tour, Mylan assigned each of them a room on the second deck. Night was not far off, so Mylan decided to put off going ashore for wood until morning. Trina and Reardon disappeared inside separate rooms. Sam was about to enter his, as well, when Mylan asked him to wait a moment.

"I wanted to ask a favor of you," he explained. "Poor Urban has suffered quite a shock, and I don't like to leave him alone. Would you mind letting him stay in your room till he manages to come around?"

"You mean he's still unconscious? In that room?"

"I imagine he is. Among the Rangels, such seizures are not uncommon. They may last for weeks at a time."

Sam received the impression that Urban wasn't really what Mylan wanted to talk about; it was just an excuse—a subterfuge. "If you want him to stay with me, I don't mind, but I can't help wondering. Do you have any idea what happened to him back there? It seems to me he had his attack when Reardon mentioned that woman—what was her name?—Nerdya, the vampire."

Mylan got a strange, haunted look in his eyes. "Yes, that was it. Nerdya, you see, was the woman who seduced Urban away from his own people. He nearly died at her hands, but despite that, in his way, I actually think he loves her."

"He's not like Reardon, is he? He's not trying to find her again?"

Mylan smiled thinly. "Is that what Reardon's up to? A man as old as he ought to know better. You don't find Nerdya—she finds you."

"You talk as if you know her."

Mylan nodded ambiguously. "No better than you, Sam." He shrugged his shoulders. "It was all a hell of a long time ago."

"Then you did know her," Sam said.

"So what if I did?" Mylan glared. "You seem awfully interested in something that's really none of your business."

"I only meant to ask if . . . if she was as beautiful as Reardon says."

"Beautiful?" Mylan's voice sounded abruptly far away. "I'm not sure if a word like that is capable of describing a creature such as Nerdya."

"You sound almost like you loved her yourself."

"Loved her?" He shook his head. "No, I never knew her that well."

Sam went into his room. A short time later, with

Reardon's help, Mylan brought the unconscious Urban into the room and placed him on an empty bed.

After that, long days passed aboard the riverboat, and the harder Sam worked, the more sweat he shed scrubbing decks, washing windows, shining brass, cooking meals, chopping wood, feeding engines, the more he enjoyed it. The past routine of life aboard the raft had grown increasingly boring, he now realized. Too many identical days spent doing identical things—drifting, thieving, singing, foraging, fishing. Perhaps that was another reason why he had joined up with Trina when he had. He needed a change, any alteration in a pattern that through repetition had become as constricting as a jail cell.

The four of them—Sam, Trina, Reardon, Mylan—stood pilot watch in turn through the day and night. At first, Mylan had stood cautiously by, coaching the others, but with the passage of time, had left them largely alone. The boat, in spite of its size and apparent complexity, was not difficult to operate. There was a big wooden wheel in the pilot's compartment that controlled almost everything. When you wanted the boat to go left, you jerked the wheel that way; when you wanted to go right, you turned it to the right. For speed, there was a throttle stick connected to the steam engines in the lower deck. For stopping, there was a brake handle that froze the paddlewheel. Much of the actual mechanics of the boat—the engines, for example—was too complicated for Sam to understand. Sometimes he almost believed that Mylan had told the truth: maybe he really had put the boat together with magic.

Sam's favorite time for standing watch was the period right after midnight. With the shore concealed from sight, the river took on the aura of an even vaster and more mysterious entity. There were only occasional obstructions in the deep water near midriver, a few logs and other floating debris. Navigation was never difficult. It was a time of peace and contemplation.

As the days and nights stretched into weeks, Sam spent most of the time when he wasn't working either in Trina's room or Reardon's. It was odd, but now that he didn't have to be around him every minute of every day, Sam thought Reardon was a lot less obnoxious than he had been. Reardon explained why he had acted so surprised when he'd first set eyes on Mylan aboard the boat. "I guess I didn't pay enough attention when we were still in the water, but he's changed, changed enormously. The last time I saw Mylan he was still a young man. Look at him now."

"You said yourself it was twenty years ago," Sam said.

"Sure, but he's aged a lot more than that. Look at his skin, look at his eyes. I know what it must be. It's the magic. Using it is a great strain. I know he told me that when I knew him before. It takes a lot out of a man."

"How old do you think he actually is? Seventy? Eighty?"

Reardon shook his head grimly. "No, that's what bothers me. I don't think he can be a day more than forty-five."

"You're kidding."

Reardon frowned. "No, ask him. It's true."

Despite its high rate of speed—many times that of the raft—the riverboat had not passed a single settlement of any size since the three of them had come aboard. The nature of the land had also changed dramatically. As Mylan had said, the forest was soon gone, with only a few bare trees scattered here and there along the shore. It was like a great, flat, broad desert; nothing alive seemed to grow here. Mylan explained that it would be necessary to reach some sort of settlement soon. Already, their supply of wood was getting dangerously thin. "And I'm restless, too," Mylan admitted. "On a long voyage like this, I start to get bored after a while. I'm eager to see how you three work out in the show. It's always a challenge to pull off a successful magic act. The trick lies in the quickness of the hand. Without that, I'd be nothing."

It was Sam's turn to stand watch in the pilot's compartment. Mylan claimed it was too hot for him to sleep. Sam had seen a lot of the magician. Mylan often sought him out in his room to engage in long, rambling conversations. "I thought you were a real magician. What does a quick hand have to do with real magic?"

Mylan shook his head. "More than you might imagine, Sam. I'll tell you a secret. Real magic is a far too precious commodity to be squandered frivolously. In the course of my act, I admit I sometimes use shortcuts."

"Is it because, when you use magic, it tires you out and makes you grow older?"

"I'll bet Reardon told you that, didn't he?" Mylan lifted an eye quizzically but did not pursue the point. "Well, it's partially true, but the significant factor is that none of us really knows what magic is. Maybe it's some sort of cosmic force. Maybe it has something to do with the Earth's magnetic belts. I do know one thing, though: whatever it is, magic is very much a limited resource; it can be used up. That's why I try to be selective. That's why I don't use magic every time I want a hangnail removed from the tip of a finger. Long ago at the dawn of time, the amount of magic present in the Earth must have truly been enormous. But that era's long gone. Too damn many magicians for too damn many centuries have used ninety-nine percent of it up. In another hundred years, maybe less, there won't be anything left. That's why I try to preserve what I can when I can."

It was the eleventh night after they had first boarded the riverboat when Urban, the Rangel, at last awoke. Sam happened to be in the room at the time.

Mylan had given him a harp to replace the old one lost with the raft, and he had it balanced on his chest, playing a gentle tune, when he realized that someone else was listening and watching.

He turned his head slightly to one side and saw the Rangel's eyes regarding him. "That was most excellent," Urban said. "You will continue please?"

"You're all right?" Sam laid his harp aside. "Do you want me to bring anyone?"

Urban shook his head. "I am quite fine. Your music awoke me. It was so stark and beautiful."

"Why, thank you, but . . . well, do you realize you've been unconscious for nearly two weeks?"

"I slept, yes—but I was tired. Don't you humans sleep, as well?"

"Why, yes, but for only a few hours at a time."

"It is different with us. We always do it the way I did."

Sam decided he ought to go tell Mylan what had happened. Not finding the magician in his room or study, he decided to try the pilot's compartment. Reardon was standing watch. He said that Mylan had been there earlier and might be returning.

"The Rangel woke up," Sam said. "I thought Mylan might want to know."

"If I see him, I'll tell him. Did anybody ever figure out what made him pass out like that?"

Sam didn't think it was a wise idea to tell Reardon about Urban and Nerdya. "I asked the Rangel. He said it's the way they always sleep."

Reardon kept his eyes fixed on the dark river ahead. "Well, maybe it's true. In spite of the years we've shared this planet, neither one of us really knows a thing about the other. Look at how long I've been alive. Urban is the first Rangel I've really been associated with in a hundred and fifty years, and he's been asleep ever since we first met."

Sam was watching the sky. It was a clear night, and the stars glowed with particular boldness. One of those twinkling pinpoints of light, he realized, must shine upon the Rangel home world. Which one? Of course, he had no idea. "I've never heard what made them come here in the first place."

"I've heard various reasons. One I like better than the others. I don't know if it's true or not."

"Tell me."

"Well, it's an old story." Reardon tugged the wheel to the left, avoiding a log suddenly revealed by the moonlight. "According to it, everything dates back to way long ago when we humans had our own ships capable of traveling between the stars. It seems we found the Rangel home world, settled down there, and made virtual slaves of the inhabitants. We exploited the planet, stole their natural resources, and left a wasteland where we had found green fertility. All of this happened in a period of a few hundred years. It didn't take long to destroy a planet, I guess. We'd honed our methods through centuries of practice."

"Who told you this?" Sam said. "Was it the man who bit you?"

"No, it wasn't him. He was a werewolf, and werewolves were never much interested in what went on outside the Earth."

"But you still haven't explained how the Rangels got here."

"Well, they were patient. That and vengeful, too, I guess. It took them thousands of years to rebuild what we had destroyed and thousands more to reach the point where they had ships of their own capable of reaching the Earth. What happened after that you know as well as me. They came, they found us weak and decadent, and they conquered."

"But they stayed," said Sam. "That's what I still don't understand. If it was vengeance, why didn't they just kill everyone and go home?"

"That's a question the story doesn't bother to try to answer. Want to hear my personal opinion?"

"Sure."

"I think they stayed to keep an eye on us. I think they were afraid it might happen again—we might reach space once more—the human plague begin to spread. Frankly, I think they've given us way too much credit. We're too old and weary to reach the heights—or depths—where we once lived. But the Rangels are careful—and cautious. They built their watchtowers, and they're watching us."

"But you don't know that any of this is true."

"No, I don't. I wasn't alive then."

"But the person who told you was."

Reardon looked sharply past his shoulder. "What makes you say that? I told you it wasn't the person who bit me."

"No, but it was Nerdya, wasn't it?"

"It could have been. I don't really remember now."

Sam nodded silently. He continued to watch the sky, feeling a special sort of shame. It wasn't for anything he had done—not him or anyone he actually knew. It was a shame he felt for deeds committed and acts accomplished by men whose bones had turned to dust long centuries past.

XI

MAGIC SHOW

Word of the magic show must have spread through the area like a raging fire, for as night descended slowly in the west, the crowd in the village square overlapped the boundaries established for it and moved into the residential streets beyond. Standing with Trina and Reardon to the left of the wooden platform that served as a makeshift stage, Sam made only one serious attempt at counting the audience and gave up after his finger passed the five hundredth bobbing head without touching more than a fraction of those gathered. Sam realized what life must be like for these villagers. For them, this show represented one of the few wonders they would ever experience in their lives.

Sam glanced at the sky and then at Reardon. He couldn't help feeling some degree of nervousness, though Mylan had insisted there was nothing to be concerned about. Tonight was the first night of the phase of the last moonchunk—it hardly seemed possible that a month could have passed since the last one— and Reardon would surely be undergoing his transformation in a very few moments. Reardon seemed no more bothered by this than Mylan. The two of them had spent an hour secreted in Mylan's study earlier in the day, and Sam only hoped that they had somehow managed to settle the problem then. How? He shrugged mentally. Maybe Mylan could use magic to prevent Reardon from assuming the form of a savage beast.

At present, in the center of the stage, Mylan was beginning his act. Proceeding rapidly, he moved

through a quick succession of tricks. Reaching in a
pocket, he pulled out a live, kicking rabbit. Tapping
his skull cap with a finger, he let loose a flock of flut-
tering yellow birds. Borrowing a crimson sash from a
woman in the front row, he tore the garment into tiny
shreds and then quickly recreated the whole with a
shake of his hand. It was a damned impressive per-
formance—something even Sam could not fail to admit—but it wasn't magic. It was illusion. And that
wasn't the same thing at all.

"What do you think?" Trina asked, leaning close to
be heard above the loud applause of the audience. "He
is good, isn't he?"

Sam nodded. "Do you have any idea how he does
it?"

"Is that important?"

He shook his head. "I suppose not."

"I do have an idea, though."

On stage, Mylan removed his cap and placed it in
front of him. Stepping back, he lifted his hands over
his head and then slowly approached the cap again,
stepping softly, like a stalking cat. When he was only
inches from the cap, he threw himself in the air and
clapped his hands together. For a moment, it looked as
though he would land directly on top of his own cap.

But he didn't. He never came down. Mylan vanished in midair.

This time, even Sam showed his surprise. The
crowd, after a moment's shocked uncertainty, clapped
enthusiastically. Sam glanced at Trina. She was smiling. "What about that one?" he asked, leaning very
close.

"I think I've got that one figured, too."

"Tell me later."

"I will."

For several long tense moments, the stage remained
bare except for the cap. Then it moved. Inch by inch,
the cap rose into the air until it hung suspended more
than six feet off the ground. Sam stared, thoroughly

perplexed. Then the cap moved again. Mylan was standing under it. With a broad grin, he swept off the cap and bowed to the crowd.

The applause this time was even more deafening than before. In spite of himself, Sam joined in. Who knows, he thought, maybe it is real magic. He decided to withhold judgment until the end.

Turning toward them, Mylan crooked a finger. Sam knew what that meant. Trina reached out and took him by the hand. "That's us," she said.

Sam felt a whole lot less confident. Mylan had described his place in the act in minute detail, but talking about it and thinking about it were not the same as actually doing it. As he moved out on stage, Sam felt momentarily frozen with embarrassment. Trina gave his hand a tug and he edged forward. He knew what an absurd figure he must seem: the fat little ape man with the tall beautiful blonde. He hugged his harp close to his chest, as if the instrument might protect him. Cazie, around his neck, seemed totally oblivious to this, her first moment on the stage of the world.

Halfway across the stage, Trina let go of his hand and continued on alone. With nervous fingers, Sam removed Cazie from around his neck and placed her carefully on the floor. Then, holding his harp, crossing his legs underneath, he sat down beside her. He tried to pretend the audience wasn't even there. He battled to make himself think he was actually alone. His fingers struck a first chord. Perfect. He experienced a sudden rush of confidence. He continued to play. Then someone tittered. He never understood why. Maybe it had nothing to do with him. His fingers fumbled. He struck an obviously wrong note. There was loud laughter. His fingers felt wet. The laughter grew louder. He didn't think he'd ever be able to finish this tune.

Cazie came to his rescue. Unconcerned with such human oddities as loud laughter and bad music, she pro-

ceeded emotionlessly through the paces of her act.
First she rose on her tail. Then she spread her hood.
Then, gently, she began to sway in approximate time
to the music that now flowed crisply from Sam's harp.
It was effective. Most of the audience had never seen a
cobra before, and they fell properly silent. Sam had a
chance to steal a glance at Mylan and Trina. The nature of their act was as much a mystery to him as what
Reardon intended to do when the last moonchunk
rose. Mylan believed it was better that way. He told
Sam he couldn't enjoy the show if he knew what was
coming next.

Trina lay on her back on a table. The red velvet
gown she was wearing—a gift from Mylan—spread
around her body like a fine blanket. Mylan was
clutching a sword. The sharp silver blade glistened in
the torchlight. For some reason, Sam didn't like this at
all. His fingers struck a rapid succession of sour notes.
Nobody seemed to notice. They, too, were watching
Mylan and Trina. Cazie continued to sway, oblivious
to the whims of the mob.

Mylan raised the sword above his head. For a dramatic instant, legs spread, he held it poised there.
Then, slowly at first, the sword fell. The blade whis-
tled, slicing the air. Trina never flinched. The sword
cut through her body at the waist and jammed in the
wooden table underneath.

Beyond the rush of the wind, there wasn't a sound.
Sam had quit playing. Halfway to his feet, he stared at
Trina. She had been cut neatly in two.

Mylan backed away, leaving the sword where it had
stuck. The crowd watched him intently, unsure of the
proper reaction. Should they applaud? Cheer? Scream?
Faint? Sam tried to play. His fingers were numb; they
felt bloated to twice their normal size. He realized that
Trina's eyes were upon him. He stopped playing and
stared back.

Then she winked.

When he saw that, he knew it was all right. She was

fine—it was just another trick. Fully confident, he let his fingers dance upon the taut strings. A trick. Hell, he'd known that all along.

Mylan stepped toward Trina. Removing his cap from his head, he moved it slowly across her body from head to feet. As he did, he chanted rhythmically, his actual words indistinct. Finished, he put the cap back on his head. He clapped his hands, once, twice.

Then, stepping back, he folded his arms across his chest.

Trina moved. At first, it was just her fingers—then her whole hand—then a foot. She sat up slowly and swung her legs over the side of the table. Moving gingerly around the sword, she dropped to her feet, stood up, and bowed. As far as Sam could see, she was as whole and complete as ever.

The applause this time was more furious than ever before. Sam decided this was a good signal to quit playing. Scooping up Cazie in his arms, he waited for Trina, who came hurrying over to join him, then exited the stage. Reardon slipped past them. It was his turn to perform next.

Trina was laughing. "Sam, Sam," she said, clutching his arm. "You should have seen your face. I thought for a minute you were going to die. Why didn't you ever tell me you cared so much?"

Her laughter brought back the anxiety he had experienced when the sword fell. "I don't think it's so damned funny. How did he do it? I thought—I mean, it really looked real."

"Do you really want to know?"

"Yes, of course I do. It wasn't magic. I know that. But how—?"

"All Mylan did—this is what I saw—was take that sword of his and jam it through a hole in the table. He never came within six inches of cutting me."

"But I saw him do it," Sam insisted.

Only her eyes were laughing now. "Did you?"

"Yes. Yes, I . . ."

"Hush. I'll tell you later. I know I've got it figured out now. Let's watch Reardon."

Sam turned to the stage, but there wasn't a great deal to watch. Mylan and Reardon stood facing each other, a few inches apart. Neither said a word, made a sound, nor acknowledged the existence of their vast audience. Reardon, shifting his feet now and then, seemed plainly nervous, while Mylan, totally in command of himself as usual, calmed the crowd with his quiet strength as the empty minutes slipped past.

Finally, Sam could not control his impatience. He leaned close to Trina and whispered, "What are they doing?"

"If it's what I think, then it's important."

"Unless they hurry up, Reardon's going to be a raging werewolf before they finish." He pointed to the sky. "You can see the twelfth moonchunk rising now."

"If you're worried, we could go back to the boat. I'm sure Urban could use some company."

Sam shook his head, treating her taunt as a serious suggestion. "No, I think we ought to stay."

More time passed in silence. Another minute—two—three; it might easily have been even more. At last, Mylan moved. He tilted his head and looked at the sky. Drawn by his gaze, Sam looked, too. He counted softly. The twelfth moonchunk, a jagged pale orb, stood plainly revealed in the east.

It seemed to be a signal. Dropping his head, Mylan marched forward, leaving Reardon behind. "Ladies and gentlemen," he said, "tonight I have a most extraordinary magical feat to perform for your entertainment. Most of us are familiar with the legend of the were-beast, a creature half man and half animal, who roams the night during the phase of the last moonchunk. Most of us accept the legend as simple superstition, although I must tell you that I recently passed through a certain nameless village, where the sheriff himself was busily leading a werewolf hunt. Needless

to say, the best he managed was to imprison a few of
his own more bizarre citizens."

The audience chuckled at this stupid law officer,
and Sam joined in the merriment. What was so funny?
he wondered later. The town was Lomata, and the
werewolf was Reardon. As Sam knew from fond experience, Reardon was a lot more than simply superstition.

Mylan went on. "Tonight is, as you may have noticed, such a night as I just described." He paused
while several thousand pairs of eyes turned to the sky,
confirming the presence of a full complement of
moonchunks. "And this man who stands here with me
is, as you'll no doubt agree, a most average looking
human being. Now, please, before we proceed, let me
caution you. In spite of what you may soon witness, do
not fall prey to unreasoning panic. Should a werewolf
perchance appear among us tonight, I guarantee you
will find him no more savage than the pet cat you
keep around the house to kill mice."

"Sure," Sam muttered, "as long as you don't mind
being treated like the mouse."

"Sam, be quiet," said Trina.

He looked at the sky. Whatever Mylan planned, it
should be happening soon. The twelfth moonchunk
had climbed high in the sky. Sam glanced back at the
stage. As he did, his knees felt weak. He could see it
beginning to happen already. Reardon's face sprouted
gray fur. His forehead sloped, his chin receded, his
gums grew fangs. As close as he stood, Sam could even
see the sharp claws extending from the hairy fingertips.

Trina grasped his arm. The audience murmured
restlessly. Someone in the back let loose a loud scream.
Sam started to step protectively back. Trina held him.
"No, wait," she said. "I think I know what he's
doing."

"This isn't a trick—this is real."

"I know, but watch."

Mylan himself seemed totally unafraid. Speaking in a gentle, coaxing voice, he approached Reardon, who was growling now, flapping his arms and prancing menacingly. The audience was not reassured. A wave of fear, almost physical in its intensity, passed through the crowd. Screams were more frequent. A few people broke from the mass and fled into the night.

Still, as the minutes passed and Reardon failed to attack, a mood of calm descended upon the square. Someone near the front began clapping and others joined in. Soon, the applause resounded as strongly as ever.

Mylan and Reardon stood nose to nose. Their eyes locked; neither budged a step.

"I don't get it," Sam said. "Why doesn't Reardon kill him?"

"I'm not sure he can."

"He's a werewolf, isn't he?"

"We know that—does he?"

For all Sam knew, Trina might have been right. Mylan proceeded to put Reardon through a series of tricks. The wolf raced across the stage on his hands and knees, growling and snarling. He rolled over like a dog and sat up and begged like a puppy.

Trina tugged at Sam's sleeve. "Would you like to go now? I think we've seen enough."

Sam was willing. He felt almost sorry for poor Reardon and the dignity he had lost. "Where? Back to the boat?"

"No, let's take a look at the town."

Turning, they pushed through the crowd surrounding the stage. Free of the mob, they were caught by a surprisingly cold night wind. Shivering gently, Sam pulled Cazie more snugly around his neck. The town was dark and empty. An occasional flickering torch illuminated a deserted corner. Sam wondered if anyone in town had chosen to stay home from the show.

"Aren't you going to tell me?" he said, as they walked. "I thought you said you knew how he did it."

She nodded. "Do you know what hypnotism is, Sam? My father used it all the time—most warlocks do—but Mylan is far better at it than anyone I've ever seen."

He was familiar with the concept, although he couldn't remember ever seeing it used. "Hypnotism is when one person controls another's mind and can make them do what he wants."

"Yes, except that Mylan seems able to control more than one mind at a time. He makes the audience see what he wants them to see. I wonder what would happen to someone who arrived late. I bet they wouldn't see anything at all."

"And Reardon? Are you saying that Mylan hypnotized him, too?"

"Oh, sure. I thought that part was much too obvious. He must have done it today when the two of them were holed up in his study."

"Then I was right all along. Mylan is just a big fake."

She shrugged. "I suppose that ought to make you feel good."

Oddly enough, it didn't. Instead, Sam felt as though he had lost something valuable. He remembered what Mylan had told him about the limited quantity of magic available in the Earth. Maybe he was just conserving a resource. Maybe he used real magic only when it was absolutely necessary.

He told Trina what he was thinking.

She nodded. "It is possible, you know."

"Sure," said Sam.

They turned a corner and moved past a board fence. Behind, the sound of laughter could still be heard. The wind brought a multitude of smells with it. Sam detected old food, sweet flowers, and the scent of mown grass.

"Why have you never tried to seduce me, Sam? We've been together such a long time and you've never made a move. Even Reardon was polite enough to ask, though I turned him down right away."

Sam glanced at her curiously, surprised by the sudden turn the conversation had taken. He felt an unexpected burst of anger. "When did Reardon do that? You never bothered to mention it to me before."

"Why? Does it matter?"

"Yes, as a matter of fact it does."

"Why? What concern is it of yours?"

"Because he—Reardon—he had no business doing that."

She laughed gaily and took his arm in her hands. "Sam, I'm not asking about Reardon. I want to know about you. Is it because of that other woman, Ellen O'Denver? Are you still in love with her?"

He shook his head, pondering. "No, I don't think so. I admired her a lot—she was a fantastic person—but I don't know if we were ever in love. She was much older than me, and smarter, too, not like you."

"Are you hinting that I'm dumb?"

"Oh, no," he said quickly. "Not in that way. I was talking strictly in terms of being a vagrant, knowing how to survive along the river, and you're a lot better at that now than when I met you."

"Then answer my question. If it's not her, then what is it?"

He shrugged, unable to avoid a slight flush of embarrassment. Fortunately, because of the dark, he doubted she could see his face that well. "I guess it just hasn't come up. We were friends and partners and that seemed to be it. Besides, that first night, you warned me to keep away."

"But that was different. At first, sure, I didn't know who you were or what you wanted. And your appearance does count against you. I suppose you know that."

"I'm ugly."

"No, that's not what I mean, either."

"Then what do you mean?"

"I mean that I think you're very handsome." She stopped, turning, and faced him. For some reason, the moonlight seemed peculiarly bright. He could clearly see her pale freckled face, the silken yellow hair. With astonishing clarity, he recalled the first time he'd set eyes on her and once again blushed.

"I think you're very pretty, too."

"Thank you."

Sam took her in his arms. He felt big and bloated and clumsy. He could smell her sweet scent. She kissed him. Cazie stirred sluggishly. Sam responded to Trina's kiss.

"Come this way." She had hold of his hand. "Thanks to Mylan, we're just about as alone as anyone could be."

Hand in hand, they crossed to the nearest yard, partially circled the big stone house, and found a sheltered place in the slick grass near a brick wall. Trina lay down on her back. Sam knelt at her side. Even here, with the shadows full on her face, he felt he could see her clearly.

Trina reached behind her neck and unfastened the strap that held her red gown. She pulled the loose flap of cloth down to her waist. Swallowing hard, Sam put his elbows on his knees and stared hard at her breasts.

"You can touch me if you want."

He nodded. Her breasts were very small and, because of the way she lay, barely discernible against the smooth skin that covered her ribs. He touched her nipples and felt them grow and harden under his fingertips. She sighed. He felt like laughing. Maneuvering his body, he managed to lie down beside her.

Cazie moved away from his neck and slipped through the grass.

Trina looked up at the sound. "Now look what we've done. The poor thing is awake."

"She'll be all right. She knows where the boat is tied. Maybe she can keep Urban company."

"Better her than me," Trina said. She drew Sam down on top of her. He shut his eyes and let his lips glide firmly against her mouth. She took his hands and placed them on her legs. He lifted her gown and pushed the heavy cloth up to her waist. Trina trapped his hands between her thighs. Her body was lean but oddly compact, the muscles bunched under the taut, stretched skin.

He was sure he didn't hear the first cry and maybe not even the second or third, but finally a voice shouted so loudly that it sounded much closer than it actually was.

Sam sat up like a bolt and looked around. The yard was dark and empty, but now he could hear footsteps, too. The shouting grew in intensity—a dozen voices at least. Trina covered herself frantically. Sam helped her knot the strap around her neck. She stood and smoothed the gown around her legs. "What's wrong?" she asked. "What's everyone shouting about?"

"I don't know, but we'd better go see."

"I hope nothing went wrong with the show."

"Maybe Mylan's hypnotism slipped and Reardon broke free."

"I hope to hell not."

"There's only one way to find out."

Together, they hurried through the yard and toward the nearest street. A dozen people went running past. Sam called to them, but no one would stop. Reaching out, he grabbed a small boy and held his arm. "What is this? Why are you running? Did the werewolf escape?"

The boy shook his head violently. "It's not him. It's in the river. It's a ship."

"A ship?" Sam said, feeling a deathly chill of foreboding. "What kind of ship?"

"A terrible one. The warlock says it is an omen of our destruction. We must run to our houses and hide and pray."

Sam shook the boy. "I don't care what that old fool said. I asked what color it was. Is it a black ship?"

The boy nodded, open-mouthed. "How did you

know? It's a black ship, with no sail or paddlewheel. Smoke pours from the top of it."

Sam let him go. Turning to Trina, he said only one word: "Nerdya."

"Do you think . . . can it be on purpose? Do you think she's come for us?"

"For me at least."

"Sam, what are you going to do now? You've got to run. It's the only way out."

He looked at the dark sky. "There's no use trying that. If she could find me here, she could find me anywhere. Besides, I'm tired of running."

"You can't fight her."

"I've got to try—come on." He took her arm and headed for the square. The crowd, pouring toward them, was thick at first but thinned by the time they saw the stage.

"There's Mylan." Trina pointed to a lonely figure sitting all alone.

"Yes, but where's Reardon? He ought to be here, too."

"Maybe Mylan knows."

They hurried toward the magician, who failed to lift his head at the sound of their approach. He sat with his head supported in his hands; his back was bent and crooked.

"We've just heard what happened," Trina said, crouching beside Mylan. "You're not hurt, are you? Where's Reardon?"

Mylan looked up. His eyes were hazy, uncertain. "Is it really her—really Nerdya?"

Sam nodded. "I should have told you. She's hunting for me. It's me she's really after." He saw no reason to conceal the truth from anyone. It was too late for subterfuge.

"Looking for you, Sam?" Mylan spoke distantly. He seemed dazed.

"Sam took something from her," Trina said.

"He did, did he?"

"A map," Sam said softly. "Part of a map."

"Only part?"

"My father has the other half. It's a map showing the way to the Lair of the Free Men."

Mylan nodded and rose to his feet. Reaching out with both hands, he clutched Sam's shoulders. He started to speak but then seemed to think better of it. Dropping his hands, he turned his back. "We'd better return to the boat," he murmured "Urban's alone and he may be worried."

"But what about Reardon?" Trina said, as they walked toward the river. "Did he go back to the boat ahead of us?"

Mylan shook his head. His eyes were even sadder than before. "I tried to stop him—I really did—but it was no use. As soon as the ship appeared, he broke away and ran toward the river. Unless he drowned, I imagine he's there with her right now."

XII

Aboard the riverboat, Urban and Cazie waited in the shell of the pilot's compartment like soldiers anticipating a final enemy assault. When the others arrived, Urban described how he had observed the black ship approaching from upriver and recognized it at once. "I've tried to keep a close eye on the ship, but it's really too dark to see anything clearly. She's there, though. I can almost feel her near."

Forgiving Sam, Cazie slipped around his neck. He then told Urban the probable reason for Nerdya's presence here.

"I've heard of this place, this Lair of the Free Men," Urban said. "But where is Reardon? Why is he not with you?"

Sam explained about that, too.

"I'm afraid I can offer no additional hope," Urban said. "About an hour ago, I heard a splashing sound in the water that might have been him swimming past. When I first heard it, I admit I thought it might be Nerdya instead and failed to investigate closer."

The idea that Nerdya might attempt to board the riverboat was not a pleasant one for any of them to consider. Sam suggested that she might already have come. Mylan decided on a room-by-room search. Finding nothing, they finished in Mylan's study and decided to wait out the night there. To Sam, the room had assumed a new, almost morbid atmosphere. The old books were no longer symbols of a vanished en-

lightenment; they were bunches of decaying paper—
nothing more.

Mylan sat behind his desk and buried his head wearily in his arms. In spite of himself, Sam felt angry.
Why doesn't he bring out some of that great magic of
his? he thought. Why doesn't he make Nerdya vanish
and save us all?

Despite the way he felt, Sam waited with the others
for Mylan to speak first. No matter what, he remained
their leader; the boat that housed them was his, if
nothing else. "I wish I could tell you it wasn't hopeless," he said slowly, "but I think she's just toying
with us or else she'd be here now. We're all aware of
her strength, all except Trina. She could enter this
room at will and none of us could lift a hand to stop
her."

"There has to be something we can do," Trina said.
"Ram her—sink her ship—anything."

"Her ship is constructed from steel and mine only of
wood. We'd sink, not her."

Sam could not dispute Mylan's pessimism. Of them
all, Sam undoubtedly knew Nerdya best. Especially at
night, her powers were limitless; she moved with the
wind. Alone, he might have sided more with Trina; he
might have been eager to fight back. But he wasn't
alone. Mylan, Urban, and even Reardon had to be
considered. Above everything, there was Trina. He
had lost Ellen O'Denver to the fangs of the vampire.
Could he bear to lose in the same terrible fashion another whom he loved?

"Then what about you?" Trina cried, pointing at
Mylan. "You keep telling us what a great magician
you are. Why don't you save us? Is it because you're a
fake? Is it because all your magic is nothing but
tricks?"

"No." Mylan sat up straight, shaking his head vigor-
ously. "Say what you want but don't say that. I wish I
could help. With all my strength, I would pray for
nothing more. I was a great magician once. I could tap

the force that resides within the Earth as easily as I now speak to you. How do you think this fabulous boat came to be built? It was magic—my magic—that's what made it what it is."

"Sure, but that was long ago," Trina said. "What have you done lately?"

Mylan stared at her as if stunned by her question. He lowered his head and nodded slowly. "No, you're right. It's all gone. I met a force more powerful than I and lost my strength in the struggle for supremacy. That was my fault, too. Before, I had squandered the magic—used it for trivial ends. I deserved my failure."

"But haven't you ever tried since then, made an attempt to recapture what you'd lost?"

"Oh, yes. Many times. The magic's there. Sometimes I can feel it near me like electricity in the air. It's not mine to tap. I'm an old man, a ruined shell of what I once was."

Trina shook her head sadly. None of them had any interest in attacking the old man further. Sam had decided what he had to do. He stroked Cazie's belly, still wet from her swim. "Maybe I should let Nerdya have the map. If she got that, she might go away and let us alone."

"No, you can't do that." This time it wasn't Trina; oddly enough, it was Urban. The Rangel shook his big head violently. "You cannot allow a monster such as Nerdya to have access to the Lair of the Free Men. To do so would be to destroy it utterly."

"Do you know what it is?" Sam asked.

"Not exactly, no, but I do know that it is important, a place beyond the will of either human or Rangel. We must not let Nerdya go there."

"That's easier said than done. Eventually, she's going to come here and take the map. Mylan can't protect us. Can you?"

"No," Urban said sadly, "I cannot."

"But you can, Sam." It was Mylan. He sat rigidly in

his chair. "You're the only one of us who can fight her on a more or less equal basis."

"Me? Why me? I'm just a fat vagrant who stole a map. I was lucky once. I'm not strong."

"But you are her son," Mylan said.

While Urban stared in amazement, Sam tried to laugh. "That's a good joke, Mylan. What gave you that kind of crazy idea?"

"Nerdya herself. I knew her long ago, remember, and she had a child. I think you're that child, Sam. No one else could ever get close enough to Nerdya to steal something as precious as that map."

Sam turned to Trina, seeking help, but he saw in her eyes that only the truth would serve. "I don't know how to kill her. If I did, I'd have done it years ago, when I stole the map. The goblins guard her all day. At night, it's even more impossible."

Urban clearly had been thinking. "What if there was a way of getting around the goblins?" he asked hesitantly. "Do you think it would be worth going after her then?"

Sam had never seriously considered the possibility of attacking Nerdya directly. "You can't go around them. They sit in the room with her coffin."

"No, they don't. You forget that I was there. The goblins stand outside the door, never within the room."

Sam shrugged. "I don't see the difference. You'd still have to go past them, and they're just as unkillable as Nerdya herself."

"Not if they never see us."

"What are you talking about? Do you expect us to grow wings and fly?"

"Not fly, no, crawl. We Rangels are restless creatures. Unlike you, we do not sleep several hours out of every day. During the period I lived aboard the black ship, I had much free time on my hands. During the day, I would walk the length of the deck and then turn back again. One morning I noticed something—a pattern in the deck—the outline of a trapdoor. Curious, I decided to see where it might lead. My strength was weak from my nights with Nerdya and the door was nearly rusted shut, but somehow I managed to pry it open and slip through. There was a ladder on the other side, which led down to a narrow horizontal tunnel. Still curious, I decided to follow the tunnel. It was a tight squeeze, though undoubtedly less difficult for a normal human being. At the end of the tunnel, I found another door. I opened this, too. Beyond was a terrible, foul-smelling chamber filled with dust and filth. It was Nerdya's bedroom, where I had lain with her each night. For the first time, I was seeing it with clear eyes. There was a black oblong box. Her coffin. My fingers froze with fear, but with a burst of strength, I hurled aside the lid. I saw her lying there. She was awake, watching me, but unable to move. My heart burned in my chest like fire. I thought I might die on the spot. Her lips streamed with the blood she had drunk from my own veins. I remember screaming. I made sounds no Rangel could ever make. I was sick. Stumbling back to the tunnel, I managed to crawl inside. Somehow I found the clarity of mind to close the door after me. Eventually, I reached the deck. I never stopped running. I jumped overboard and swam to shore. I ran and ran and ran. My own people refused to have me back. I could not blame them."

"And you think you could find that passage again?" Sam said.

"I'm sure of it."

"She saw you. She may have guessed how you came and sealed the tunnel."

"I believe it's a risk we must take."

"You could have killed her then."

"I know and deeply regret that I did not. But I loved her. Can you possibly understand that? Among my people, love comes but once in a lifetime—if then. In spite of all I knew and saw, I loved Nerdya."

"And now?" asked Mylan, his voice kind.

"Now, too."

"But you'll help kill her?" Sam said.

"Without hesitation. She is a dreadful, evil thing."

"Then tell me how to find this secret passage."

"No." Urban grinned broadly. Sam was amazed; he'd never known Rangels could smile like that. "I won't tell you, Sam—I'll show you."

"I don't think there's any need—"

"Necessity isn't a factor. I'm speaking of tactics. The more eyes, the more hands, the better. Even in the day, Nerdya is not without power. I related how my fingers froze when I tried to open her coffin. For you, Sam, as her own blood, the ordeal may be even more difficult."

"Well, I want to go, too," Trina said. "I'm not afraid of her, and I've got hands and eyes of my own."

Sam wanted to object but knew both she and Urban were right. Going alone would be stupid. If he merely wanted to take his own life, it would be kindest to do it now and avoid the need for a trip to the black ship.

Mylan said, "I'll go, too."

Sam turned to him in surprise. This was something he had not anticipated. "Are you sure? Three of us should be enough."

"No." Mylan's eyes were firm and unwavering. "I think I may be able to help."

"How?" asked Trina, bluntly.

"I imagine I'll find a way."

"Then it's decided," Urban said. "Come dawn, the four of us will embark for the black ship. We can use one of the small rowboats below."

"And we'll need certain other articles," Mylan said, his words ripe with meaning. "I'll see that they're brought."

"What other things?" said Trina.

"A hammer and a stake. In order to kill a vampire, one must drive a wooden stake through the creature's heart."

"Oh," said Trina, suddenly pale.

Mylan glanced at the window and the dark night beyond. "I fear this night may be a very long one for all of us. If Nerdya fails to come before dawn, then it will be our good fortune."

Sam went out on deck. A narrow walkway led around the circumference of the boat and he decided to follow it. The night had grown even colder. Cazie snuggled at his neck. His gaze swinging between the river and the sky, he paused on the opposite side of the deck, where the jagged smudge of the black ship showed dimly beneath the blazing illumination of the stars. From across the river, he heard a sound that made his blood run cold. What was it? A moan of agony? A cry of passion? A howl of pain? It was Reardon—he was sure of that. As long as he listened, the sound was not repeated.

He had heard a sound like that once before. He rarely recalled his early life, when as a young boy he had lived aboard the black ship, but he did remember a man who had once been his friend. Not at all like his mother's usual lovers, who died and were made into goblins within days of boarding the black ship when Nerdya grew bored with their tedious selves, this man was young, blond, handsome, well-spoken. Every day at dawn, he would stop at Sam's room, sometimes remaining the entire day, and the two of them would talk for long hours about every subject conceivable under the sun. From this man, his first true friend, Sam had learned of the geography of the planet, the history of humanity, the existence of the Rangels, the myth of the Lair of the Free Men. Still, every night, the man went to serve Nerdya and as the weeks passed, he grew pale, thin, and weak, until one night, as he wrestled with a terrible dream, Sam jerked wide awake at the sound of a horrible moaning howl that made his blood run cold. Stiff with fear, he sat rigid in his bed and listened intently. The sound never came again, but in the morning, for the first time, the man failed to appear at his usual time, and then Sam realized what it was he must have heard: the man was dead; Sam never saw him again.

Removing his gaze from the black ship and his thoughts from an even darker past, Sam looked down at the river below. Something peculiar was happening there, he realized; the water was swirling, bubbling. Grasping the hand rail, he leaned away from the deck and tried to see with more clarity. It was a toothfish. As Sam observed, the huge white thing rose to the surface, water spilling off its broad back in great roaring streams.

Sam held in his breath. He had never seen a toothfish this close before. Its bulk stood clear in the water and Sam believed, if he had wanted, he could have reached out and touched the white skin. He saw things he had never noticed before. The beast's hide, for instance, which he had always assumed to be as pure as the sky, revealed, everywhere he looked, literally thousands of tiny red creatures like fat worms clinging ferociously to the skin. These were parasites, Sam quickly comprehended, leeches whose sole purpose in life was to drink the blood of the great white fish.

The toothfish appeared to notice nothing. In absolute serenity, it floated beneath the star-flecked sky. Observed from this perspective, from above where the mouth did not show, the beast no longer seemed such an embodiment of malevolence. It was the parasites, the bloodsuckers, who disgusted Sam. The toothfish was a great planet; the parasites were the insignificant entities who dwelled upon the surface.

And they were dying. Sam watched closely, understanding the beast's motive for remaining on the surface. Exposed to an alien environment and unable to breathe, the parasites died by the hundreds, sliding mutely into the waiting water. Sam laughed aloud at the benign indifference of the great murderous fish. It knows the cosmos, he thought; it grasps the riddle of death and life. He saw the big round eye of the beast watching him and waved, suddenly delirious with joy.

When its flesh was clean, the toothfish submerged. Sam peered down into the water as the white shape receded toward nothingness. A whirlpool formed in its wake. Around and around, the parasites floated. Then they, too, were sucked below.

"What was that noise?"

Sam turned. Trina stood behind him. "A toothfish. One just surfaced right here."

She peered past him at the now smooth surface of the river. "The water isn't deep enough, is it?"

"I know but I saw it. There were thousands of water leeches all over its body and it killed them all. It was a fantastic sight to see."

Trina was watching the black ship. "What do you think? Will she come tonight?"

Suddenly, he was sure. "No. She's playing with us. She won't come until tomorrow."

"Then that gives us time—time to strike first."

"It should."

"You don't sound happy. Mylan said the same thing. I was just talking to him, before I came here. Sam, who do you think he is?"

"He's just . . . Mylan, I guess. Why? Is there any reason he should be somebody else?"

"No, I suppose not. It's just—well, doesn't it seem odd to you? He seems to know everything about her."

"He admitted he knew her."

"I know, but . . ." Her head jerked. "Look. Do you see that? It wasn't there before, was it?"

Sam looked across the water at where she was pointing. A square of yellow light shone aboard the black ship. A lantern, he guessed—a light in a window.

"I wonder what it means," she said. "Do you think it could be Reardon?"

Sam shivered. It was such a cold dark night. He took hold of Trina's hand. "Let's go below."

She looked at him oddly. "Why? You can't be tired can you?"

He nodded slowly. "I think I really am."

She smiled thinly. "Believe it or not, me too."

"We can sleep together," he said impulsively.

"Is that what you want?"

"Sure."

She gazed across the water for the last time. "Then let's go."

XIII

GOBLINS

As Sam thrust the oars deep into the river, struggling mightily against the raw strength of the current, he could see the dark hulk of Nerdya's ship looming ahead. The sun stood low in the western sky. Were they any closer now than a minute ago? Had something gone wrong? Had they somehow managed to get turned in the wrong direction? The oars raised blisters on his palms. He couldn't seem to row quickly enough.

"Sam, take it easy," said Mylan, from his place in the stern of the small rowboat. "We've got time. Be patient. We don't want you exhausted before we even reach the ship."

Sam knew Mylan was right, but he still couldn't control his feverish pace. He had to believe that it was not impossible: there was still time—they could kill Nerdya. His arms strained against the weight of the oars. His back groaned with agony. He glanced at the sun. It hung close to the horizon—too close. He tried to increase the rapidity of his strokes.

He remembered waking up. It was Urban who had roused him from Nerdya's spell, which had put them all asleep. Being a Rangel, Urban had avoided complete contamination and wakened quickly. Still, by the time he succeeded in stirring Sam, Trina, and Mylan from their slumbers, the sun was well along in its course of final descent. Of them all, only Mylan refused to give up hope.

He laughed when Urban explained what must have

occurred. "So she wants to be clever, does she? Well, I wouldn't worry. She's tried her damnedest and failed. Thanks to Urban, we're wide awake. The sun is shining. Let's get below. I think it's time to show her what she's up against." Mylan had grabbed hold of a small black bag and led the way to the bottom deck.

Now the rowboat banged against the hull of the black ship.

Sam jumped in surprise. He had not realized they were so near.

Mylan looked intently around. "We'll have to find some way of reaching the deck. Sam, maneuver us around toward the stern. We'll try to climb the anchor chain."

"Yes, Mylan." Sam rowed quietly. The sun, hidden by the bulk of the ship, could no longer be seen directly; its light shined everywhere.

When the boat slid close to the anchor, Sam let go of the oars and caught hold of the chain. Urban helped tie them securely.

"Well, who wants to go first?" Mylan said. "That looks like a hell of a climb. I'd hate to have anyone fall off now."

It was decided that Urban should ascend first. Mylan followed immediately, clutching his black bag and climbing with surprising ease. Trina kissed Sam before leaving. He waited until her feet passed the level of his forehead, then removed Cazie from around his neck and placed her on the floor of the boat. "I want you to wait until dark," he said. "If I'm not back by then, swim like you've never swam before." He patted her head, believing that Cazie understood. Then he climbed, too.

Reaching the deck, he stood for a moment, peering at his surroundings. Not unexpectedly, the black ship bore a powerful air of familiarity for him. He tried to shake the feeling off. The deck was clean and neat, with a number of wooden crates piled nearby. The ship rocked gently in the current. There was no one in sight. Sam watched the sun as it dipped hesitantly toward the horizon.

"Urban will lead us to the trapdoor," Mylan said.

"It's this way," Urban said, pointing toward the sun. "Not far, I hope."

They followed him, moving in a swift, silent line. Urban wisely kept to the edge of the deck where they were far less apt to chance upon a goblin emerging from the gloom below. Sam tried to calculate the amount of time they had remaining in which to reach Nerdya's lair. It was a fruitless exercise but helped pass the time. A cool breeze, harbinger of the night, wrinkled his hair. Twenty minutes, he guessed—at the most, thirty. He tried to picture Nerdya dead but the vision refused to develop. I just don't believe it, he thought; I don't believe she can really die.

"Look out!"

It was Trina who screamed the warning. Spinning on a heel, Sam brought up his arm just in time to ward off the initial blow. The force of the goblin's rush sent the pale, thin, almost transparent creature rocketing past him. Wheeling, Sam saw a half-dozen more goblins hurrying toward them. Sam put up his hands in self-defense. Two of the goblins went for Urban and two more for Trina. Sam jumped the remaining two. Swinging his fists, he hit both. It was like punching a bag of water. The flesh gave way in an instant; there was no force of impact.

The goblins must have seen them coming and lain in wait. Sam tried to believe this wasn't the end. How could you hurt something you couldn't even hit? Urban lay pinned to the deck. Two goblins held Trina tightly between them. Sam tried to go to her assistance. He took a step and an arm went around his throat. The touch was ghastly cold. He struggled, gagging. The arm around his neck was like a steel chain.

What had happened to Mylan? As he struggled to break free, Sam searched for the missing magician. Finally, through hazy eyes, he spotted him. Mylan had somehow evaded the notice of the goblins. He squatted on the deck, partially concealed by the bulk of a wooden crate. He looked funny. His eyes were shut, his head thrown back, his face creased with tension. He acted as if he were in some kind of trance. His fingers clawed at the air.

The remaining two goblins grabbed hold of Sam's dangling arms. He was thoroughly caught now. Desperately, he tried to talk to them. He admitted why he had come to the ship and begged their assistance. "She killed you. Don't any of you know that? As long as she's alive, you'll never be free." It was useless. If the goblins heard—or cared—they made no sign.

But then it happened. The goblin with his arm around Sam's neck cried out first. It was an inhuman sound. Releasing its grip, the goblin slid to the deck. It lay there, kicking, rolling, shouting, squirming like a man on fire.

Then the two holding his arms did the same. Farther away, two more goblins dropped to the deck, screaming. Free, Trina rushed to Sam and threw her arms around his waist. He hugged her. Urban was also loose. On the deck, all seven goblins lay squirming in agony.

Mylan moved toward them. His step was halting and his hands trembled. "Hurry," he said, gasping. "We haven't much time. We . . ." He started to fall.

Sam caught and held him. Mylan was like a dead weight in his arms.

Slowly, the old magician righted himself. He stood on his feet and shook himself violently. "Don't worry about me. I'll be all right. Let's go."

"But what about them?" Sam said, pointing to the goblins. "Shouldn't we . . . ?"

"They're not hurt. They'll live—if you can call it that."

"But did you . . . ?"

Mylan grinned weakly. "I told you I was a magician, didn't I? Well, that was it. I found it again, Sam.

I took it from the Earth and made it do my bidding."

Urban led them away. The trapdoor was only a few yards farther beyond the point of the ambush. Urban knelt down where the outline of the door showed clearly on the deck. Using both hands, he tried to get a grip. Sam held his breath as the hinges creaked. What if the door wouldn't open? He looked at the sun. It was either go now or die. There was no time to return to the riverboat before dark.

Unexpectedly, the trapdoor heaved open. Sam stifled an urge to cry out in triumph. Urban dropped his long legs through the opening. Sam remembered that there was a ladder, then a tunnel. "Keep in direct contact with the person in front of you," Urban said. "Once inside, we won't be able to see a thing. Sam, you come last and close the door tight."

Sam kept glancing around. If more goblins came and found them now, it might be worse than anything; they would be caught in their own trap. As first Urban, then Mylan, then Trina disappeared beneath, Sam kept his ears cocked. He could still hear the goblins moaning behind. Then it was his turn. Using a bare foot, he felt for the first rung. When he found it, he went through. Reaching up, he gripped the heavy door and drew it down from above. The door clanged firmly shut. It was dark. Sam edged down the ladder. At the bottom, he felt solid floor under his feet. Crouching down, he moved his hands through the air. He touched something soft. Trina. She laughed. "Sam, not there."

"Now listen," said Urban. He was whispering. "I'm inside the mouth of the tunnel, so just follow me. Place a hand on the individual preceding you and keep it there at all times. Say nothing unless it's absolutely necessary. Whether she can hear us, I cannot say, but the risk is there."

Sam put his hand on Trina's spine. When she moved, he moved, too. The tunnel ran in a straight line, sloping gently downward, without curves or bends or sharp changes in direction. The height of the shaft gradually lessened until, after a time, Sam dropped to his stomach and moved by squirming forward like a snake. He kept a hand on Trina's trailing foot. The slick tunnel floor provided little firm traction. Progress was slow and painstaking. A great deal of time seemed to pass. It was difficult to conceive, surrounded by such darkness, that the sun still shined outside. What if the day had actually ended? What if, when they reached Nerdya's chamber, she was awake and waiting for them, with blood-stained, smiling lips?

"Hold on a minute." It was Urban at the head of the line; he whispered. "I think we've got a problem. I can't remember—maybe I just didn't notice it before."

Sam had stopped with the others. "What is it?" he asked, in a heavy whisper.

"The passage seems to divide. I can feel the break with my hands."

"Then which way do we go?"

"That's the problem. I don't remember this at all." A rising note of panic entered his voice.

Mylan spoke soothingly. "Then there's no problem. We'll simply have to divide our forces. Urban and I will take the left fork. Sam, you and Trina swerve right."

"What if we find her and you don't?" Trina said.

"Do what you can. As soon as it's obvious, Urban and I will turn back. Remember, there's time, plenty of time."

Sam could hardly believe that. Still, no other course of action made sense. If he and Trina found Nerdya first, he might be able to delay her. He didn't think she'd kill him right away. She'd want to find out about the map first. If only he could hold his tongue. For a time.

The right-hand passage that he and Trina followed seemed wrong from the beginning. There were too many twists and turns, curves and corners, things that failed to match Urban's description. Still, Urban hadn't remembered the fork in the tunnel, either; there was still a chance this was the right path.

The tunnel ended with a blank wall. Trina spoke over her shoulder, telling Sam what she could feel.

"You're sure there's no opening? It might be the door Urban talked about."

"I'm feeling with my fingernails, but it seems solid. It could be a blind end, Sam. Maybe we ought to turn back."

"Try to force it."

"All right." He heard her grunt.

"Anything?"

"I'm not sure. It may have moved."

"Then let me try." Sam tried to slide beside her, but there wasn't room enough, so he moved on top of her, balancing with his hands. It was an awkward position, but he managed to touch the blank wall. Trina was right: It seemed solid. Sam pushed hard with both hands, resting his weight on Trina. At first the wall didn't budge. Sam strained and all at once the wall fell inward. A bright light blinded his eyes. He clawed at his face, struggling to see.

Trina, trapped beneath him, screamed.

Sam still couldn't see a damn thing. He assumed it had to be Nerdya and figured he was doomed. When his vision finally cleared, he realized it couldn't be her room; he knew this place. It was where he had grown up. He couldn't say why he recognized the room, for it was not distinctive. Still, he was positive.

A small wooden bed occupied one corner. The figure of a man lay sprawled upon it, his arms flung out. Sam squinted to be sure. Now he understood what had made Trina scream.

The man was Reardon.

"He's dead, isn't he?" Trina said.

"Let's see." Sam dropped into the room. Turning, he assisted Trina through the square hole. Reardon's eyes were open and staring. Sam waved a hand in front of them. Twin wounds on each side of his throat dripped blood. His skin was as white as a cloud. Sam picked up Reardon's wrist and felt for a pulse.

Reardon's head jerked spasmodically. "Sam?" he said, through pale swollen lips.

"You are alive."

"Am I?" He chuckled deep in his chest. "Prove it."

Sam let go of Reardon's wrist and knelt down to be close to his lips. "We'll get you out of here. Don't worry. She'll never get you again."

Reardon moved his head back and forth on the blood-splattered mattress. "I'm going to die. Don't you understand? This is the way I wanted it."

"You let her kill you," Trina said, from behind Sam's shoulder, her voice choked with disgust.

"She can be very kind. I didn't stop her."

"We will," Sam said. "That's what we're doing here. We've come to kill her."

"I knew you would. That's why I let it happen. All night I kept her busy. She drank and drank and drank. She wanted to go to you, but I wouldn't let her."

"Then you saved us, Reardon."

"It was the least I could do." He smiled, searching for Sam's hand, pressing it gently. "Now go to her. Let me alone and let me die. We're all driven by our own particular circumstances, Sam. My life's been too god-damned long as it is. Do you understand me?"

Sam nodded. "Sure."

"Then forgive her, too."

"Nerdya?"

"Yes. She's lived even longer than I have." Reardon winked. As he did, his shoulders shook. He gasped for air. Sam reached out to comfort him, but Reardon knocked his hands away. He gurgled and a small quantity of blood came out of his mouth. His chest stopped heaving. He was limp.

Sam stood up. "He's dead now."

"Look at him," said Trina. "Look at his face. He almost seems . . . happy."

"At the end," Sam said, "I think he was—he was glad."

Sam looked at the door. He couldn't let the shock of Reardon's death slow them down.

Trina was looking that way, too. "What do we do now?"

"Find her room. We can't go back through the tunnel. It'll take too long. She's got to be around here somewhere."

She looked at Reardon, wiping her eyes with the back of a hand. "Give me one minute."

Sam waited. He needed the time, too. "Better now?" he asked.

She shook her head. "We'd better get out of here."

Sam heard a scream. It reminded him of the cries the goblins had made up on deck when Mylan turned his magic on them; this scream was very close.

"What was that?" said Trina.

"Let's see."

Sam threw open the door. Directly in front of him, a goblin lay squirming in agony on the floor. Across the corridor, a door stood open. Through the gap, Sam saw Mylan and Urban. Mylan stood just inside the doorway, his face twisted, head thrown back, eyes shut. More magic, Sam guessed.

Deeper inside the room, Urban knelt beside a black wooden oblong box.

Nerdya's coffin!

The realization hit Sam like a fist. This was her room—they had found it.

Sam vaulted across the goblin on the floor and dashed into the room. He heard Trina following him. "Close the door," he called to her. "Shut it and lock it if you can. We don't want them—"

He looked at Urban. The Rangel was like a statue rooted to the floor. His hands were raised in front of him, as if in prayer. In one hand he clutched the hammer and in the other he gripped the stake.

But he wasn't moving.

Sam made himself approach. All the time, he was conscious of the coffin's proximity—the box and what it must contain. He grabbed Urban and shook him. "Are you all right? Can you hear me?"

He heard a noise, a hiss, like a snake. Involuntarily, his eyes moved to the coffin. He looked inside. She was there, all right. All at once, the years since they had parted vanished into nothingness. Nerdya had not changed. He saw her lean face, cheeks pink and flushed, black hair like a raven crown around her skull. She wore a pure white gown that reached to her ankles. Through the transparent fabric, Sam could see her heavy brown breasts and the dark triangle of her pubis.

Her eyes, black and hollow, caught and held his gaze.

Sam fought to turn away. He groped blindly for Urban and somehow managed to grip the hammer and stake. He held them, raised them, but could not strike.

He felt her laughter. "Sam," she said soundlessly. "Sam, you have returned."

He knew he couldn't speak, couldn't fall victim to her spell. With a tremendous expenditure of strength, he raised the wooden stake above the coffin's edge.

"The map, Sam. You have it. Give back what you stole."

His tongue trembled, wanting to answer, wanting to obey. He bit down hard and tasted his own blood. He couldn't kill her. The wooden stake in his hand was like a dead weight. For a brief instant, he managed to break free of her eyes. He looked at the room. Urban remained frozen to the floor. Trina stood just inside the door, unmoving. Mylan, kneeling, held his head in his hands; that last act of magic seemed to have drained him.

"Sam, look at me!"

Her voice in his mind cracked like a whip. His head jerked back. She was old—so terribly old. Her eyes reflected the maelstrom of the past, a tunnel whirling back through centuries toward ultimate oblivion.

She moved in her coffin.

As she did, Sam realized that the end had come. Outside, unseen, night had fallen at last. Her lips parted in a smile of triumph; she rose in the air. A torrent of blue-black blood jetted from her mouth in a stream, soaking her gown like rich paint. Reardon's blood—poor dead Reardon—his friend. Sam screamed in silence. He held out his arms to her, offering the hammer and stake. She laughed, bleeding more. It was over: done. Nerdya floated serenely toward him, dream creature, her gown billowing like a cloud.

A hard hand struck Sam on the shoulder and knocked him to the floor. Free from Nerdya's eyes, Sam fought to clear his mind. The hammer and stake were wrenched from his grasp. He heard the sound of a terrible struggle. Someone screamed. A familiar voice. She was screaming in terror.

It was Nerdya!

Sam reached his knees. Uncovering his eyes, he stared at what they revealed. Looming above him, Mylan and Nerdya struggled, locked in combat, each with a hand on the other's throat. Mylan held the hammer and stake in one hand and slowly forced Nerdya back toward her coffin. How could he do it? Was it magic? Some vast untapped reserve of strength? Screaming, Nerdya clawed at his back, ripping his shirt, savaging the flesh underneath with her nails. Her gown flapped in the air like the beating of giant wings. Mylan gasped, setting his feet. With one hand, he hurled Nerdya into the coffin and held her pinned there.

Carefully, he shifted the hammer and stake so that he could use them.

"You!" cried Nerdya, laughing. "I should have known—I should have looked."

Mylan pressed the stake against her heart.

"You'll kill me? Don't you know? You were the one—the only one I ever loved."

He raised the hammer.

"I love you!" she shrieked.

The hammer fell.

"*Yes, yes, yes!*"

From out of the coffin, a geyser of blood spurted a yard in the air.

There was a groan of agony.

Sam stumbled to his feet, raced to the coffin, grabbed the edge, and peered inside.

Nerdya lay, bathed in blood, the stake protruding from her chest.

She belched, emitting a cloud of gas. The odor forced him back.

She was dead. He was sure. Truly and finally dead.

Sam tripped over something. He looked down. Mylan lay on the floor, the hammer still locked in his hand.

Urban and Trina ran over. "She's dead," Urban said. "You killed her, Mylan."

Something was very wrong with the old magician. "Sam," he said. "Sam, are you here?"

Sam knelt right beside him. "I'm here, Mylan."

"Come close—bend down."

Sam put his ear close to Mylan's lips.

"In my study," Mylan said. "Go there and look. An old book with a green cover and gold lettering. Turn to page one hundred. Can you remember that?"

"I'll remember. What is it?"

"Something you've been seeking."

"But I—"

"I couldn't give it to you before because of her. As long as she lived, you had no chance. Now it's different. I knew you were strong enough as soon as I finally recognized you. I knew you had learned enough. Now . . . go."

"But, Mylan, who are—?"

"Good-bye, Sam."

"Good—" Sam raised his fist and put it close to his mouth. He turned his head.

"I think he's dead," Urban said.

"He is." Sam stood slowly.

Trina had the door open. "The goblin's gone," she told them. "Maybe we can go."

Sam nodded. "They should all be gone. When she died, they were released."

"Doesn't it feel different now?" She took a deep breath. "Even the air tastes pure."

He nodded.

"Look here." It was Urban, standing beside the coffin.

Sam went and looked inside. All that remained of Nerdya was a pile of white dust.

Then Trina cried out. Sam turned.

Mylan had changed, too. The lines in his face were gone; his hair was blond.

Sam suddenly realized that he had seen this face before. Long ago. On the black ship.

The dead man on the floor—Mylan—was the same man who had visited him in his room so long ago.

As soon as they reached the riverboat, Sam hurried to Mylan's study and found the book with the green cover and gold lettering. He turned to page one hundred, shook the book, and a folded sheet of paper dropped out.

Sam smoothed the paper open on the desk.

At first glance, he knew what it was. There was no need to compare this portion of the map with the one he had stolen from Nerdya.

Sam realized that both his mother and his father had died on the same day.

Trina laid a hand on his shoulder. "We'll go there right away, Sam. We'll find the Lair of the Free Men and discover the secret behind all the riddles. We'll take the riverboat. I think Mylan meant it that way."

"You knew, didn't you?" he said, turning.

She shook her head. "I guessed. Especially last night. When Mylan knew who you were. Who else could have?"

Sam nodded. "Here, let me show you something."

"What?"

"The other half of the map—my half. I guess it's safe to show you where I hid it."

"I've always wondered."

Sam reached to his throat. Removing Cazie, he turned her over so that her soft underbelly showed. He pointed to a broad rectangle of color just below her jaw. "Remember how I told you I got that tattoo. Well, Cazie got one at the same time."

"The map," she said.

"Could you think of a safer place? Cazie really does bite the people I don't like," he said, trying to smile. But it wouldn't come. He could still see Mylan—both faces—the withered old man and the strong young one. Sam's eyes filled with tears. He hadn't wept in years and years. Now he did—for the father he had known, after all.

XIV

LAIR OF THE FREE MEN

Even with a complete map, more than three years passed before Sam, Trina, Urban, and Cazie reached the Lair of the Free Men.

In the course of their journey, many strange, terrible, joyous, and wondrous events occurred.

For nearly a full year, Mylan's magical riverboat served them well. It was wrecked on the high rocks that guarded the entrance to an underground channel.

Sam constructed a large raft from wood salvaged from the accident. They piled their few belongings on this new raft and continued their journey.

Trina slipped and fell off the raft into a swift river current. She nearly drowned before Sam managed to pull her back on board. Using a special Rangel technique, Urban forced clean air into her lungs so that she could breathe again.

The complete map gave them a definite course to follow: they went south along the Long River, turned east on a small tributary, passed through a deep underground channel, and reached the surface at a second broad river.

A Rangel airship intercepted them a few miles along the Second River. When Urban explained where they were going, the Rangels went away without further comment.

The shores of the Second River contained no towns. Most of the inhabitants of the area lived in primitive tribal villages. Trina said these people were more like animals than the men she had known in the past.

A marauding band of tribesmen armed with spears and axes captured Trina and held her prisoner. With considerable daring, Sam and Urban effected her rescue.

Another time, a group of men wearing the fur of wolves attacked Urban. Sam and Trina saved him.

During the fourth month of the second year, Trina delivered her first child. It was a boy, who died five months later from a contamination that not even Urban could cure.

Antelope, bison, and wild cattle roamed the banks of the Second River in great herds. Hunting was easy and good.

The river carried the raft through a high plateau, where white snow twice fell upon them. Sam lay flat on his back and let the cool flakes strike him gently on his upturned face. He opened his lips and swallowed some of the snow. Melting on his tongue, the flakes tasted pure and sweet.

Many other strange, terrible, joyous, and wondrous events occurred during their three-year journey; most were forgotten by the end of the voyage.

The river carried them between high mountains and down into a wide valley. Several months had passed since they had last set eyes on another human being, although the herds of wild game remained plentiful. Sam studied the map diligently. He lifted Cazie in his hands and peered at the spot just beneath her jaw. Nodding to himself, Sam drove the raft toward shore. "This is it, all right," he told Trina and Urban. "This is the Lair of the Free Men."

The valley was a pleasant place. They beached the raft and began to explore. The sun shined brightly on their heads, and the air was nectar sweet. The only other living creatures they saw were a few harmless furry animals who resembled plump, tailless rats. Although all of them were hungry, not even Sam felt in the mood for killing anything. Instead, they ate raw fruit off short bushy trees. The fruit had a sour taste but was very filling. Sam ate three fist-sized berries and wasn't hungry again for hours.

On the fourth day after entering the valley, they came upon a broad lake. Sam considered whittling a fishing pole, but Trina said she'd eaten quite enough fish to last a lifetime. Urban pointed out something Sam had missed: in a clear space near a curve in the lake stood several small grass huts.

"People?" said Sam. It seemed surprising because, since reaching the valley, Sam had experienced a sense of overwhelming aloneness.

They went to investigate. Sam wasn't frightened—fear was an impossible emotion in this peaceful valley—but his belly felt as tight as a stretched drum. Now what's wrong? he wondered.

As they approached the nearest of the huts, a squat figure appeared in the doorway. At first Sam thought the man must be a dwarf wearing furs. As Sam drew closer, he realized that the creature wasn't a man at all.

Nor was it a Rangel—or anything else Sam had ever seen.

The three of them faced the strange creature. It made a sudden barking sound deep in its throat.

"I think I know what it is," Urban said. "I saw one once before. A supervisor of mine kept a pet."

"A pet?" said Sam. "But it's . . ." He had been going to say human, but that was obviously not correct.

"It's a dog," Urban said.

"But I thought dogs were an extinct species," Trina said.

"Not completely," Urban said. "And not here."

Two more of the dogs appeared from within the hut. One was female and the other a child, female also.

Urban walked down among them. "Mutants," he said, after a brief inspection. "They've lost their tails and facial fur. And look at their teeth—the canines have vanished. They're herbivorous, I think."

"I thought dogs walked on four legs," Sam said.

"They did; these don't. That's easily enough overcome, given sufficient time. Your ancestors did it—and
so did mine. Why not theirs, too?"

"How much time?"

"Who knows how long these creatures have thrived
in this valley? Since we Rangels came—perhaps before."

"Then you know about them?"

"Not me, but somebody does—I told you that."

Sam felt that he understood. The Rangels knew
about the dogs but never came here. This was the Lair
of the Free Men because the creatures who dwelled
here were not really men.

"It would be easier if we could talk with them," he
said.

"I'm sure they have a language," Urban said. "We
could probably learn it—or teach them ours. You don't
build houses as complex as these until you possess a
sufficiently abstract language system."

"Birds build nests," Trina said.

"These are more than nests."

As if to confirm Urban's opinion, the male dog uttered a series of sounds, his voice gruff and guttural.
Listening closely, Sam thought he could actually make
out distinct word units.

The other huts were emptying now. The dogs gathered curiously around their visitors.

Sam turned to Urban. "They're our replacements,
aren't they? I think I've got it figured out now. When
we're all dead, when the human race is finally gone,
these creatures will inherit the earth."

"If they're ready. Does that bother you?"

Sam shook his head. He really wasn't sure how he
felt. "I don't . . . I think I'd better be alone." He
turned to move off.

"I'll go with you," said Trina.

The two of them walked away from the grass huts
and the dogs. They moved along the sandy shore of

the lake until Sam spotted a broad smooth rock. He sat on one side and Trina sat on the other. Sam stroked Cazie underneath her chin. The surface of the lake was like a sheer flat mirror.

"It was a mistake," Sam said. He glanced at Trina out of the corner of an eye, wondering if her reaction was different from his. "We should never have come."

"We don't belong," she said. "We're aliens—like the Rangels."

"It's because we aren't worthy. We're old and tired and spent. We're going to die—all of us."

"Then you think we should go."

He nodded. "We have to."

"It is a beautiful place—the most beautiful place I've ever seen. We gave up so much to get here. We worked so hard and so long. Poor Reardon. And Mylan. It's as if they died for no reason."

"Mylan must have known what was here. I wonder why he wanted us to come. We have no right to stay. This place belongs to them." He made a sweeping gesture at the huts still visible past a low rise. "Dogs, not men."

Urban approached them. He came alone. There was an unexpectedly grim expression on his face.

Sam told Urban what he and Trina had decided.

Urban frowned. "I think you're wrong, Sam. You should stay."

"But don't you see what this means? This isn't a place for human beings."

"Who are you to decide?" Urban acted genuinely upset. "What's the problem, Sam? Are you feeling sorry for yourself—you and your human race? Don't do that. You had your time and now it's nearly done. How can you ignore everything that's happened to us? You're a person, too, Sam—an individual."

"I don't understand what you mean."

"I'm talking about the same thing you are—about being worthy."

"We're not worthy," Trina said. "No ordinary person can be. That's what this place is all about."

"I doubt that," Urban said. "I think that's just what your self-pity wants it to be. You're not ordinary—neither one of you. If you were, do you think Mylan would have entrusted you with the map? Look at what we've been through since we left the river. If you two aren't worthy, neither am I, and I've already decided I'm going to stay."

"You are?" said Sam, with surprise.

"Yes." Urban nodded firmly. "A person is the direct result of his own life and experience. Your life, your experience, has been good—and worthy. You've achieved a dignity through effort that transcends that of your species. You've nothing to be ashamed of. You've proven yourselves a hundred, a thousand times over."

"I wish I could believe that," Sam said. His voice lacked conviction. Was it possible that, even as he denied it, he was already coming to believe?

"Come," said Urban. "Let's go back."

The three of them went down to the huts.

As they walked, Urban said, "As far as I'm concerned, it's only right—and fitting—that you both stay. These are dogs, remember. They used to be your domestic pets. If it wasn't for the human race, they'd have been extinct centuries ago."

"So?" said Trina.

"So who else is better equipped to teach them? Who else is better able to explain the mistakes of the past so that they won't be repeated through sheer ignorance? I think that's why Mylan wanted you to come here. He knew you could help—help get them ready for when their time comes."

"And protect them, too," Trina added musingly. "We know about the world out there; they don't. Look. Here comes one of them now."

Sam thought it might well be the same dog they had

first encountered. The dog shambled toward them and held out a hairless, five-fingered hand. Balanced in the palm of the hand was a fresh ripe red fruit.

"It's making a gift," Trina said.

"Or an offering," said Urban. "Take it—it's yours."

Trina nodded. Bowing and smiling, she accepted the fruit from the dog's hand. "Thank you very much," she said.

The dog uttered a single sharp barking sound. He, too, seemed to smile.

Urban turned to Sam. "I think he just told you he's glad you're here."

"Why should he be?"

"Because he remembers. He knows what you and your race have done for his."

Sam let out a long sigh. "And you really think he wants us to stay?"

"Yes," Urban said.

Sam looked at the dog and then at himself. It was like seeing the same thing in a slightly distorted mirror. All right, he thought. I'm not ordinary—none of us is. I'm not unworthy.

Sam looked at Trina, and she looked at him. In her eyes, he saw a reflection of his own thoughts.

"We'll stay," he said softly.

AFTERWORD
by F. Paul Wilson

I have this flaw in my character: I invariably read the
Afterword before the story itself. Not a major flaw,
I'm sure you'll agree, but one that can backfire on you
when the Afterworder gives away some of the plot
twists. So, in deference to those readers afflicted with
a similar aberration, I'll do my best to guard against
such slip-ups.

Another thing I won't be doing in this Afterword is
telling you what a great and good friend Gordon Eklund is, or call him "Gordie," or prattle on about how
far back we go, or how many tankards of ale we've
hoisted at the countless science fiction conventions
we've attended together, or relate embarrassing personal anecdotes. We've never met, at least not in person. I've encountered him often, however, in the pages
of his novels and magazine fiction—we're old friends
in that milieu. Perhaps someday soon this East Coaster
will bump into that West Coaster at one of the many
sf cons around the country, or at a Nebula banquet,
and the man I've met in print will finally be realized
in the flesh.

Until then, I shall know him only by his work . . .
which brings us to the preceding piece of fiction. For
two men who have never met, never communicated directly, and who were not given a common theme for
their novellas, we appear to have come up with
strikingly similar works of fiction. *The Tery* and *The
Twilight River*: each has a post-holocaust setting in
which humans are divorced from pre-existing technol-

ogy; each has a misshapen outcast for a central character. Dreadful Sam and the Tery share a common bond
of circumstance in their lonely lives on the periphery of
a rigid, autocratic society, and in their desire to move
inward toward humanity.

But there the similarities end. As individuals they
could not be more different. Dreadful Sam has traveled and experienced more than most of the people in
his world; wiley and worldly, he knows how to live
within the spaces between human and Rangel law,
knows the value of subtlety and a low profile. Con-
versely, the Tery is an innocent, familiar only with a
small area of his forest and supremely capable there,
but knowing nothing of humans beyond the fact that
they've hurt him and tried to kill him; he stumbles
and blunders through relationships, assuming everyone to be as open and above board as he, learning the
hard way. The two protagonists view themselves and
existence from separate perspectives—note, for instance, their radically divergent responses to the notion of collective responsibility.

Personal observations: Numerous images passed
through my forebrain while reading *The Twilight
River*. The one with the brightest after-image is Nerdya's black ship. At its first mention early in the story,
I immediately flashed on a drawing I had seen in a
copy of *Unknown Worlds* from 1942 (before my time,
I assure you). Hannes Bok had done it for his own
novella, *The Sorceror's Ship*—a two-masted galley,
black against ruggedly detailed mountains interlaced
with white, stylized clouds. From that point onward,
Nerdya's ship became inextricably entwined with
Bok's drawing. I could not separate the two. No matter how Eklund described the former, I always saw the
latter. Still do.

And how about that suspenseful crawl through the
bowels of Nerdya's ship? The tension was palpable at
that point, proof that the author had managed to
make you care about his characters. I was reminded of

BINARY STAR #2   133

Jonathan Harker's exploration of his host's castle in the early chapters of *Dracula*.

The Twilight River is all Eklund, however. And although not your typical science fiction yarn (if such a thing still exists), it does utilize a certain classical sf motif. It's a trek, a quest, and its travelers come in all shapes and sizes. There's the paunchy, floppy-eared Dreadful Sam and the graceful Trina—a gnome and a wood nymph; there's a Karloffian alien, a near-senile wizard, and an existential werewolf. I defy anyone, even Clifford Simak, to come up with a motlier, more bizarre crew of pilgrims than that!

So much for the superficialities.

It has long been my contention that more serious writing exists in the guise of science fiction than dreamt of in the philosophy of *The New York Review of Books* and its ilk, wherein sf is reflexively dismissed as pulp writing, mere genre fiction of no literary value. Have you looked into some of the travesties being touted as major Literary Novels? More often than not they are hollow things, easily deflated; readers willing to see a naked emperor will find themselves in possession of a word-balloon patinaed with style.

Ironically, it is the ghettoized sf writer who is presented with the opportunity to tackle important themes. A significant percentage of modern science fiction contains solid writing, richly textured on a number of levels despite the cloak of derring-do. For the sf writer can play god—he can manipulate not only events, but the very physiology of his characters, their milieu, even history itself. And in so doing, he can approach the human condition on his own terms and lay it bare more deeply than in any other branch of fiction.

Consider the story you have just read. In *The Twilight River*, Eklund has presented us with a truly pessimistic vista. Humankind is on the wane. We've seen our day of glory, acted like fools and monsters, reached our peak. We've been knocked down, but we're not bouncing back. We now lie shattered into countless petty, servile, conformist factions, without hope, without a goal, without an identity as a race.

But bright spots burn within the gloom. There are renegades who still carry glimmers of the old human spirit and who cannot sit still and wait for everything to whimper to an end. And there is a Promised Land— the Lair of Free Men—that lures the renegades onward.

Promised Lands, unfortunately, are never what they're cracked up to be. When the remnants of the original band of wayfarers attain their goal, they find not milk and honey, but pathos and, perhaps, the ultimate irony. Even then they refuse to despair. They are no longer the people who started the journey. They have run the gauntlet of the human-alien hybrid culture along the river and have been redeemed. Not religiously, but as individuals. For it is as individuals that we ultimately exist and survive and achieve self-esteem. When all men are brothers in despair, there will always be some bastard who'll swear he's an only child and who'll pull himself out of the mire to go see what's on the other side of the hill. Or so I hope. And so, apparently, does the author of *The Twilight River*.

For those of you familiar with the bulk of Gordon Eklund's work, the solo pieces and the collaborations with Gregory Benford, *The Twilight River* probably held a few surprises. It treads the borderpath between science fiction and fantasy, keeping the reader in delicate disequilibrium by never fully entering either realm. Not an easy road for a writer to travel without losing his footing, but Gordon Eklund pulls it off admirably.

THE TERY

by F. PAUL WILSON

PROLOGUE

It had become a subvocal litany—
A whole planetful of Christians
Too good to be true
Bound to be disappointed
                            —running through his head in
a reverberating circuit until all other considerations
were blurred to indistinction. But the defeatism inher-
ent in the phrases could not dampen the anticipation
that grew tingling throughout his body as he approached the chapel.

The descendants of the original settlers of the
planet, now newly opened to trade, were divided into
two nations. The smaller island country—inhabited, it
was said, by "Talents," or something like that—wanted
nothing to do with the Fed and so were left quite
alone. The larger nation, however, welcomed the
chance to rejoin the mainstream of interstellar humanity, and it was in this segment of the population that
Gebi Pirella, S.J., was interested.

His mission was one of critical importance to the
Amalgamated Church of Unified Christendom because the inhabitants here had been described as fol-
lowers of a distinctly Christian-like religion, complete
with crucifixes and all. It had been mentioned by earlier trade envoys who had been permitted a brief glance
inside one of the chapels that the crucifixes were somehow *different*, but no specifics were mentioned.

No matter. News of the existence of a planet-wide
Christian enclave would prove to be incalculably im-

portant to the stagnating Unified Church—spreading its name and inevitably drawing converts from all over Occupied Space.

"The cross is just a symbol, of course," Mantha was saying as he pointed to the top of the chapel. He was a big, fairhaired man wearing only a loincloth in the heat. His grammar and speech pattern carried an archaic ring. "Not an object of worship. We revere the one who died upon it and hold to the lesson of brotherhood he taught us."

"Of course," Father Pirella replied with a concurring nod. Not only was that heartening to know, but it was the largest piece of religious information he had been able to pull from this taciturn native human who seemed to serve as some sort of ecclesiastical administrator to the locale.

The Jesuit had pushed their initial conversation toward a discussion of theological concepts but soon discovered that he and Mantha did not share the same vocabulary on religious matters. Beyond determining that the religious sect in question was less than two centuries old—unsettling, that, but surely not without a satisfactory explanation—his most basic questions had been met with an uncomprehending stare. The easiest and most logical solution was to suggest that they go to the nearest religious structure and start there with concrete articles. After establishing a little common ground, they could then progress to abstractions.

Mantha held the door open for him—hinges . . . the technological level here was startlingly depressed—and Father Pirella entered the cool dim interior.

There was no altar. Stark and alone, a huge, life-size crucifix dominated the far end of the chamber. He moved toward it eagerly. Merely to find the Christ figure here on this isolated world would be quite enough; but to demonstrate that it holds a central position in the culture would be more than anyone in

the order of the Church had ever dreamed. It would
be the consummation of—

"Mother of God!"

The words echoed rapidly, briefly in the dimness.
Father Pirella's feet began to slide on the polished
floor as he recoiled in horror at the sight of the figure
on the cross.

Crushing disappointment fanned his indignation.
"This is sacrilege!" he hissed through clenched teeth
framed in tight, bloodless lips. *"Blasphemy!"*

The priest for a moment looked as if he were about
to hurl himself at the astonished and totally confused
Mantha, then he shuddered and rushed out into the
bright, wholesome daylight . . .

"I did not know what you were looking for," Mantha said when he finally caught up to Father Pirella,
"but I knew you would not find it in there." He gently took the priest's arm and began to lead him down a
path through the trees. "Come. Come with me to
God's-Touch and you will perhaps understand things
better."

Father Pirella allowed himself to be led. God's-
Touch? What was that? Couldn't be any worse than
what he had just seen.

"Everything starts a long time ago," Mantha was
saying. "One hundred and sixty-seven of our years, to
be exact. It begins in a field not too far from
here . . ."

They hadn't left him for dead. They knew he was still alive, could see the shallow expansion and contraction of his blood-smeared rib cage as he lay on his face in the grass. But there were other stops to make and he took such a long time dying. A tery didn't merit a final stroke to end it all, so they left him to the scavengers.

Consciousness ebbed and flowed, and every time he opened his eyes it seemed that the world was filled with flies and gnats. He found he was unable to lift his arms to brush them away. The effort involved in attempting to do so dropped him into oblivion again.

The creak of a poorly lubricated wooden axle pulled him up. He heard stealthy footsteps through the ground against his left ear and allowed himself to hope. Summoning whatever reserve was left in his body, he pushed against the ground with his right arm and tried to roll over. The daylight suddenly dimmed and he knew he was losing consciousness, but he held on and managed to get a little leverage from his left arm, which had been pinned under him. He moved. A shift in his shoulder girdle and suddenly he was rolling onto his back amid a cloud of angry flies.

The effort cost him a period of awareness, and when he came to again, the creaking was gone. Despair crushed him. The furtiveness of the footsteps he had heard was proof enough that they belonged to another tery, for stealth simply was not the way of the human soldiers. Now they were gone and with them his last hope of rescue. He was dying and knew it. If the hot, drying sun and his festering wounds didn't kill him by nightfall, one of the large nocturnal predators would finish the task. He couldn't decide which he—

Footsteps again! The same ones, light and stealthy, but much closer now. The passer-by must have seen some movement in the tall grass as he rolled and come over to investigate, then stood at a cautious distance and watched. The tery lay still and hoped. He could do no more.

The footsteps stopped by his head and suddenly there was a face looking down at him—a human face. He lost all hope then. If he could have found his voice he would have screamed in anguish, frustration, and despair.

But the human neither ignored him nor further mistreated him. Instead, he squatted beside him and inspected the near countless lacerations that covered his body. His face grew dark with . . . could it be anger?—the tery was not adept at reading human expressions—and he muttered something unintelligible as his inspection progressed.

Shaking his head, the human rose to his feet and moved around to a position behind the tery's head. He bent down and hooked a hand under each of the tery's arms and tried to lift. It didn't work. The human lacked sufficient strength to move the considerable weight, and the slight change in position he accomplished served only to send searing jolts of pain throughout the wounded creature's body, eliciting a low, agonized moan.

The human loosened his grip and stood up, uncertain of his next step. After a short pause, he tore a strip of cloth from the coarse shirt he wore and laid it over the tery's eyes. Then he strolled away. The sound of his retreating footsteps was soon joined by the creak of the wooden axle. Both eventually faded beyond perception.

It was a small act of kindness, that strip of cloth,

and totally incomprehensible to the tery. Why a human should want to keep the flies off his eyes while
the rest of him died was beyond him, but the comfort
it afforded was appreciated.

The sun blazed on him and he felt his tongue grow
thick and dry during the periods of consciousness
which seemed to be growing progressively shorter.
Soon, one of those periods would be his last.

He was brought to again by minute vibrations in
the ground at the back of his head. Trotting hooves,
and something dragging. The soldiers were returning.
He was almost glad. Perhaps they would trample him
as they passed and end it all quickly.

But the hoofbeats stopped and footsteps approached. The cloth was pulled from his eyes with an
abrupt motion and the faces that leaned over him
were human but didn't belong to soldiers. There were
four of them and they glanced at each other and nodded silently. One with blond hair turned and moved
from sight while the others, much to the tery's surprise, bent over him and began to brush the flies and
gnats from his wounds. All this without a single word.

The blond man returned with one of the mounts.
From a harness around its neck, a long pole ran along
each shaggy flank to end on the ground well beyond
the hindquarters. Rope was basket-woven between the
poles.

Still no word was spoken.

Their silence puzzled him, for they were obviously
on their guard. What was there to fear in these woods
besides Kitru's troops? And what had these humans to
fear from Kitru, who slew only teries?

Further speculation was delayed by the appearance
of a water jug. Its mouth was placed against his lips
and a few drops allowed to trickle out. The tery tried
to gulp but succeeded only in aspirating a few drops,
which started him coughing. The jug was withdrawn,
but at least his tongue no longer felt like dried leather.

With the utmost gentleness and an uncanny coordination of effort, the four men lifted the tery and placed him across the webbing of the drag. All without speaking. Perhaps they were outlaws. But even so, the tery began to think them overly cautious in their silence. . . . The soldiers were long gone.

The humans mounted and ambled their steeds toward the deep forest. The uneven ground jostled the drag and caused a few of his barely clotted wounds to reopen, but the tery bore the pain in silence. He felt safe and secure, as if everything was going to be all right. And he hadn't the vaguest notion why he should feel that way.

The path they traveled was unknown to the tery, who had spent most of his life in the forest. They passed through dank grottos of huge, foul-smed fungi that grew together at their tops and nearly blocked out the sun completely, and skirted masses of writhing green tendrils all too willing to pull any hapless creature within reach toward a gaping central maw. After what seemed to be an interminable length of time, the group passed through a particularly dense thicket and came upon a clearing and a camp.

The tents were crude, all odd shapes and sizes, and scattered here and there in no particular arrangement. The inhabitants, too, offered little uniformity of design, ranging from frail to obese. This was hardly what the tery had expected. He had envisioned a pack of lean and wolfish outlaws—they would have to be to hold their own against Kitru's seasoned troops. But there were women and children here and a number of them took leave of their working and playing to stare at him as he passed. These people hardly looked like outlaws . . . and the silence was oppressive.

His four rescuers stopped and untied the drag from the mount, then lowered it gently until the tery was lying flat against the ground. One of them called out the first and only word spoken during the entire episode.

"Adriel!"

A girl emerged from a nearby hut. She was young—seventeen summers, perhaps—slightly plump but not unpretty. Seeing the tery, she rushed over and dropped to his side to examine the wounds.

"He's cut up so bad!" she said. Her voice was high and clear and full of empathy. "How'd it happen?"

"Those are sword wounds," one of the other men said with some impatience. "That can only mean Kitru's men."

"Why'd you bring him back?"

The first man shrugged. "It was Tlad's idea. He found the beast and somehow convinced your father that we should help it. So your father sent us after it."

Adriel's brow furrowed. "Tlad did that? That doesn't sound like him."

The man shrugged again. "Who can figure Tlad anyway?" He indicated the hut. "Your father inside?"

"No." Adriel rose and pointed to a far corner of the camp. "He's over there somewhere."

The men left in silence as the girl ducked back inside the hut. She re-emerged with a wet rag and knelt beside the tery. He was riding the ragged edge of consciousness then, and the last thing he remembered as everything faded into blackness was the cool, wet cloth wiping the dirt and dried blood from his face and a soft voice cooing.

"Poor thing . . . poor thing . . ."

"Think he'll live?" said a voice behind Adriel.

She looked up. A bearded man, tall and muscular, stood there. "Oh. Tlad. Yes, I think so. If his wounds don't fester too much, he should do fine."

"Good," the man said with a quick nod and started to turn away.

"Why did you tell my father to bring in a wounded tery?" she asked.

"He needed help and I couldn't help him."

She looked at him closely. His light brown hair hung lankly against the darker brown of his beard. He was dirty and he smelled bad and she didn't much like him. He returned her stare.

"That was nice of you," Adriel said.

"You and he are running from the same thing—I thought you might want to help him out a little. And he looked like he needed all the help he could get. Do a good job."

"I don't need you to tell me that!" she said sharply, letting her annoyance at his remark show.

He barked a short laugh and strolled to his wagon. With a single, smooth motion, he bent, grasped the two handles, and started off into the woods, trailing the wagon behind him. A few shards of broken pottery rattled in the back; the left wheel squeaked on its axle.

She watched until the thicket swallowed him up, then returned to her work with a scowl. Tlad had risen in her estimation today by his show of compassion for the poor beast unconscious before her, but she still did not like him. She couldn't pin it down, but there was something about that man that caused her to mistrust him.

She went back into the hut to get some clean rags to bind the tery's deeper wounds, and when she returned, she saw her father approaching her across the clearing.

"That thing still alive?" he said when he reached her side and stood surveying the bulk of the tery. Komak was a man huge in height, girth, and spirit. His shaggy red hair and beard encircled his head like a mane; his skin was the type that never seemed to tan—it was always red from exposure to the sun despite the fact that he spent all of his time outdoors these days; and his eyes were a clear, pale blue. Adriel shared his coloring in hair, skin, and eyes, but was shorter and had a smaller frame.

"Of course he's alive! Can't you see his chest moving?"

Komak nodded. "So this is Tlad's tery. Now that we've got him, what're we going to do with him?"

"I want him as a pet. And don't you ever call him 'Tlad's tery' again. He's mine now."

"I don't know about that. Look at the size of him. If he should turn on you . . ."

"He won't," she said assuredly. "He knows I'm his friend. I could see it in the way he looked at me when I started washing off his wounds."

"Well, we'll see."

"Father," she said after a pause while she tied a knot in a bandage, "are Kitru's men exterminating the forest teries, too?"

Komak squatted beside her. "Yes, I'm afraid they are. Overlord Mekk's decree applies not only to us but to the teries and even to some of the more bizarre plants—at least that's what Rab told us."

"And where is this Rab fellow everybody talks about?"

"I don't know." He let his body slip back and rested

on his buttocks. "But I wish he'd get here." With a slow, almost painful motion, he lay back on the ground and closed his eyes.

"Tired?" Adriel asked, stopping her ministrations to the tery and looking at her father with concern.

"Exhausted. I'm not cut out for this. I didn't want to be leader of the group. When I agreed to the position, I thought it was only for a few days . . . until Rab showed up. Now it's been months."

"Where could he be? Think he got caught?"

"Possible. He said we didn't have much time to get away from the keep when he warned us. Maybe he tarried too long trying to make sure everybody got out."

Adriel remembered the day vividly. Her father had come home from Kitru's court, where he served as an advisor on matters of design and construction around the keep, in a state of great agitation. An unknown Talent who called himself Rab had whispered to his mind about secrets in old books and about a messenger on his way from Overlord Mekk with a new proclamation—a rider to the old Tery Extermination Decree that would include possessors of the Talent as offenders against God. Possessors of the Talent would thereby be declared anathema and summarily condemned to death without trial.

Word spread rapidly among those with the Talent—Rab, whoever he was, had contacted many of them—and the majority believed him. The Overlord had long been under the spell of a fanatical religious sect which worshipped the True Shape. All deviations from True Shape were considered unholy. Apparently the sect's dogma now excluded possessors of the Talent from True Shape.

There were doubters, of course, who claimed that it went against all existing laws to order their deaths merely because they possessed the Talent. These few stayed behind while Komak, Adriel, and the others packed whatever they could and fled into the woods. If they were wrong in trusting Rab, they reasoned, all it cost them was a few days of inconvenience and perhaps a little embarrassment. If they were right . . .

The wisdom of their choice became horrifyingly evident on their third night in the woods when the anguish, pain, and terror of the other Talents left behind in the keep leaped through the darkness to wake them from their sleep. The agonized emotions slowly dissipated as those Talents were systematically slaughtered in their homes. Only Adriel slept through it all.

"Maybe Rab is right here in this camp and we don't know it," she told her father.

Komak opened his eyes and raised himself up on one elbow. "Not possible. I don't know how to explain it to you but . . . but once you've communicated with someone via the Talent, you'll always recognize him again. Rab isn't here."

"Maybe he's Tlad, then. We don't know anything about him."

"But Tlad doesn't have the Talent. You said so yourself. And you should know—you're the Finder."

Yes, she was the Finder, all right. Sometimes she wished she weren't. "Still," she said, "there's something about that man I don't like."

"Don't like? He's never harmed you or any of us. As a matter of fact, he's been a good friend to us."

"Perhaps that's not the right word. I don't know. He's sneaky. He always seems to be watching us. Maybe he's working for Kitru, spying on us."

"If that was his plan, my dear, he could have led the troops here long ago. And don't forget how he acted on behalf of this tery here—no man of Kitru's would do that."

But Adriel would not allow her suspicions to be put to rest. "I can't explain what he did today, but—"

"Don't try to explain Tlad," her father cut in. "He's not like us. He lives alone out here, makes his pottery, and doesn't bother anyone. Doesn't seem to be much afraid of anyone, either. But forget about him now. We have more pressing matters at hand."

"Oh?" She finished up the last dressing on the tery and looked at him.

"Yes. It's rumored that Overlord Mekk is planning a personal inspection of all the districts soon and that's probably why Kitru is sending his men out into the bush to kill off the teries: He wants to make a good impression on the Overlord." He paused for a moment, then: "This creature was found much too near the camp for comfort. Kitru's men might happen on us next. We must move on. And soon."

He rose to his feet and stood with hands on hips, letting his eyes rove the weirdly silent camp. All motion ceased abruptly as everyone turned to face the big man. After a short pause, he turned back to Adriel and the camp dissolved into a flurry of activity.

"As soon as you finish with him, start gathering your things. We move at daybreak tomorrow."

III

They numbered near fifty, these strange, silent folk. The tery watched their wordless coordination in fascination: with incredible swiftness they broke camp at first light, loaded their pack animals and started off through the sun-filtered forest toward a new and safer location.

Still weak from his wounds, the tery found himself beset by blurred vision and nausea every time he tried to raise himself to an upright position. He had passed the night in a deep, exhausted, untroubled sleep to awaken alert and chilled in the dawn.

Adriel, however, was up before him and ready. "There, now," she said softly, pressing his shoulders back against the drag on which he had spent the night. "You don't have to go anywhere and you shouldn't." Her voice was soft and reassuring, its tone meant to convey the meaning of the words she didn't know he could understand. "See if you like this."

She placed a shallow earthen bowl filled with milk and bits of raw meat before him. With two or three brisk movements, he shoveled all the meat into his mouth, swallowed convulsively, then drained the milk.

Adriel watched in awe. "You must be famished! But that's all for now—you'll get sick if I let you eat as much as you want." She poured some cool water into the empty bowl. "Drink this and that'll be all until later."

When they were all set to go, the tery's drag was bound again to one of the mounts. Adriel covered him with a blanket and walked beside him, a reassuring hand on his shoulder, as they began to move.

The tery considered his benefactrix. She had a clear, open face in which he could read little. She appeared neither happy nor unhappy, neither contented nor frustrated . . . lonely, perhaps? He thought that for the daughter of a chief—at least her father *seemed* to be the chief—to be lonely was unusual. Perhaps she wasn't pretty by human standards.

As they moved through the trees, a young man came up and matched his step to hers. He was well built with curly brown hair and an easy smile. A wispy attempt at a beard mottled his cheeks.

"How's the Finder today?" he said.

She sighed. "How do you think, Dennel?"

"Same old problem?"

Adriel nodded.

"Will you ever understand?" he asked with a grin. "Speech is such a burden for us: thoughts flash as entities between us, whole concepts transfer from one to another as a unit, in an instant! We converse in colors and emotions and mixtures I can't even begin to describe! We don't leave you out on purpose. It's just . . . well, why walk when you can fly?"

"I know all that, Dennel. We've been over this before, but it doesn't help. It doesn't keep me from feeling left out. Back at the keep I could at least go and find somebody to talk to. But here . . . here I'm the only one who was born without the Talent."

"But the Talent came out in you in a different way! You're a Finder!"

"I can *find* possessors of the Talent, sure! But I can't communicate with them. I'm cut off!"

"But your ability to find makes you the most valuable member of the group. Through you we can find new members to add to our ranks. And we need everyone we can get." He glanced up and down the column of travelers. "Every single one."

"That still doesn't keep me from feeling like a cripple," she replied sulkily.

In the silence that followed, the tery had time to ponder what he had just heard. He now understood why these humans were fleeing Kitru. They, like the teries, were products of the Great Sickness of long ago and were thus on Mekk's extermination list, too. His mother had explained all that to him. She had also spoken of these people once: they were called *psipeople*. That explained the eerie silence of the camp—they spoke with their minds. All except Adriel.

"How's the tery?" Dennel asked casually. Adriel immediately brightened.

"Coming along, poor thing. He heals fast. Some of his smaller cuts are almost closed up already."

Dennel leaned over to get a better look at the wounds, then quickly turned away. "That could be you or I some day if the troopers ever catch up with us."

"But they won't," Adriel told him, her optimism genuine. "My father can keep us one step ahead of Kitru's men without even trying. But let's not worry about it—it's too early in the day for that."

"All right," he laughed, and looked at the tery again, this time from a greater distance. "At least he's not a talker and not *too* ugly. Looks like a cross between a big monkey and some wiry breed of bear!"

The tery disliked Dennel's tone but had to agree with the comparison. He was about the height of a man when he walked upright, although he much preferred to go on all fours. His hands were large, twice the size of a man's, and he was covered from head to toe with coarse black fur which was short and curly everywhere except the genital area, where it grew long and straight.

"Talker?" Adriel said, glancing between Dennel and the tery.

"Sure. Some teries can be taught to speak, you know. I saw one with a traveling music troupe that came through the keep a few years ago. Some of them sang, some of them danced, and one even gave dramatic readings of poetry. But that was before Mekk declared them—and us—'unholy.' "

"Really? Do you think maybe I could teach this one to talk?"

Dennel shook his head. "I doubt it. First of all, I've been told that you've got to start them young if you're going to have any success. And secondly, you have to be lucky and get one who can be taught. The degree of intelligence varies greatly from one to another."

"Oh," she said with obvious disappointment. "I thought I might have someone to talk to."

"They can't *think*, Adriel. At the very most, all they can do is mimic sounds. And I'm not so sure you'd want a talker around anyway. Some of them are so good you'd actually think they had a mind."

"I guess it would be a little frightening at that," Adriel admitted.

The tery could have destroyed Dennel's misinformed theories in an instant, for he was a "talker" and had no doubts about his ability to think. But he kept to himself. If these humans found the thought of a talking tery repugnant, how would they feel if they knew that this animal was listening in on their conversation and understanding every word? He needed them now—especially now—while he was wounded, alone, and helpless, and couldn't risk alienating them.

"By the way," Adriel asked, "just what does the word 'tery' mean?"

Dennel shrugged. "I haven't the faintest idea. As far as I know, they've always been called teries. The name probably originated during the Great Sickness."

Dennel excused himself and walked toward the front of the train. As the tery scrutinized the psi-folk around him, he began to understand Adriel's predicament. Glances would pass between individuals, someone would smile, another would laugh, but speech was used only on the pack animals to keep them moving.

Adriel was indeed a lonely girl.

When the train halted at dusk, the tery was finally freed from the drag and allowed to take a few painful steps. Adriel had done an excellent job of cleaning and binding the wounds; his animal vitality would do the rest.

She appeared carrying two bowls. "Hungry?" she asked as he limped toward her. He had been given small amounts of milk during the day and now there was another portion of raw meat in the second bowl. He ate slowly this time, savoring the flavor. It was the flesh of a fleet grazing animal called *mas*. They were hard to catch and it occurred to him that there must be some good hunters among the psi-folk.

Adriel examined his bandages and murmured soothingly as he ate.

"Looks like you're coming along fine. You'll be back to your old self in no time." She sobered suddenly. "Then I suppose you'll take off into the bush again. You don't have to go, you know. We'll treat you well here, really we will. You'll have food and shelter and a friend: me."

The tery considered this.

Later, well fed and freshly bandaged, he followed Adriel to the community dinner table but remained at a respectful distance. The progress of the meal was an awe-inspiring sight: Bowls crisscrossed the table, hands reached and were filled, portions were dispensed in precisely the desired amount—all without a single word. Only Adriel's tiny voice broke the silence at odd intervals.

When bellies were full, the tables and pottery cleaned and cleared away, the group gathered around the central fire for what appeared to be some sort of conference. Adriel hung back, indecisive, unaccountably hesitant. Finally, after two or three deep breaths, she strode forward to where her father sat in silence. The big man smiled as she knelt beside him. The tery remained in the background at the perimeter of the firelight, watching, listening.

"We were just discussing the future," her father told her, "and it looks as if we'll be spending years in these forests." He glanced sharply at Dennel, whose face flickered on the far side of the flames. "Haven't I asked you to use your tongue when my daughter is present? If not out of kindness, then at least out of courtesy!"

Grudgingly, Dennel spoke. "But you haven't given my idea due consideration, Komak. We could make ourselves very useful to Kitru—and to Overlord Mekk himself. Think of the intelligence network we could form for him. Why, he could know what was going on in any one of his provinces at any time!"

"You're dreaming," Komak said. "Practicality can't touch Mekk these days. He's become a religious fanatic. The priests have poisoned him against anything that does not bear True Shape—and that seems to include our minds. No, Mekk is unreachable, I'm afraid. And Kitru—Kitru fears Mekk and dares not disobey him. I should know after spending years as his advisor: Kitru is a cruel, venal, greedy man; but he's a coward where Mekk is concerned. He won't question a single aspect of the extermination decree."

"But we could be useful!" Dennel insisted.

"You mean 'used,' don't you?"

"No—"

"A man is only what he proves himself to be," Komak said with an abrupt note of finality. "Right now we're fleeing for our lives, but your alternative strikes me as worse. Should we prove ourselves to be slaves? Tools of a tyrant? I think not, even if he permitted us to live that long. We can only run for now, but Rab promised that someday we'd return—and on our own terms!"

"But where is he?" Adriel said. "The answer means more to me than the rest of you. Most of you heard from this man by way of the Talent. I only have second hand knowledge—yet here I am in the middle of the forest, fleeing from everything I know. Where is he? I thought he was supposed to join us out here."

"He was. I don't know what happened to him. It's quite possible he met with the very fate he warned us all against. If only we knew something about him, maybe we could learn if anything happened to him."

"I'm leery of this fellow Rab," Dennel said. "Where did he get all his advance information? And why haven't we ever heard from him before?"

Komak shrugged. "I can't possibly answer those questions. Perhaps he comes from Mekk's fortress—maybe that's where he got his information. One thing we do know: his warning was timely and correct. Need I remind anyone of what we experienced on the third night after fleeing the keep?" No one met his searching gaze.

"I'm still suspicious," Dennel said finally. "How did Rab manage to contact those who were not publicly known to possess the Talent? Adriel is the only Finder in the province. . . . I fear a trap, Komak."

"Well, if there's a trap, Rab will have caught himself—because he contacted us via the Talent, which puts him on Mekk's extermination list along with the rest of us. And don't forget: There are still a few Talents hiding undiscovered in the keep. Rab contacted them, but Kitru hasn't found them yet." He shook his head. "So many unanswered questions. It's best we learn to like the forest. I fear it will be home for a long, long time."

On that depressing note, Adriel retired to her tent and verbal conversation ceased. The tery dozed off.

IV

He was well enough to travel the next day and left
the train of the psi-folk as it moved deeper into the
forest. He was not deserting his rescuers; he intended
to stay with them, for he had nowhere else to go now
and they seemed well organized. The raw meat and
milk of the night before and again this morning had
restored his strength. Moving steadily, if not quickly,
through the lush foliage, he knew where he was going
and what he would find. He hadn't wanted to leave
Adriel. It would have been so easy to stay by her side
and leave all the pain behind. But he couldn't. It was
the way he was.

The hunting had been particularly good two days
before. The tery hunted with a club and a club was all
he needed. He was early in returning to the clearing
around the cave that served as home for him and his
parents, and intended to surprise them with the two
large *dantas* he had bagged. But it was he who was
destined to be surprised: Steel-capped, leather-jerkined
strangers had invaded the clearing.

Keeping low, he had crept through the small plot
where they tried to grow a few edibles. Halfway
through the garden, the tery noticed something huddled among the corn stalks to his left and crawled over
to investigate.

His father lay there. A big, coarse brute who was
happiest when he could sit in the sun and watch with
eternal wonder the growth of the things his mate had

taught him to plant, he had been pierced by a dozen or more feathered shafts and the red of his life was pooled on the ground beside him.

Rage and fear fought for dominance within the tery, but he dug both hands into the ground and held on until the dizzy sick feeling that swept over him had passed. Then he grabbed his hunting club. Holding it tightly, he kept low to the ground between the rows of stalks and moved slowly toward the cave, hoping . . .

His mother, her head nearly severed from her body, lay in the mouth of the cave.

All control had shattered then. Screaming hoarsely and swinging his club before him, the tery charged. The utter berserk ferocity of his attack was almost as startling to the tery as it was to the soldiers.

Almost. The archers were caught off guard, but the troopers' swords were already bared and bloody. The first of the group lifted his blade as the tery closed, but the creature batted it aside and swung his club for the trooper's head. The man ducked but not quickly enough, and the tery had one less opponent facing him. His club swung again and connected with the shoulder of an archer, who went down screaming.

But there were too many of them, and all were seasoned warriors. Before he could inflict any more real damage, the club was sliced from his hands and a sword point bared three of his ribs.

Wounded, weaponless, the tery ran. And he would have escaped easily had not the captain thought to order his men to their mounts.

"Don't run him through!" he heard the captain yell. "Just keep slicing at him!"

It was great sport. The troopers were all excellent riders. They would cut him off, then surround him and slice away. When each had added fresh blood to his sword, they would let him escape the circle and run a short distance, only to cut him off and start slicing again. He was an exhausted bloody ruin by the time he finally collapsed in a field of tall grass.

"If he's not dead now," the captain panted as he stared down at the tery from his mount, "he soon will be. Let the carrion eaters finish him!" And so they left him for the scavengers.

The tery remembered that captain's face.

The clearing was much as he had left it—except for the scavenger birds. He chased them away from the decomposing, partially devoured things that had been his parents. At the risk of reopening some of his deeper wounds, he went about the task of placing the cadavers inside the cave. It was grisly work, and the stench, combined with the knowledge of what he was handling, made him retch a number of times before the task was completed.

His father had been a wild, bearish creature, born of equally wild parents and raised in the forests where he spent all his life. His mother was different in both appearance—no two teries are alike unless directly related—and social history. Graceful in a simian way, she had been captured as an infant and brought up in the keep when Kitru's father was lord there. That was in the time before Mekk issued his proclamation calling for the extermination of everything that did not bear True Shape. It was considered fashionable then to have a tery or two around the court who could speak and recite.

His mother was one of those teries. She would delight visitors with her singing, her recounting of history, and the reciting of the many poems she had memorized. But she tired of being a pet and escaped to the forests in her early adulthood.

There she met her mate, who could speak not at all and who could not learn to speak with any fluency—for although he had the intelligence, he had gone too long without ever speaking. He did manage to communicate in other ways, though, and soon a child was born to them.

The little tery's mother taught him to speak and

taught him of his origin—how the Great Sickness had caused changes in many of the world's living things. His ability to think was one of those changes. These were things she had learned during her stay at the keep, and the cub absorbed everything she could pass on to him. He was bright, curious, and eager, and readily learned to speak, although his voice had a gruff, discordant tone.

He said nothing now, however, as he climbed the hillside above the cave and pried loose stone after stone until a minor landslide covered the mouth of his former home. When the dust had settled and the rumble of the slide had echoed off into the trees, he sat alone on the cliff and surveyed the clearing that had been home for as long as he could remember.

It was difficult for the tery to understand the turbulent emotions that steamed and roiled within his chest, making it hard to draw a deep breath without its catching halfway down. His placid life had not prepared him for this, and his emotions were in turmoil.

He had been wronged—*his parents* had been wronged! Injustice. It was a concept that had never occurred to him before, and he had no word for it. For there was no justice or injustice in the forest, only the incessant struggle to go on living, taking what was needed and leaving what was not. Things tended to balance out that way. Carelessness was redeemed in mishap, vigilance rewarded in safety and, often, a full belly.

Stealthy images crept unbidden from the past as he sat there. He had managed to hold them at bay while going about the task of interring his parents' remains, but now that that was done and he was gazing at the cold, dead, empty piece of earth that had once held warmth and security for him, he began to remember hunting and swimming lessons from his hulking father, and sitting curled up at his mother's side in the cool of the evening.

His chest began to heave uncontrollably as a low,

broken moan of unplumbed sorrow and anguish escaped him. He suddenly began to scramble blindly
down the cliffside, nearly losing his footing twice in
his haste to reach the clearing.

Once there, he ran from one end to the other, sob-
bing and whimpering, frantically casting about for
something to break, something to hurt, something to
destroy. As he approached the garden area, he grabbed
one of the crude hoes his father had used for tilling
and scythed his way through the stalks of maize and
other vegetables growing there. When that was in
ruins, he raced back to the base of the cliff and picked
up any stones that would fit into his hands and hurled
them with rage-fueled ferocity at the rubble-choked
mouth of the cave. Some caromed crazily off the pile,
others cracked and shattered with the tremendous
force of impact. Whining and grunting, he threw one
after another until a few of his wounds reopened and
his strength was completely drained. Then he slumped
to his knees, pressed his forehead against the ground,
and sobbed.

After a while, he was quiet. After a while, he could
think again.

Another new concept for which he had no word
grew in his mind: revenge. Had his parents been killed
for food by one of the large feline predators that
roamed the forests, he would never have thought of
retribution. That was the way things worked. That
was existence in the wild. His parents would be dead—
just as dead as they were now—but the balance would
not have been disturbed.

The tery raised his head. Neither his mother nor his
father had ever threatened or harmed a human; in
fact, they had avoided any and all contact with them.
Yet the soldiers had come and slaughtered them and
left them to rot. Such an act was not part of the balance. It skewed everything, and nothing would be
right again until the balance was restored.

The tery vowed to remember that captain's face.

He stood and surveyed the ruins of what had once been his home. He would cut all ties with the past now. He was a fugitive tery and would stay with the fugitive humans he had met. His parents would be left behind, but he would never forget them.

Nor would he forget that captain's face.

It was midday when the tery started back. The psi-folk would have been on the move all day, so he traveled on an angle to his earlier path in order to intercept them. He was moving along the edge of an open field when something made him stop abruptly and drop to his knees. The skin at the nape of his neck drew taut and he sniffed the air for a scent.

Something had alerted his danger sense—his muscles were tensed and ready to spring, his jaw was tight, and his gaze darted across the field and in among the bordering trees.

Nothing.

Taking a few hesitant steps forward, he felt the sensation increase. Fear . . . dread . . . foreboding. All without visible cause. His mind rebelled. There was nothing to fear! Yet something within him—deep within him—was warning him away from this place.

He strained his vision into the shade at the bases of the nearby trees. Perhaps one of the big meat-eaters had a lair there and a subliminal effluvium of death and dung was being carried toward him on the gentle breeze.

He saw nothing. Perhaps . . .

There—in the darkness between the boles of two large trees—something shimmered. It wasn't something . . . it wasn't anything, really. Just an area of shadow that shimmered and wavered as if seen from afar through the heat of a summer day.

Keeping to the open field, he made a slow semi-

circle, at all times maintaining his distance from the spot. It looked no different from the new angle and he saw nothing particularly threatening there. Unique and beyond anything he had ever experienced in his short life, yes. But nothing overtly dangerous.

Why, then, did it terrify him so?

He decided to find out. Slowly, with one reluctant step after another, he forced himself to approach the spot. And with each advance the terror within him grew and gripped him tighter and tighter until he felt as if lengths of vine were coiling around his throat and chest, suffocating him. His heart was beating in his ears, the air pressed against him. A cloud of impending doom enveloped him until his legs refused to respond to his mental commands, until his mind itself refused to go forward and he found himself running, gasping, clawing his way across the open field, away from the shimmering fear.

When he could finally stop himself from running, he had reached the far side of the field. He leaned against a tree trunk, panting while his sweat-soaked fur dried in the breeze.

He had never known such fear. Even when the troopers had chased him and sliced him and he had been sure he was going to die, he had not been so afraid.

He waited until he was breathing easily again and his heart had resumed its normal rate. Then he moved away into the trees. He still wanted to know what lay within the shimmering fear and was determined some-day to find out. There were many odd things left be-hind in the world after the Great Sickness, and the shimmering fear was certainly one of the most bizarre. Perhaps he could move through the upper levels of the trees and look down on it from above. . . . That might work . . .

But not today. He was too tired and emotionally spent today. All he wanted to do right now was to find the psi-folk, eat something, and settle near the fire for the night.

Keeping the sun to his left, the tery moved further into the trees. He had not gone far when he came across an isolated hut. It was deserted. He noticed a kiln off to the side, cold, with clay pots and trays piled all around it. He looked inside the hut . . . clean, with a pallet on the floor and a small stone fireplace in the corner.

This must be the home and work place of the one who found him after the troopers were through with him, he decided. The man they called Tlad. The tery briefly debated whether or not to sit and wait for Tlad to return, then decided against it. He owed the man a great deal more than gratitude. But how to show it? From listening to conversations between Adriel and some of the psi-folk, he gathered that this Tlad was a solitary sort who did not make friends easily and had little need for the company of other humans. He certainly would not want a tery around, then.

The tery moved on through the forest, the only place where he truly seemed to belong.

As he continued toward the presumed location of the psi-folk, the physical and emotional stresses of the day were beginning to take their toll. Entering a grassy copse, he stopped to rest and thought he heard low voices ahead. It was too soon yet to be intercepting the psi-folk—and idle chatter was certainly not one of their traits—so he silently slithered along the ground to investigate.

A scouting party of six troopers was resting in the shade as their horses grazed nearby. All his fatigue suddenly evaporated as the tery felt a blinding rush of hatred. But he held his position. He knew his reserves were low, and even under optimum conditions the headlong rush his emotions demanded would have been suicidal. The tery circled them and continued on his way. His hour would come, he knew. He had only to wait. And besides . . . the captain was not among them.

He came upon the psi-people very shortly thereafter. For reasons not apparent, they had stopped their march early and were busily setting up their camp. Adriel spotted him first.

"It's the tery!" she cried, leaping to her feet and almost upsetting the mixing bowl in her lap. "He's come back!" She rushed forward, fell to her knees beside him and threw her arms around his neck. "You came back!" she whispered as she hugged him. "They said you were gone for good but I knew you'd come back!"

Pleasant as it was, the tery had no time for such a welcome. He had just realized that the probable line of march of the scouting party would lead it close to this site . . . so close that discovery would be unavoidable. The troopers numbered only six, so there was no danger of an attack; but should they be allowed to return to the keep with even a general idea of the whereabouts of the psi-folk, extermination would swiftly and surely follow. He had to warn them.

But how? He dared not speak for fear of letting them know he was a talker . . . *and* a thinker—such a warning would indicate reasoning ability. The tery could not be sure that their sympathy for his loneness in the vast forests would overcome their repugnance at having a talking, thinking, *comprehending* animal in their midst. There had to be another way.

He broke from Adriel and ran to her father. Wrapping long fingers around the leader's arm, he tried to pull him away from the central pit he was helping to dig.

"Adriel!" Komak shouted, angered at being disturbed. "Get your pet away from me or we won't have a fire tonight!"

"I'll bet he's hungry," she said, and went to get some meat.

This approach obviously wasn't working. Short of a shouted message, only one recourse remained.

Bolting toward the trees, he ignored Adriel's pleading calls and disappeared into the brush. It didn't take him long to find the scouts—they were dangerously close and headed on a collision course. He searched the ground briefly and came up with a fist-sized stone, then climbed out on a limb that overhung their path and waited.

They were walking their mounts single-file through the dense undergrowth and grumbling about the heat and difficult traveling. As the last man passed below, the tery hurled the rock at his head and leaped from the tree. The missile drove the trooper's steel cap into his scalp with a dull clank, and his horse reared as the tery grabbed the helmet off the sagging form and disappeared.

Hopefully, the loss of a man—whether temporarily or permanently, the tery could not be sure—would throw the scouts into sufficient confusion to allow the psi-folk time enough to prepare a move against them.

Gripping the rim of the helmet between his teeth and running as fast as his four aching limbs would carry him, the tery burst upon the campsite and went directly to Komak. The sight of a steel cap with fresh blood around the rim was all the big man needed to set him into action. He shot to his feet and glanced around. In an instant the camp was thrown into frenzied activity.

"What is it, father?" Adriel asked, aware that an order had been given.

"Troopers! Your pet's brought us a warning." He guided her ahead of him toward their half-erected tent. "I never expected to see one of Kitru's men this far into the forests . . . but the tery was gone only a few minutes. They must be nearly upon us!"

She blanched. "What'll we do?"

"There's only one thing we *can* do." He bundled the tent fabric into a careless wad and shoved it out of sight behind a bush. "We haven't got time to run—

although Dennel seems to think that would be the best course."

He glared across the clearing at the youth, who stood uncertainly amid the flustration. "But finding a recently abandoned campsite is the next best thing to finding the group itself. They'd run to the keep and soon a whole company would be charging after us. This is probably just a scouting party. All we can do is set a trap and hope there aren't too many of them."

Komak's plan turned out to be fiendishly simple. The tents were quickly struck, and the women and children were sent from the clearing along with everything they could carry. Twenty men with strung bows concealed themselves in the surrounding bushes. The tery traveled with Adriel and the other noncombatants for a short distance, then doubled back to the campsite.

As he watched from a nearby tree, the scouting party—one member with a bare and bloodied head—entered the clearing in a cautious single file. They made a careful inspection of the half-dug central fire pit and conversed in low tones. The earth had been freshly turned and they were wary now.

Komak watched until he was certain the entire party had revealed itself, then used the Talent to assign each archer a target. When each trooper had been assured of three arrows, the remaining two archers were held in reserve. His mental command caused eighteen bows to *thrum* in perfect unison. Five of the scouts twisted and fell immediately. The sixth had stooped suddenly to examine the ground and received only a superficial wound in the fleshy part of his upper right arm. Seeing the fate of his companions, he turned and ran for the brush. The two reserve archers stopped him before he had covered six paces.

There had been no word during the entire episode, and no cheering at its close. If not for the rustle of the leaves, the noises of the birds and insects, the tery would have thought he had gone deaf. It dawned on him then that with greater numbers and a greater desire to fight, these psi-folk could rule the forests completely and pose a real threat to Kitru . . . and perhaps to Overlord Mekk himself.

Before the women and children were brought back, the bodies of the troopers were carefully buried in the brush and their horses added to the psi-folks'. Then they hastily set up camp for the night, and just as hastily broke it the next morning. Dennel was absent. No one had seen him since Komak's decision to ambush the scouts instead of flee from them. The group left without him on a long forced march into the depths of the forest.

"He'll find us again," Komak told Adriel as they packed their tent. "He can no more take care of himself than he can fight for himself. He needs us—we don't need him."

"He was always nice to me."

Komak put an arm around his daughter's shoulders and laughed. "For that reason alone, I'll welcome him back!"

"But is he really such a coward? He says he's mostly concerned with preserving the Talent."

"I know what he *says*. But I also know that he's scared to death. Last night when we set the ambush, I was supposed to have twenty-*one* archers. But Dennel ran off. Still running, I'll bet. He claims we'd be better off if we split up into smaller groups. That way, in the event of an all-out attempt to do away with us, we could be fairly sure that some would survive to carry on the Talent."

"That sounds reasonable."

"On the surface, it does. But I really don't think Dennel's all that interested in preserving the Talent. Preserving Dennel is his main concern."

Komak paused, then grinned pointedly. "Besides— last night proves that there are definite advantages to moving with a large group of individuals who can communicate silently and instantaneously. I think the lad just wants to run and I wouldn't worry too much about him. I'm sure he's not worrying about us. Your tery is a better friend—worth three Dennels."

Adriel turned her head and saw her pet ambling on all fours among the psi-folk. Instead of ignoring him or swatting him when he got in the way, they smiled at him, called to him, scratched his back, or gave him bits of food. He had become a hero of sorts and had earned his place in the tribe.

His behavior of the night before was rationalized as a natural response to the merciless treatment he had received at the hands of the troopers when they had cut his flesh to ribbons: The tery came upon the scouts and instinctively attacked one of them, bringing back the helmet as a trophy. He was now considered a valuable watch animal.

The sun was tangled in the trees by the time they stopped that day. Some of the psi-folk didn't even bother to set up their tents, but ate small amounts of dried meat and fell asleep under the stars. A light drizzle awoke them next morning.

It was a tired, cold, achey group that held silent conference in a tight knot near the central fire. Finally Komak broke away and strode angrily to where Adriel sat with the tery. The group gradually dissolved behind him.

"What's wrong, father?"

"They want to stay here. We should be moving further away from the keep than this, but the women are tired and the children are crying and it was the consensus that this is far enough."

"I'm tired, too."

"We're *all* tired!" he snapped, then softened. "Sorry. I told you I never wanted this job. But one thing I'm going to insist on is sending out a few scouts of my own to see what the surrounding area is like before we get too settled."

VI

"*Food* . . ." she said in a plaintive voice, holding a small piece of meat before her. "Come, now. Say it: *Food* . . ."

The sun was half way to its zenith and Adriel had been coaching the tery since breakfast. The girl was determined to teach her new pet to speak. The tery finally decided to gamble and try to please his mistress by following her persistent example.

Pretending great effort, he rasped, "Food."

Adriel sat frozen in wide-eyed wonder.

"Food," he repeated.

Komak was sitting nearby and turned his head at the unfamiliar voice. "Was that . . . ?"

"Yes!" Adriel said breathlessly. "It was him! He spoke! Did you hear him? He spoke!" She quickly gave the tery the piece of meat she had been holding and held up another. But further demonstration of his newfound ability was halted by the arrival of one of the point men Komak had sent out.

After a few moments of telepathic conversation, her father turned to her.

"Looks like we'll be needing you."

"Oh?" She had been half-expecting this.

"Seems there's a tiny village a little ways off to the east. Perhaps twenty or thirty inhabitants, and one or two may have the Talent. It's up to you to find them."

* * *

Twelve mud-walled domes sat in a circle around a wide area of bare earth. Adriel motioned the tery to stay back out of sight in the brush, then walked forward toward the circle of huts, holding tightly to her father's arm. He stopped at the perimeter and let her proceed to the center alone.

No one understood the Talent, least of all Adriel. Her mother, before she had sickened and died, had tried in vain to explain it to her. Half of the Talent was another voice, a separate voice that did not automatically accompany vocal speech. It had to be volitionally activated. The other half was the receptive faculty that operated continually unless it was consciously blocked out. Most Talents learned of their ability first through the receptive facet.

Adriel understood none of it. The Talent was a tingling in her mind, a vague sensation she could home in on and almost touch. To those who possessed the full Talent, reception was nondirectional. Images appeared behind their eyes, words sounded between their ears, concepts exploded within their minds. But from where?

Adriel knew where.

She stood now and watched as the inhabitants of the miniscule village came out of their huts and stared curiously at the newcomer, whispering but not straying far from their doorways. Adriel turned in a slow circle. Once. Twice. Then stopped and faced a man, a woman, and what looked like a ten-year-old boy.

There was a faint, familiar sensation of the Talent off to her right that she knew was her father. There was another sensation, a strong tingling in the forepart of her brain, emanating from the trio before her. She moved forward and the sensation became stronger with every step until she stood within arm's reach.

The man was blank, but the woman and boy were definitely Talents. Strong ones. She placed one hand on the woman's shoulder and the other on the boy's head, then looked to her father.

The two Talents followed her gaze to Komak and that's when he contacted them. With a reassuring smile beaming through his red mane, he motioned them toward him. The woman whispered something to her uncomprehending husband, then the trio followed Adriel to where her father waited.

"Now tell us what this is all about!" the woman demanded sharply when they were out of earshot of the village. Her features were pinched and her jet hair was drawn back severely. "And use your tongues so my husband will understand."

"We're traveling with a group of Talents," Komak said, "the only survivors after Kitru slaughtered all the rest of our kind in the keep. We want you to join us. We number fifty-three now and need every Talent we can find."

"Why?" the woman asked, suspicious and overtly hostile.

"For safety, of course. Overlord Mekk will be visiting the keep, and Kitru has been scouring the forests for teries and Talents in preparation for his arrival."

The man shook his head. "We'll stay right here."

"That could be dangerous," Komak told him. "What's to prevent some of Kitru's men from coming through here with a Finder and ferreting out your wife and child as we did?"

"We're isolated out here," he said. "Almost lost. I've been to the keep two or three times in my life and nobody there even knew this village existed. And no one here knows that my wife and son possess the Talent except me. I think we can risk staying where we are."

"Very well," Komak said after a pause. He was obviously disappointed. "We'll be camped toward the sunset for a while. If you should change your mind . . ."

"Thank you," the man said. "But the forest nomad life is not for us. We'll take our chances here." He put one arm around his wife and the other around his son as the trio walked back to their hut.

"Isn't it rare for a psi to marry a non-psi?" Adriel asked her father as they returned to the forest.

"Very rare. The rapport between two lovers with the Talent is far and away more intimate than anything a non-psi can experience. But the woman and her son were the only psis around so it's possible she never had a lover with the Talent. Doesn't know what she's missing." His eyes seemed to glaze as if he no longer saw the forest through which he was walking. Adriel wondered if he was remembering her mother.

"I wish them well," she said at last in an attempt to bring her father back from his reverie. "It must take a lot of courage to risk extermination as they're doing."

"Or a lot of foolishness. The dividing line isn't always clear."

VII

It wasn't until four days after the ambush that Dennel returned. He kept to himself, however, no doubt ashamed of his behavior.

Adriel and the tery became inseparable and took no notice of him. She "taught" him more words and devoted most of her day to him. Resting her hand on his back and talking to him as they wandered side by side through the leafy glades near the camp, she hadn't the slightest suspicion that he could understand her every word. His ears were for her alone, that she knew; he wasn't secretly carrying on a mental conversation with someone else as she spoke—something which the tery gathered had happened more than once in the past.

"You're lucky, you know," she told him as they sat on a grassy knoll and watched the brightly colored tree-things go about their daily routines. "Nothing holds you down. You can come and go as you please and you're at home with us or away from us. But me . . . I'm stuck here with a bunch of people who feel insulted if they have to use their tongues!"

She laughed. "I thought I was going to be a lady once—can you believe that? A nobleman's son took a fancy to me and I thought I'd someday be living in the upper quarters of the keep. Then Mekk went and issued his decree and I've spent the past few months living like a savage."

The tery came to think of Adriel as a wonderful creature—fresh, young, ready to burst into womanhood at any moment, and only a fanged, barrel-chested beast at her side to share the experience. She wanted to love and be loved, to stop running; she longed for the stability she would have had had she not been born a Finder.

And the tery became a substitute for everything she desired. A thousand tiny kindnesses were showered upon him. She would put much time and effort into preparing the meat for his dinner, and carved and painted a bowl from which to eat it. She learned the use of the loom so that he wouldn't have to sleep on the bare ground.

The two were driven closer and closer together by the void of silence that separated them from the rest of the tribe. Life became an idyll for the tery, a series of sun-soaked days of easy companionship . . . until the morning by the river when he discovered a dark and frightening hunger lurking within him.

Adriel was modest by nature. Every morning she would retrieve a jug of water from the stream that passed not too far from the camp and sponge herself off in the privacy of her tent. This particular morning was an exception, however, for she left the jug empty and led the tery along the bank of the stream until it widened and emptied into a river.

Pushing through the brush, she stepped down the bank and up to her ankles in the water. The far shore was further than the tery could throw a small stone, but floating leaves moved by at a leisurely pace, indicating a gentle current.

"There," Adriel said with a self-satisfied air, "I knew we'd find a river eventually. This looks deep enough." She pulled off her blouse and the knee-length pants she had recently made after finally deciding that a skirt was impractical in the forest. She wore nothing underneath.

Without the slightest hesitation, she made a shallow dive into the clear water, then bobbed to the surface and turned to face the tery.

"Ohhhhh, that feels good!" She dunked her head

again and came up gasping. "I thought I was never going to feel clean again!" She motioned to the tery. "Come on—it's only water!"

But he stayed behind the bushes lining the bank. That much water made him uneasy. He had often waded to his knees while fishing with his father, but the thought of immersing himself to his neck was frightening. And there was something else . . . the brief glimpse of Adriel's nude form had stirred something within him, something pleasurable and yet uncomfortable. He stayed where he was.

Adriel splashed the water in front of her. "Oh, come on in! You'll like it! Really!" But her pet made no move to join her. "Looks like I'm going to have to drag you in," she muttered and kicked her way closer to shore.

When she could feel the river bottom beneath her feet, she stood up and waded toward the bank. Her skin was white and smooth and glistened wetly. Water ran from her hair over her rounded, budding, pink-tipped breasts, down across her abdomen to the red-gold fuzz that covered her pubes.

That same pleasurable something washed over the tery again as he watched her. It was a warm something that seemed to be centered in his groin. She was completely out of the water now and climbing the bank in his direction. The warmth in his groin increased and the erratic fleshy part of him that usually hung awkwardly between his legs became large and stiff. His breathing was rapid as he tried to look away, but he could not. . . . This was wrong! He wanted to leap upon her, paw her, press the hungry distended flesh into her. . . . *Wrong!*

Adriel leaned over the bushes and extended her hand to him. "Come on," she said in a coaxing voice. The sunlight caught the myriad droplets of water that had formed on her bobbing breasts, and the cooling effect of a gentle breeze had caused her nipples to harden and stand erect. "I won't let you drown."

With a sudden motion he wrenched himself around and tore headlong back into the trees. He kept running, concentrating all his physical effort on moving his four limbs as fast as his muscles would allow. Leaping over fallen branches and around earth-sunk boulders, he raced past Tlad's empty dwelling, across the field that bordered the shimmering fear, and didn't stop until he stood in the ruined clearing that had once been his home.

Exhausted, he slumped on the rubble choking the mouth of the cave that held his parents' remains and desperately wished for them to rise and live and comfort him. Life had been so simple then. . . . His mother had all the answers. She would explain this blazing turmoil within him, explain why a tery should have such an unnatural desire for a human.

He waited, but his mother did not rise.

As his strength returned, so did memory of Adriel's glistening naked form, reaching for him. He felt the warmth return, felt himself grow erect again. Enclosing the stiff, enlarged member within both of his fists, he began moving them up and down until a spurting spasm brought a relief of sorts . . .

The tery returned to the psi-folk camp in the late afternoon. He did not approach Adriel's hut immediately as he would normally do, but wandered the perimeter, wondering if she had guessed what had happened down by the river bank. Near the center of camp he saw a cart loaded with pottery. He searched for Tlad and found him squatting beside Komak in the shade, dickering.

"Then it's settled," Tlad was saying. "A hindquarter of *mas* for the load. And fresh—none of this dried stuff."

"Agreed," Komak nodded. "You drive a hard bargain, Tlad. You'd never get such a price if we hadn't broken so much pottery in that forced march we had to make from the old campsite." His eyes narrowed.

"But what I want to know is how you found us here?"

"I've lived in the forests longer than you. I have ways."

"I'm sure you do. But we waded down a stream most of the way. We left no trail."

Tlad shrugged. "I have ways."

Komak broke off further interrogation when he caught sight of the tery loping toward them.

"Looking for Adriel?" he said, rising and affectionately roughing up the fur at the back of the tery's neck. "She told me about you—afraid of the water, are you? Well, we're all afraid of something, I guess."

"Where is Adriel, anyway?" Tlad asked. "I want to ask her a few things about this pet of hers."

Through his beard, Komak's mouth could be seen tightening into a grimace of distaste. "Off walking somewhere with Dennel. Don't know what she sees in him."

"You don't think too much of him, I take it?"

"I like him not at all and trust him even less. But that is a problem between Adriel and myself. As for you—there's a hunting party out now. Should be back with a *mas* or two by sundown."

Tlad nodded. "I saw them setting up on my way here. Think they'd mind if I watched?"

"Just stay back and out of sight," Komak warned and strolled away.

The tery was about to follow him but was stopped by Tlad's voice.

"So you're a hero around here now, eh? Coming up in the world. Komak says Adriel's even managed to teach you some words." He rose and then squatted again before the tery, putting their eyes on the same level. For an uncomfortably long time, Tlad looked into the yellow feral eyes until the tery finally turned away.

The man rose and mumbled a few unintelligible words, then he walked off toward the trees. Looking

over his shoulder as he moved, he slapped his thigh
once and called to the tery.

"With me!"

Lacking anything better to do, he drew along side
and kept pace. He felt strangely drawn to Tlad. The
fact that he had been instrumental in saving his life
was a definite factor, but there was a feeling of kin-
ship with the man, a certain undefined sharing of a
common ground.

They moved side by side through the forest until
Tlad suddenly stopped and motioned the tery to stay
where he was. Alone, he moved cautiously and silently
ahead, briefly disappearing into the undergrowth,
then returning with a satisfied smile on his face.

Without a word, he chose a tree and began to climb.
The tery followed. When they were five or six man-
heights up the tree, Tlad made himself comfortable on
a limb, and shielding his eyes against the late afternoon sun to his right, peered ahead in the direction
they had been traveling.

In a small clearing, eight Talents, five men and
three women, stood in a semicircle with arms linked.
No one moved, no one made a sound. They stood that
way for what seemed an interminable period and the
tery began to get restless. Not so Tlad, who watched in
silent fascination.

The tery was about to climb back down to the
ground and find something more interesting to do
when he noticed a movement in the brush surrounding the clearing. The head of a large buck *mas* appeared. Slowly, hesitantly, it moved forward until it
had fully emerged from the brush. *Mas* were vegetari-
ans—grazers and leaf-nibblers—and their only defense
against the carnivores that craved their flesh was
speed. A graceful neck held the creature's snouted
head on a level with those of the Talents who faced it;
a sleek, short-furred body tapered down to four delicate legs. *Mas* were skittish and bolted at the slightest

provocation, which made the sight of one standing not five paces from a group of humans almost incomprehensible . . . unless the Talents were exerting some sort of influence over the beast. It moved forward slowly until it stood within the semicircle. Then with one abrupt motion, the male Talent on the near end of the semicircle raised a heavy club and brought it down against the slim, sloping neck where it joined the skull. The *mas* crumpled, instantly, painlessly dead.

The men were lifting the hind legs in preparation to drag it back to camp when suddenly all the Talents froze in their places momentarily, then dropped whatever they were doing and ran back toward the camp, leaving their prize game animal where it had fallen.

Tlad started to scramble down the tree. "Something's wrong!"

The tery followed him to the ground, but once on all fours, he left Tlad behind as he raced for the camp. He found it in a shambles with silent, grim-faced people running in all directions, grabbing weapons and harnessing mounts. He immediately looked for Adriel and could not find her. A chill of foreboding stole over him as he hunted up Komak.

He finally found him at the weapons wagon, filling a quiver with arrows. He hesitated, fearful for Adriel, yet unable to learn a thing about her. Tlad arrived then, calling for Komak. The big red-haired man ignored the call and strode toward his tent without answering. Tlad, however, would not be put off. As the tery watched in the growing darkness, he intercepted Komak and matched his stride. After a brief exchange, Tlad stopped short and grabbed Komak's arm. They seemed to be arguing. Komak finally wrenched his arm out of Tlad's grasp and hurried away.

The tery approached Tlad, hoping to learn something from him.

"There you are!" Tlad said. He squatted before him and put one hand on his head. "Listen, my furry friend, and listen well: Adriel has been captured by

Kitru's troops. No one knows how it happened but there are tracks to the south that show Adriel and Dennel walking right into the arms of a squad of troopers."

The tery felt every muscle in his body tighten and he started to turn away, but Tlad pulled his head back around and looked into his eyes.

"Listen to me! These fools are going after her—they have some crazy idea about storming the keep. That may be just what Kitru wants. Not only will he have a Finder in his control, but he'll be able to slaughter all the Talents who escaped him when the proclamation first came through. *You*"—he slapped the tery's shoulder—"must get to the keep first. Get in there and get her out. I don't know how you're going to do it, but try! Not only does Adriel's life depend on it, but the lives of everyone in this camp. Now, get!"

The tery needed to hear no more. Without a backward glance he turned and trotted into the forest, pacing himself for what he knew would be a long and dangerous journey through the night-darkened forest. With easy, loping strides, he left the scrambling psifolk far behind. He was well on his way to the keep before he realized that, without the slightest hesitation, Tlad had told him what had happened, what he should do, and why he should do it—*fully expecting him to understand every word!*

VIII

The keep was a darker blot against a darkened sky when the tery reached it. He stood at the base of the high outer wall, far from the gate, and gathered his strength and wits. He had never been in the keep before, but that didn't bother him—he had often hunted unfamiliar sections of the forest, and come back with game over his shoulder.

This would be like a hunt—the keep would be an unknown section of forest, the troopers would be the big predators with which he was always in competition, and Adriel would be the prey. He geared up his confidence. He could do this. He had been raised in the forest with a club as his only weapon—he either learned to use his strength with stealth and cunning or he went hungry. The tery had seldom gone hungry.

He began to climb. The outer wall was crudely made of rough stone, and his long fingers found easy holds as he scuttled upward. He reached the top and raised his eyes above the ledge. There was a narrow walkway all along the outer wall with wooden stairs leading up to it. Sputtering torches and oil lamps placed at odd intervals within the wall showed a number of irregular buildings that made up the keep, one standing noticeably higher than the others.

A bored-looking sentry approached along the walkway. The tery lowered himself and hung just below the ledge until the guard had passed, then slithered over the top and dropped to the ground where he crouched in the deep shadow under the walkway.

He waited. No alarm was sounded, no troopers came running. He had successfully penetrated the first line of defense. The next step was to decide which building to search first. His gaze was drawn to the tall, imposing structure that stood over the other buildings. That would be where Lord Kitru would reside—it seemed logical that a man who believed himself above other men would want to live where he could look down on them.

With neither weapons nor clothing nor accouterments, the tery was a fleeting shadow among other shadows as he made his way to the base of the tower. Yes, Kitru would dwell here. And who would better know the location of the captured Finder than the lord of the keep? Perhaps he had even quartered her here to assure her safekeeping.

He looked up the face of the tower wall. It was made of the same rough stone as the outer wall, so climbing it would be no problem. The surface was pierced here and there by narrow windows which the tery judged wide enough to allow him entrance. He started up. He had traveled only three man-heights when a shout from below caused him to freeze and hug the wall.

"Ho! You there on the tower! What are you doing?"

The doors to the trooper barracks flew open and there was the sound of many running feet in the darkness below.

The same voice spoke again. "You! Come down from there! I've got a crossbow now . . . start coming down! No tricks or I'll spit you with a bolt!"

Glancing up, the tery saw the lowest window not far above him and made a sudden frantic effort to reach it. True to his word, the guard below loosed a bolt. The missile grazed the tery's ear and smashed against the wall in front of his face. Fragments of stone and mortar peppered his eyes. Recoiling, he lost his precarious grip and fell. He landed on all fours but found nowhere to run—the wall was to his back and two full squads of troopers faced him with drawn weapons.

"Someone get a light and let's see who we've got here!"

A torch was quickly brought and the troopers recoiled in surprise at the nature of their captive.

"It's one of those damned beasts!" exclaimed a burly guard with a pike. He drew the weapon back and the tery readied to dodge. "This'll finish—"

"*Stop!*" cried a voice from behind them and the troopers turned to see who had dared to tell them to spare a tery. A young man dressed in civilian clothes stepped into their midst with an imperious manner. It was Dennel.

"Just who are you to be giving orders around here?" the man with the pike asked belligerently.

"Never mind that," Dennel said. "Just let me tell you that if this tery is killed, Kitru will have your head. This particular beast could be very valuable to him."

The trooper paused, uncertain. He resented being told what to do by some unblooded, baby-faced, non-combatant upstart; but if this newcomer were telling the truth, he might well end up on the receiving end of Kitru's wrath—and that was not a place he wished to be.

He turned to the man beside him. "Get Captain Ghentren."

There followed a short period of tense waiting during which the tery put aside his surprise at finding Dennel free within the keep and looked for an avenue of escape. There was none. The troopers formed a tight, impenetrable semicircle around him.

Half-dressed, his eyes puffy from sleep, the captain arrived and the tery felt an involuntary growl escape his throat. His body crouched to spring. This was the officer who had ordered his men to slice but not to kill . . . this was the parent-slayer!

One of the troopers who was watching him more closely than the others recognized the tery's stance and raised his crossbow.

"Watch him!"

The tery forced himself to relax as the troopers pointed their bows and pikes at him, ready to kill at the slightest move. He would never reach the captain.

The officer glanced at the tery without the slightest hint of recognition in his eyes, then turned to his men. "This had better be important enough to wake me— I'm to leave on a mission for Kitru before first light."

The burly trooper with the pike stepped forward and pointed to Dennel. "This stranger says Kitru will have my head if we kill the tery."

The captain turned to Dennel. "Oh, so it's you. Since when do you speak for the lord of the keep?"

"Because I know this beast!" Dennel replied. "It's the girl's pet and she's very attached to it."

"I care nothing about the Finder's pet!" he snarled and turned away. He threw a command over his shoulder as he began to walk away. "Kill the thing and hang the body out by the main gate."

"You'd *better* care about the Finder's pet!" Dennel shouted. The captain whirled around, rage blazing in his face. "The Finder is immensely important to Kitru," Dennel said quickly. "He can try the drugs first, but if they fail, he'll need a lever to get cooperation from the girl. This beast might just be that lever."

The captain pondered this briefly. It was obviously to his advantage to keep the tery. If the drugs worked on the Finder, the beast could be slain at dawn; if the drugs failed—and they weren't too reliable—then he could let Kitru decide the beast's fate . . . and take full credit for its capture.

"Perhaps you are right," he said with sudden mildness and turned to the troopers. "Take the creature below and throw it in with the crazy one. . . . They'll make good company for each other!"

This brought a laugh from all the men and broke the tension. Dennel turned and departed, a satisfied smile on his face.

"Who was that?" one of the pikemen asked as they watched him go.

"A coward and a traitor to his own kind," Ghentren replied in a low voice. "He thinks he's got Kitru's ear, but the lord told me himself that as soon as he has no further use of the whelp, I can do what I wish with him." The tery saw the captain's smile and knew from experience what kind of torment it could spell.

A pikeman gave him a poke with the sharp end of his staff and he was prodded toward a sunken stairway that led under a building adjacent to the main tower.

"Below" consisted of a small underground chamber broken up into three tiny cells. It was apparent that there was little need for incarceration facilities at the keep. Executions were far more economical and certainly less time consuming. Sharp, jabbing pike tips herded him into the middle cell and the lone guard locked the door behind him.

Amid harsh barks of laughter someone yelled, "Company for you, Rab!"

The laughter faded as the tery watched the troopers file out. The guard reseated himself by the door and tried to doze. In the wan torchlight that filtered through the grate in his cell door, the tery tried to figure out why the door wouldn't open. He had never seen a lock before. He was peering through the key-hole, trying to see the inner works, when a gentle voice startled him.

"You're a man, aren't you." It was not a question.

The tery whirled to see a filthy, bearded, bedraggled man standing behind him, watching him intently.

"I can tell by the way you examine that lock." He looked old at first, but as he moved forward and came into the light, he appeared to be somewhere between youth and middle age. "Can you speak?" he asked.

"I can speak," the tery said in a slow, harsh, grating voice. "But I'm not a man."

It was odd, speaking to this man. He had never really spoken to anyone but his mother and father in his entire life. He had repeated words and sentences to make Adriel happy, but that was hardly speech.

"Oh, you're a man, alright," the dirty one said, looking the tery over carefully. "It's just that nobody ever told you so. My name's Rab, by the way."

"The troopers called you 'crazy' twice," the tery said pointedly.

"And I must look the part, too!" Rab laughed. "But anyone who's been locked up in a hole for months without a bath, clean clothes, or decent food will start to look a little crazy"—his voice lowered briefly, almost as if speaking the next phrase to himself—"and perhaps even *feel* a little crazy at times"—then rose again—"but I assure you I'm not! And I also assure you that you're quite as human as I am."

The tery snorted. "Do not play with me. I may not be human but neither am I a fool!"

"But you *are* human!"

"I know what I am: I'm a tery, a product of the Great Sickness."

"And I'm a heretic for knowing that you're not!" Rab shouted, then eased his tone. "Sit down and let me tell you what I've learned. You'll find it hard to believe because it goes against everything you've been taught since birth. But I can prove it—at least I could when I had my books. Sit. We've plenty of time."

Reluctantly, the tery complied, easing himself down onto the damp, hay-littered floor. He had tried the door and knew it was proof even against his strength. The conversation he had overheard between Dennel and the captain had eased his fears about Adriel being in any immediate danger . . . and perhaps this deranged human could help him if humored.

"First off," Rab began, "I've suspected since my early youth that the tery is not the mutated beast tradition tells us he is. In fact, I more than suspected it—I knew it."

"How could you 'know' it?"

"Never mind how; let it be enough for the moment that I did. I was raised a scholar in Overlord Mekk's court and had the training and time to search into the past. I found old manuscripts from as far back as the time of the Great Sickness. Our language has changed much since then but I did manage to decipher them and found many references to a group of people called 'the Shapers'. Just who they were and what they did was never explained. . . . It seemed to be taken for granted that the reader knew.

"All this whetted my appetite for more, so I searched deep into the caves and ruins that surround Mekk's fortress. In one I chanced across some old—very old—volumes. They were different from all the others . . . in perfect condition . . . printed on incredibly thin sheets of metal . . . five volumes . . ."

His voice trailed off as he briefly relived the find, a scholar's ecstasy beaming through the grime and matted hair that covered his face. Then he shook himself and resumed his tale.

"Yes . . . five volumes. I finished translating four of them a few months ago and was so caught up with what I'd learned that I ran to tell Mekk himself."

He paused and smiled grimly. "That was a stupid thing to do—for that act alone I deserve to be called Crazy Rab. I didn't get to see Mekk, of course. No one gets to see the Overlord these days since the True Shape priests took over as his advisors. I was shunted off to one of the high priests and should have had sense enough then to keep quiet. But no! Crazy Rab had to lay the entire translation out before him. I was so excited about what I'd found that I never considered what a threat it was to the political power the True Shape cult had acquired.

"You see, I had learned some incredible things in those volumes. I learned that we are just a tiny colony of a larger race, that our ancestors came from the sky and that there are hundreds of other colonies of humans on the other side of the sky. It's crazy, I know, but those volumes are real and obviously not a product of our culture.

"It seems that our ancestors were banned from the mother world and settled here to build their own culture. They were called 'teratologists' and toyed with the stuff within that gives a thing its shape, that makes a child resemble its parents. They set out with the mission to create a perfect race of perfect humans, each with the power to speak mind-to-mind; the Talents were the high point of the teratologist art before it was corrupted. But a perverted element came to power and a being's shape became a plaything for the ruling clique. They created monstrous plants, made beasts look like men and men look like beasts."

"Talents and teries came to be in the Great Sickness," the tery said.

"Not true. That's a myth. Someone like you and someone with the Talent are both human, and both *teries*—products of the teratologist culture."

The tery's expression was unreadable, but his tone was frankly skeptical. "And where is this culture now?"

"Dead. Gone. Wiped out in the Great Sickness. In fact, the five volumes I found were apparently written at the height of the Great Sickness. Their author says in the fourth volume that the teratologists—he calls them 'Shapers'—accidentally caused a change in something called a 'virus' and a monstrous plague swept the world, reducing our ancestors' civilization to rubble. We are the survivors."

The tery regarded his fellow captive thoughtfully. The man did not rave—seemed quite sane, in fact, and spoke with utter conviction. But it was all so preposterous, so contrary to common knowledge! Everyone knew . . . and yet . . . if those volumes truly existed . . .

"Where are the volumes now?" he asked.

"Kitru has them. It's a complicated story involving incredible stupidity on my part. But briefly: In Mekk's fortress, the high priests tried to get the volumes from me—were ready to kill to silence me. So I fled, but not before learning of the proposed addition to the old Tery Extermination Decree that would mark all Talents for extinction. I took the volumes and came here, hoping to find someone in power who would listen. I went to Kitru with my translation and he threw me out. I'm ashamed to say that I went back again and that's when he had me thrown in here to await Mekk's arrival, which has been twice postponed—thankfully. So I've moldered for months. When the Overlord finally does arrives I'm to be burned as a heretic."

He paused, then sighed despondently. "At least I managed to warn the Talents of the extermination decree. Most of them got out in time."

The tery's mind made a delayed correlation: "You're Rab!" he said in an excited growl.

"Yes. I believe I told you that a number of times."

"You're the one the psi-folk have been waiting for!" He had heard the name mentioned many times among the Talents but had failed to connect it with this man.

"How do you know that?" he asked, rising slowly to his feet.

"I've been living with them. But that must mean—"

"Yes . . . I'm a Talent. And a Finder, as well. But Kitru doesn't have a Finder of his own so he does not know that."

"But he does have a Finder!" The tery briefly recounted the day's events.

Rab was frantic. "You mean the Talents are coming here? Now? They'll be wiped out!" He began to pace the perimeter of the tiny cell. "We've got to stop them!"

The tery stood in the center of the cell and watched Rab move around. "Can we dig out?"

Rab stopped pacing and shook his head. "No. The keep is built on solid rock. The only way out of here is through that door." He paused, thinking. Then: "You know . . . I never had the opportunity to get the advantage on one of these guards when I was here alone, but now that there's two of us—and only one of us thought to be human . . ."

IX

The dozing guard at the outer door was startled to wakefulness by shrill cries of fear and pain from the central cell. Grabbing a torch from its wall brace, he rushed to the door and peered through the grate. The flickering light revealed the tery in ferocious assault upon the screaming Rab. The guard hesitated briefly, then decided it might be wisest for him to intervene. Kitru only imprisoned those whom he thought might prove useful at some time in the future. And such must be the case with Crazy Rab. Even though it wasn't his idea to put the two of them together, if the prisoner were killed, the guard knew it would mean his head.

Unlocking the cell door, he entered with the torch held before him. His plan was to back the tery away from Rab and then drag the man out and put him in a separate cell.

"Back!" he yelled, thrusting the torch toward the tery's face. "Back, you ugly beast!"

The tery looked up and shrank away from the flames.

"Don't like fire, aye?" he said, pressing his advantage. "Didn't think you would!"

What he didn't expect, however, was that Crazy Rab would grab his sword arm after he had separated the struggling pair. The guard turned to strike the man with the torch but felt it wrenched from his grasp by the tery who had suddenly lost his fear of fire. In one motion the tery lifted him into the air and hurled him against the stone wall. The guard rolled to the floor and lay still.

Rab bent over him, then rose and regarded the tery uneasily. "He's alive, but barely. You're quite as strong as you look, my friend, but you'll have to learn a little restraint."

The tery's only reply was a low growl. He wanted to find Adriel and could not concern himself with the well-being of those who would harm her.

Rab sensed his companion's impatience and led him from the cell. "Now to the tower. I got to know this area of the keep fairly well while awaiting audiences with Kitru and I think I know how we can gain the stairs of the main tower without being seen. After that we'll have to depend on luck."

Cautiously, they emerged into the courtyard and noted the positions of the sentries. Rab darted along a deeply shadowed wall with the tery close behind; he paused at a flimsy wooden door, peered within, and found it dark and empty.

"This is the kitchen," he whispered, once inside. "They prepare the food for the keep's higher-ups here." He pointed to a narrow door off to the left. "That leads to a passage which opens directly onto the stairs of the main tower. The scullions use it to deliver food at mealtime. I doubt very much if anyone will be watching it now."

They opened the door and felt their way along the inky passage. Torchlight filtered through cracks in another door far ahead and they soon found themselves on the massive circular stairway of the main tower.

Rab glanced above and below, than smiled with relief. "No guards. No one's looking for danger from the inside. Come. We've got to get to the top if we're to find Kitru."

Wordlessly, the tery assumed the lead. Adriel was near now—he could feel it as he glided up the stairs. He halted as he heard the sound of descending footsteps above, around the curve of the stairway before him. Whirling, he motioned to Rab to stay where he was and went ahead alone. A window opened through the outer wall above him. The tery reached it with a powerful leap and concealed himself within its shadow.

A young man, alone, rounded the curve and came into the light of the sputtering torch attached to the wall. Dennel.

As the youth passed the window, the tery leaped from his niche and landed behind him with a whisper of sound. Dennel spun in surprise and fear, then recognized the tery. He peered into the darkness beyond the torchlight, looking for signs of a guard or a keeper. But there were none.

He approached the tery slowly, cautiously—not out of fear for himself, but to avoid frightening the animal off.

"How'd you get out, boy?" he said in a coaxing voice. "Don't worry. I'm not going to hurt you. I'll take you to your friend." He edged closer, talking continually in a soothing, gentle tone. "You want to see Adriel? That's who you're looking for, aren't you? She's right up those stairs and you'll probably get to see her tomorrow. That's when—"

The tery's right hand shot out and closed on Dennel's throat as he rose on his hind legs and lifted him clear of the steps.

"Traitor!" he rumbled in his grating voice. "To save yourself you betrayed all of your kind!" He shook him like a limp doll.

Dennel was unable to utter a sound. Even without the tery's huge hand half-crushing his larynx, the sound of coherent speech from the lips of what he had considered a stupid beast, coupled with the naked fury he saw in that beast's eyes, would have struck him dumb.

"Just hold him steady," Rab said, ascending into the light. "He's a Talent and I'll communicate with him that way to save us time."

Dennel locked pleading eyes on Rab, obviously looking for a way out of the tery's grasp. But Rab's face remained stony until he had learned the answers to whatever questions he was asking.

"All right," he said finally. "Set him down and he'll lead us to the Finder."

The tery complied and hovered impatiently over Dennel as the young man leaned against the inner wall, gasping and rubbing his throat. Rab pushed him upward.

"Move. It'll be light soon."

Dennel took two steps, then lurched away and started to run down the steps. The tery caught the back of his tunic in his fist and raised Dennel into the air again. He was about to hurl him against the stone steps when Rab caught his arm and stopped him with an urgent whisper.

"*No! Put him down!*" He caught Dennel's wide, terrified eyes. "He won't try that again—will you?"

Dennel shook his head, fully convinced now that he was not quick enough to elude the tery's reach.

Rab scrutinized the tery as he put Dennel down. "You frighten me, friend."

"You have nothing to fear from me," the tery said in a rough whisper. "Only the captain named Ghentren and those who would hurt Adriel need fear me." He pushed Dennel between them and pointed upward. "Lead."

Rab paused before moving. "I think I'd know you were human now even if I hadn't found those ancient volumes. Since we entered this tower you've displayed craft, deceit, loyalty and outrage at betrayal. For better or for worse, my friend, you're as human as I am . . ."

The tery pondered this in silence as a thoroughly cowed Dennel led the ascent. Following almost absently, he tried to sort the confused jumble of thoughts within his mind. Could Rab be right? Could he be truly human after all? Was it really so preposterous?

He thought back on his life with the psi-folk and realized that he had accepted their company with such a
natural ease, despite the fact that he had had no previous close contact with humans. Not only had he felt
at home with them, he had been drawn back to them
after initial contact. He didn't need them for food or
shelter—he simply enjoyed being in their company.
Perhaps the desires awakened in him by Adriel the
day before were not so unnatural after all . . .

Further speculation was terminated by Rab's hand
on his shoulder. They had reached the top of the stairway and a great wooden door barred their way. Hearing a voice within, Rab elbowed Dennel aside and gently pushed it open.

A lean, graying man stood in the center of the room,
a wine cup in his hand. He was dressed in a soiled
tunic girded with a leather belt from which hung a
short sword in a scabbard.

The tery heard Rab mutter, "Kitru."

The lord of the keep swayed as he poured red liquid
from a silver flagon. Adriel was bound to a chair before him, her back to Rab and the tery.

"Fool doctors!" Kitru shouted at the girl. "Told me
the drugs would make you totally subservient to my
will—fools! I wasted the entire night waiting for them
to work!" He sipped noisily from his cup. "But when
it's light and I've had some rest, we'll try a new approach—the howls of your beloved pet should make
you more compliant. And if that fails, we'll make sure
to capture your father alive when he arrives to save
you. But I *will* have a compliant—no, *enthusiastic*—
Finder by the time Mekk arrives! Do you understand
me?"

The tery dropped all caution at the sight of Adriel
and burst into the room. Startled by the intrusion, Kitru instinctively reached for his sword. The blade was
out of its scabbard by the time the tery reached him,
but before it could be put to use, the tery knocked it

from his hand and closed long fingers around his throat.

"*Don't!*" Rab cried, knowing what was coming. "Just hold him there until I check the girl."

He leaned over Adriel. Her expression was blank, her pupils dilated. Rab shook her shoulder and her head lolled back, but no sound escaped her throat.

Hearing a menacing growl from the tery, Rab turned. "She's all right. I've seen the effects of this drug before. She'll be like this until about midday, then she'll be sick, and after that she'll be herself again." He looked at Kitru's face which was turning a mottled blue under the tery's grip. "Let him go for now but watch him—we'll use him for safe passage through the gate."

"Who are you?" Kitru rasped as he slumped to the floor and clutched his bruised throat.

"Remember the man you called 'Crazy Rab' and threw into the dungeon?" Rab said with an edge on his voice as he untied Adriel. "I was a much more presentable member of humanity then, but beneath this beard and filth I am that same naive scholar."

"How did you get up here?"

"The same way we'll get down," Rab said, untying the last knot. "The stairs." He rose to his feet. "There! Now, where are my books?"

Kitru jerked his head toward a dark corner of the room. "But only four remain."

"I know," Rab said, striding to the indicated spot. "Dennel told me you're sending one off to Mekk with news that you have a Finder. Your messenger will be wrong on both counts—when Mekk arrives there will be no books and no Finder. And he won't like that."

"Ah! Dennel, is it?" Kitru said, his eyes coming to rest on the young man cowering in the doorway. "You betray *every*one, it seems."

"No, sire! I swear—they forced me into this . . ." His voice trailed off as he sought but found no hint of understanding in Kitru's face.

The tery glanced at Adriel slumped in her chair. She looked . . . dead. He took a step toward her, just to check—and that was when Kitru made his move. With a quick roll he grabbed his fallen sword and gained his feet. The tery pivoted to find himself facing a sharpened length of gleaming steel.

"Rab," Kitru said with a tight smile on his face, "you're not only crazy, you're a fool as well. You should have fled when you had the chance. I'll see you, your traitorous friend, and this beast roasted alive before morning!"

The lord of the keep had lost all trace of fear now. He knew he was a good swordsman, and all that threatened him here were an unarmed scholar, a coward, and an animal. The wine he had consumed further bolstered his confidence.

"We are leaving with the girl," Rab stated coolly.

"Oh?"

"Yes. This fellow"—he indicated the tery—"is a friend of hers. He's going to take her back to her people."

Kitru laughed aloud. "Friend? Oh, I'm afraid you're crazier than anyone ever imagined, Rab! This is her pet!"

"*I am a man!*" the tery said and Kitru took an involuntary step backward. The tery was not quite sure why he had said it; he could not truly say he thought of himself as a man. The declaration had escaped him involuntarily.

"You're not a man!" Kitru sneered after recovering from the surprise of hearing words from the beast's throat. "You're a filthy animal who can mimic a few words."

"How strange," Rab said in a goading tone. "I was just thinking the same thing about you."

In a sudden rage, Kitru roared and aimed a cut at the tery's throat, figuring to catch the beast off guard and then dispose of the others at his leisure. He lunged wildly, however, and the tery leaped aside and aimed a balled fist at the back of the keep lord's neck. Kitru went down without a sound and lay still, his head at an unnatural angle.

Rab came over and nudged the body with his toe. "I wish you hadn't done that. I was going to trade his life for safe passage out of here."

"There'll be no safe passage for us anywhere now!" Dennel wailed.

"We can still get back to the forest," Rab told him.

"The forest! What good is that? It's a living hell out there! I–I'm not like the others . . . I can't live like an animal, scrabbling about for food and shelter. The forest has always scared me. I'm frightened every day out there, every minute. I can't eat, I can't sleep."

"But out there you live as a man," Rab said. "Here, you live as a tool, and only so long as you prove yourself useful."

"No—you don't understand." A thin line of perspiration was beading along Dennel's upper lip. "I can reason with them . . . make them accept me!"

Rab turned away. "Suit yourself." He indicated Kitru's inert form. "Think you can make them accept that?"

Dennel's knees buckled and he had to clutch at the doorjamb to support himself. His voice cracked from the expanding pressure of a sob. "There must be a way!"

The tery had already forgotten Kitru and was kneeling beside Adriel. The girl stared vacantly, unseeingly ahead of her, but did not appear to be physically injured. The tery lifted her, one arm across her back, one under her knees, and held her tightly against him. She was breathing slowly, regularly, as if sleeping. After a long moment, he turned to Rab.

"She will be all right?"

"She'll be fine." Rab was busy wrapping the four remaining books in a wall drapery. Even from across the room the tery could sense something strange, *alien*

BINARY STAR #2   203

about those volumes. "*If* we get out alive. And I've got an idea of how we might do that. If we can get downstairs unseen—"

"There is one debt yet due in this keep," the tery said. He had tasted vengeance blood tonight and craved more. One more life needed to be brought to an end before the balance would be restored. The parent-slayer dwelt below in the barracks.

"What are you talking about?"

"A captain named Ghentren must die before I leave tonight."

"Ghentren left a little while ago," Dennel said from the doorway. "He was sent to Mekk's fortress with a sample of the books and news of the captured Finder. He's gone."

"Forget him," Rab said, swinging the sack of books over his shoulder.

The tery said nothing, but knew he could not forget him. Balance would not be restored until Ghentren's blood had seeped into the dirt like his mother's and father's.

Rab headed for the steps, pulling Dennel after him. "Come. We'll get you out of here alive."

The tery brought up the rear, carrying Adriel's limp form as gently and smoothly as possible. He kept his eyes on Dennel, directly ahead of him, and as they rounded a curve in the stairway, he noted a subtle change in demeanor. The young man's slumped, dejected posture gradually straightened. He stole a quick glance over his shoulder at the now-burdened beast behind him. Without warning, he leaped for one of the window openings in the wall.

"Guard! Guar—!"

With one quick movement, the tery's right arm snaked out and lifted Dennel into the air by his throat. He swung him in an arc and smashed the man's head against the stone wall, cracking it like an egg. A grisly stain remained on the stones as he loosed his grip and let him drop.

Rab's face blanched. "Did you have to do that?"

"If his yelling brought the troopers, we'd all be dead," the tery growled. "Now only he is dead; we still live, and there are no troopers." He clutched Adriel closer. "If he wishes to be killed, he should not include us."

Rab sighed. "He didn't think he'd be killed. I caught a flash from his mind in the instant he called out—he thought he could use sounding the alarm as a show of loyalty. Poor Dennel . . . he feared the forest, and they wouldn't let him stay here."

Continuing the descent, Rab grabbed a torch out of its holder on the wall and led the way to the kitchen. The scullions had not arrived yet. Rab found the wood pile for the stove and shoved the torch into it. After assuring himself that the wood was catching, he looked outside.

The stars were fading and the sky was lightening beyond the wall. Pre-dawn—that hour of the day when consciousness has ebbed to its nadir, when the man awake finds it most difficult to remain so, and when the man asleep is most inert.

Rab and the tery were two wraiths skimming across the courtyard to stand and wait in the shadow under the walkway on the outer wall, each with his own precious burden. They did not have to wait long. The initial whisps of smoke from the kitchen went unnoticed and it was not until the flames caught the door and licked upward that a groggy sentry sounded the alarm.

All available hands rushed to quench the conflagration. As a bucket brigade was formed from the well to the kitchen, Rab and the tery crept up the steps to the walkway. Rab threw his books over the side, then held Adriel as the tery climbed down the outside of the wall. Reaching the ground, he caught Adriel when Rab dropped her over the side, then caught Rab himself.

"Now run!" Rab whispered. "Somebody's sure to

spot us before we reach the trees, so run like you've never run before!"

The tery found the going difficult. He was built to travel on all fours, yet with Adriel in his arms he had to run in an upright position. Her weight threw his balance off, but he still managed to outstrip Rab in their race for safety.

They were half way to the trees when a call went up from one of the few sentries remaining on the wall. But before many arrows could be loosed, they were out of accurate range for even the best of the keep's archers. The trees closed in on them and they were safe.

After putting a little more distance between themselves and the keep, Rab called for a halt and dropped his bundle of books to the sward.

"I don't think there'll be much pursuit, if any," he panted, leaning against a tree trunk. "Once they find Kitru dead, there'll be nothing but chaos in the keep." He noticed that the tery still held Adriel in his arms. "Why don't you put her down and we'll see if we can bring her around."

There was a long pause before the tery answered. All the while, he held Adriel's inert form against his chest, tightly, possessively. Her warmth, her softness, her scent were all awakening a timeless ache deep within him. He had never been so close to her. Holding her like this . . . he had come to a decision.

"That won't be necessary," he told Rab in a dry voice.

"What's that supposed to mean?"

"We're not going to rejoin the psi-folk. We'll find a life of our own in the forest and no one will ever harm or threaten her again."

Rab studied his companion. "I don't think that would be wise," he said softly.

The tery spoke in a rush, more in an effort to convince himself than Rab. "I'm human, am I not? You told me so yourself. And right how I feel very human! She's human, too. And she's lonely and unhappy living with the psi-folk. I could make her happy. She loves me—she's told me so, many times."

"She loved you as a beast!" Rab said, straightening and approaching the tery. "But will she love you as a man? It's a choice that only she can make. And if you try to make it for her, then you're no better than Kitru and the captain who killed your parents!" His voice softened. "And there are some hard facts you must accept: If by some wild chance she did accept you as a man and a husband, the offspring of your bonding would carry your shape—or at least a good part of it. Your ancestors were deformed at the whim of some diseased mind and this atrocity has been perpetuated for generations. It might be best for you to decide to bring their colossal joke to an end—let it go no further than you."

The tery's voice was thick as he spoke. "I would find that easy to say if the only mark I carried was the ability to speak with my mind—a gift rather than a deformity! It is easy to speak of letting the curse go no further if someone else must make the decision!"

A grim smile played about Rab's mouth. "Why do you think I've spent most of my life looking for a link between teries and humans? I told you I *knew* there was a link—how do you think I knew?"

"You . . . ?"

Rab nodded. "I was born with a tail, as were my mother and her brother and sister, and their mother before them." He shook his head sadly. "What amusement my ancestors must have caused some depraved Shaper! Normal in every way except for a tail! But my family has seen to it that the tail is cut off flush with the body immediately at birth—there's virtually no scar left if done that early in life. And so they passed for generations as humans, yet all the while thinking of themselves as teries, lower life forms somehow altered by the Great Sickness so that they looked and acted like humans. I'm sure some of my forebears suspected that they might be human, but none was ever so sure as I. For I had another birthright besides a tail—I had the Talent. Neither my mother nor father was so gifted—perhaps each carried an incomplete piece of the Talent within and those pieces fused into a whole when I came to be. . . . I don't know. . . . There's so much I don't know! But I did know I was a tery with the Talent, and only humans had been known to possess the Talent. So I decided to prove I was human.

"I also decided that the Shapers have laughed long enough. I shall father no children."

The tery stood unmoving, eyeing Rab intently. He had known the man only a short while but had come to trust him. He sensed he was telling the truth. . . . Yet he could not put Adriel down. He felt he would explode if he did not have her.

"You cannot stop me, Rab," he said finally.

"That's true. You've killed two men tonight, nearly killed a third. You could kill me easily. But you won't. Because I sense something in you . . . something better than that. I sense in you most of the good things that are human. And you won't force yourself upon the girl who befriended you."

Rab emptied his ancient metallic volumes from the drapery that had served as a sack, and spread it on the ground. After a brief, tense moment, the tery gently placed Adriel on the cloth and folded it over her. Straightening up, he turned and started to move toward the forest depths.

"Where are you going?"

"Away. I don't belong here."

"Yes, you do!" Rab said. "Or at least you will. The Talents won't accept you as a man right away, and they may even reject you if we push your humanness on them too forcefully. So we'll start slowly. You'll talk more and more; you'll start to use tools. I'll guide you. Before I'm through I'll have them thinking of you as a man before I ever get around to telling them! And the first thing to do will be to give you a name."

The tery had turned and watched Rab's eyes as he spoke. Only one other man had even looked at him that way.

"Will you stay . . . brother?"

The tery said nothing. Moving slowly, almost painfully, he returned to Adriel's side. Lowering himself to his right knee, he buried his face into the palm of his left hand. He remained in that position for a long time. Rab moved away and sat quietly with his back against a tree.

The tableau was broken by the sound of someone crushing through the underbrush nearby. Both were on their feet immediately: Rab half-hidden behind the tree trunk, the tery crouched over Adriel, ready to spring.

A lone man broke into view. It was Tlad.

X

Tlad looked at Adriel's inert form.

"Is she hurt?" There was obvious concern in his voice.

"No," Rab replied, cautiously stepping out from behind his tree. "Just drugged. But who are you?"

"I'm called Tlad. The tery here can vouch for me."

Rab glanced sharply in the tery's direction. "He knows?"

The tery nodded—a very human gesture—and lowered himself to all fours next to Adriel. "He is a good friend. I don't know how he knows, but he does—perhaps for a long time. Maybe he is a tery, too."

The tery's voice showed the physical, mental, and emotional strain of the night's events. His mind and body were numb. A great weight seemed to be pressing down on him, making it hard to breath; but he didn't care. He merely wanted to lie down and let everything pass. He felt adrift . . . lost . . . stripped of his identity. His place in the world had been torn away from him: He was no longer a tery, he was a human. But he could neither live as one nor be accepted as one. He knew Tlad should not have been able to find them, yet he had. The tery did not have the will to wonder how.

Not so Rab, who wasted no time in satisfying his curiosity. "How did you know to look for us here?"

But Tlad did not answer. Instead, he walked to where the ancient volumes had been spilled from the

drapery and knelt to inspect them in the growing light.

"These yours?"

"Yes."

"Then you must be the one the Talents have been waiting for. Rab, isn't it?"

"You're one of us?"

"No." Tlad continued speaking as he flipped through each of the volumes. "But they're not far behind me, heading directly for the keep. I suggest you let them know where you are. They're in range."

Rab looked off into the forest for a moment, then returned his attention to Tlad. "There. They know we're safe and where we are. Should be here soon. Now, tell me wh—"

"Where's Volume Five?" Tlad said in an agitated voice. He quickly ran through the four volumes a second time. "Did you lose it?"

Rab sat down with a jolt on the other side of the pile of books, a dumbfounded expression on his face. "Who *are* you? I'm the only one who can read these things! How could you know that Volume Five is missing? This is the only set!"

"Wrong," Tlad replied. His voice was low, his words hurried. "I come from a fishing village but never had much of a bent for the sea. So as a boy I used to comb the ruins up the coast. I found a similar set and brought it to the village elder who knew how to read some of the ancient writing. He kept the books for a long time, and when he was finally through with them, he made me row him out past the reef. As we sat in the boat, he swore me to secrecy and told me what the books contained. Then he threw all five overboard."

"So you know about the Shapers and the truth about the teries."

"I also know the contents of Volume Five."

"Then you know more than I do," Rab said. "I never got to translate that one."

"Then it's lost?"

"No. One of Kitru's officers is on his way to Mekk's fortress with it now."

Tlad shot to his feet. "NO!"

The violence of Tlad's reaction startled Rab and even managed to penetrate the mental fog enveloping the tery. He rose and padded toward the pair.

"What's in the fifth volume?" Rab asked.

Tlad hesitated, then seemed to reach a decision. "Volume Five tells of the final days of the Shapers and how they gathered all their records, their techniques, and their hardware into a huge underground cache. Among the items they hid were the superweapons they used to keep the underclasses in line. Volume Five gives the location of that cache."

Rab, too, was on his feet now. "And it's on its way to Mekk!"

"If that madman gets his hands on those weapons, there won't be a forest to hide in. He'll have everything that doesn't bear True Shape—whatever that means—hunted down and destroyed. And a lot of other things will get destroyed along the way . . . maybe everything. Is there any way we can intercept that officer?"

"No," Rab said with a quick shake of his head. "Dennel told me that the messenger was scheduled to leave before first light. He's long out of reach by now. Where is the cache?"

"Right under Mekk's fortress, if the maps were accurate. The Shapers seemed to think it was pretty safe—you had to go through the Hole to get to it."

Rab blanched. "The Hole? Then it's unquestionably safe."

"Surely the Hole is empty now!"

"No. The offspring of the original inhabitants still dwell there—no one dares to let them out. And no one enters the Hole willingly. Don't worry: The cache is safe."

"I wouldn't count on it. If Mekk learns that the

Hole stands between him and the power to destroy anything that displeases him, he'll find a way around it or through it. He'll get to that cache. We've got to get there first!"

"And how do we do that?"

Tlad tugged at his beard. "I can't say. I'm from the coast . . . I don't know much about Mekk's fortress."

"You certainly know your way around the forest!"

"I *live* in the forest now—I'm a potter, not a fisherman. But there must be some way we can get into the fortress and retrieve that book."

"There is none, I assure you. Mekk dwells in mortal fear of assassination—that's why he's postponed his inspection tour of the provinces so many times. The walls of his fortress are sheer and high—not even our tery friend could scale them."

"How about the main gate? There's got to be traffic in and out of the fortress!"

"All civilians must have passes to enter the fortress, and all are sent home at dusk. Mekk's tower is surrounded by troopers day and night. I'm afraid we're lost."

"No," Tlad said with a certainty that seemed unfounded, "we're not lost. There has to be a weak spot, and I'll find it."

He turned and walked off into the trees.

The psi-folk arrived soon after Tlad's departure, and it was a silently joyous event. They all recognized Rab by his Talent and crowded around him, slapping him on the shoulders and back. Adriel was laid on a drag and had regained consciousness by the time they all returned to the camp area that evening. Rab, Komak, Adriel, and the tery sat apart during the celebratory feast that followed.

"This is quite a fellow you have here," Rab said, indicating the tery, who had not strayed from Adriel's side during the entire journey.

"That he is," Komak agreed. Rab had made sure to

impress upon all the importance of the tery's role in Adriel's rescue. "Never thought he would amount to much when Tlad convinced me to bring him into the camp, but he's certainly proved me wrong. He's a smart one—smarter than some humans I've known!"

"Is that so?" Rab said, his eyes dancing as a smile showed through his freshly washed and trimmed beard. "And you say Tlad was responsible for bringing him into camp?"

"You know Tlad?"

"We've met. A most interesting man. I'm anxious to meet him again. We've many things to discuss. But getting back to our friend here—do you have a name for him, Adriel?"

The girl shook her head carefully; she had been beset by a throbbing pain in both temples since awakening. "No. I was waiting to find a name I liked for him but never got around to deciding. He's always been just 'the tery'."

"Then I shall take the liberty of naming him for you. Do you object?" Adriel was not in a condition to object to much of anything, so Rab siezed the advantage and pressed on. "Good! Then I shall name him *Jon*."

"Jon is a man's name," Komak said. It was more of an observation than an objection.

"He shall be Jon, nonetheless."

XI

Two days later, when Adriel was well enough to travel, Rab assumed the role of leader from Komak with the latter's grateful blessings. He moved the tribe in a generally eastward direction, away from Kitru's realm and toward Mekk's fortress. He would keep a respectful distance between his people and the Overlord's legions, but he had determined that the Talents' days of blind flight were over. He sensed within that the enigmatic Tlad would find some weak spot in Mekk's defenses and would need help. He wanted to be nearby to supply that help, for the same inner sense told him that the fate of his people was in some way tied to Tlad and to Mekk's fortress and—stranger still—to the tery. He felt constrained to keep all the pieces at hand until the puzzle could be solved.

The tery stayed with the tribe during its leisurely eastward trek. He avoided Adriel, however. Once assured that she had recovered from the drugs, he kept his distance. The girl didn't understand this and was visibly troubled, but the tery forced himself to ignore her hurt and spread his company among the rest of the psi-folk. He did so not only because Rab suggested it, but because proximity to Adriel had become such an achingly painful experience.

He would walk beside one of the Talents for a while and pretend that he was practicing his speech. He'd point to an object and call it by name, or point and pretend he didn't know what to call it and induce the Talent to tell him. He was fully accepted by everyone now because of his heroic rescue of Rab and Adriel, and within a matter of days the psi-folk were subconsciously convinced that he was more of a burly aborigine than an animal. Everyone delighted in increasing Jon's vocabulary.

He hated it. Before he had met Rab, it had been almost amusing to play the dumb animal. Now things were different. Now he found the role degrading. He wanted to belong, to be accepted as the thinking, feeling, rational being he was. He, too, awaited Tlad's return to give the psi-folk—and himself—a direction other than flight, a goal beyond survival.

Rab drilled the archers daily. The march would be stopped in mid-afternoon; after camp was set, targets would be raised—some were suspended on ropes with pulleys for practice against moving targets—and simultaneous volleys were rehearsed time and time again. There was some grumbling over sore fingers, arms, and shoulders, but the improvement in coordination and accuracy was significant.

Tlad walked into the camp at sunset of the eighth day and was immediately drawn aside by Rab. Jon the tery followed. He wanted to hear what was being planned and, as ever, knew that he liked being near Tlad.

"Well?" Rab said expectantly when they were out of earshot of the rest of the tribe. "Did you come up with anything?"

"Yes and no. There seems to be no way to get into Mekk's fortress other than a frontal assault, and we haven't the numbers for that. Also, there's no way to get to the weapons cache other than through the Hole."

Rab's face showed his disappointment. "So far you haven't said anything we don't already know."

"Have patience. I've been wracking my brain to remember the maps I'd seen in Volume Five, and finally came up with a crude idea of what the area around

Mekk's fortress looked like before everything fell apart during the Great Sickness." Tlad looked tired and his voice was strained, as if he had recently been under great stress. "I've found a way to get into the Hole without going through the fortress. That means we can get to the weapons."

"Go through the Hole?" Rab said in an awed whisper. "That's impossible! We'd be torn to pieces!"

Jon broke his silence. "What is this Hole? I've never heard of it."

"Mekk's fortress is built over the ruins of what used to be the headquarters of the old Shaper regime," Tlad said. "They performed most of their experiments there and all their failures went into a sealed cavern below. They let monstrosity mate with monstrosity down there to form new and even more monstrous off-spring."

"It's a man-made hell," Rab said, visibly shuddering. "I once had a glimpse of its denizens through one of the grates that provide ventilation for the Hole."

"Aparently the Shapers enjoyed watching them," Tlad said. "They built an underground corridor with a transparent wall through which they could watch the goings-on in the Hole in safety. I can get us to the Hole without Mekk's or his troopers' knowledge. From there it should not be far to the cache."

Rab was adamant. "No matter how near or far it is, it can't be done! The foulest, most depraved teries in existence live down there in constant warfare. The only thing that can bring them together is the sight of a normal human—they will act in concert to pull that human to pieces, then resume fighting over the remains!" He lowered his voice. "That is how Mekk's enemies are executed—dropped through one of the grates into the Hole."

"It's a risk that must be taken," Tlad insisted.

"Forget it! Mekk would have killed off the Hole dwellers if he could—as teries they fall under his extermination decree, don't forget. But he's left them alone. His troops won't go near the Hole and he'd risk a mutiny if he tried to force them."

"Then I can't help you," Tlad said angrily and turned to go.

Jon placed a restraining hand on his shoulder. "Wait. Perhaps a tery could reach these weapons through the Hole."

Silence followed as both men looked at the tery.

"It could work," Rab said finally. "But how could one man accomplish anything?"

"He could bring back a few weapons," Tlad replied, "and with those at hand, we could clear a path through the Hole—nothing could stand in our way—and get the rest."

"Yes!" Rab cried. "That's it!" He put his arm around Jon's hulking shoulders. "Brother tery, you're about to save the Talents once again!"

"Why must it be like this, Tlad?" Rab said as the two men sat alone by the central fire after the rest of the camp had drifted off to bed. He had a pile of small pebbles in his hand and was throwing them into the fire one by one. "Why must we be out here in the forests struggling to stay alive while Mekk and his priests and his troops are in their fortress scouring their brains for ways to find and kill us?"

"Because they believe you're offensive to the sight of their god." Tlad smiled sardonically in the dying firelight. "Who could think of a better reason?"

"I could think of a better way to use religion, I assure you! Besides numbers, our biggest disadvantage is that the religious myths have been turned against us. The True Shape faith says that the Great Sickness was an act of God, through which He altered all those who displeased him, and that all those bearing the mark of the Great Sickness are offensive to God and must be eradicated. The priests got to Mekk years ago and convinced him to order the extermination of all teries.

And a few months back they got him to add the Talents to the list. It's now an act of devotion to go out and kill a tery or a Talent."

"I'm sure Talents were included in the extermination order for political reasons as well," Tlad said. "If Mekk is as suspicious and fearful as you say, he probably wanted to eliminate those subjects who could possibly plot against him without ever saying a word."

"That's probably true. And at this point the provinces are complying with the extermination decree out of fear of Mekk's wrath. But as time goes on, the practice of killing on sight anything that doesn't bear True Shape will become traditional and customary and routine. It will continue long after Mekk is gone because it is entwined with religious myth. How do we fight that? How do you fight a myth?"

"With another myth," Tlad said.

Rab laughed at his companion's matter-of-fact tone. "Just like that? Another myth? Ah, if I had that power! I'd create a religion that could bring us all together, not drive us apart. Or better yet, I'd do away with all religion and let us live for ourselves, not for a mythical creature."

"That would be unrealistic. Myths exist because people want them, cling to them, need them. To supplant existing religions, you'll have to come up with a bigger and better god, one who will push the others aside, one who thinks teries and Talents are every bit as good as humans."

"If I can get our hands on those weapons," Rab said with sudden intensity, "I'll show Mekk and his priests just how good teries and Talents can be!"

"Is that what you want the weapons for? To make yourself the Overlord?"

"No, of course not. But we can use them to change things around to our benefit. We won't have to run anymore—from anyone!"

Tlad made no reply. He merely gazed into the fire, a worried frown on his face.

Jon sought Tlad out the next morning and learned that he had departed at first light, no destination given. He headed for Tlad's hut. It was mid-morning but he knew he could easily catch up. No human could move through the forests as fast as . . . he'd have to get used to classifying himself as human. He had come to accept that now and he wanted the other humans around him to accept it. But Rab said go slow, go slow, go slow. So he did. But it irritated him more and more each day that he had to hide his intelligence. Previously taciturn by nature, he had now developed an insatiable urge to talk to other humans. But there was no one to listen. Rab was always busy or surrounded by Talents, and when Tlad arrived, he and Rab spoke of things that Jon could not understand, and so he was forced by ignorance to remain silent.

Thus he sought out Tlad—who was human yet did not seem to require the company of other humans. Perhaps he would accept the company of a tery who desperately craved to be with another human on an equal footing. They were both aliens, outsiders, standing apart from the rest of the culture . . . Tlad by his own choice, the tery by heritage and decree of law.

Tlad was not at his hut, had not been there recently by all signs. Perhaps they had traveled different paths, the tery passing him on a parallel course. Jon waited for a while, then decided to scout through the area between the hut and the new camp of the psi-folk.

Eventually, he came to a familiar clearing. Looking to his left he saw what he had come to call the shimmering fear. And walking right up to it—*into* it—was Tlad. The shimmer enveloped him and he disappeared.

Jon ran forward. If Tlad was in danger he had to help. Had whatever was inside the shimmering fear drawn him in? Or was he immune to the fear? These questions remained unanswered as he felt the first tentacles of terror and revulsion coil around his chest and throat and begin to squeeze. But still he ran. He ran until he felt he could no longer breath, until his legs became stiff and rigid. And when he could no longer run, he walked, slowly, painfully, forcing each limb forward until he was within the shimmer and the forest was gone and all that was left was the fear that buzzed around and through him. Still he forced himself on, one more step . . . one more step—

—and the shimmer was suddenly gone. With it, the fear. He stood panting and sweating in a cool, odorless room that seemed to be made out of polished steel.

Not three paces ahead of him sat Tlad, seated with his back to him. He was staring intently at a portrait of a man on the wall above him. Jon opened his mouth to speak . . .

. . . but the portrait spoke first.

XII

I regret having to say this, Steven, but I'm going to have to turn down your request. The Federation Defense Force intervenes only in certain strictly limited areas, and your request for intervention on Jacobi IV does not meet the criteria set forth in the LaNague Charter. The imposition of a protectorate in this case would be at odds with the very purpose of the Cultural Survey Service, which is to preserve and promote human diversity. The psis you've described on Jacobi IV are well on their way to establishing a truly tangential culture; intervention by an interstellar culture at this point would stifle them. Your talented friends will have to find their own way out of this predicament, I'm afraid, and I wish them all the luck between the stars. You may help them, of course, but only with the materials at hand. Good Luck, Steve, and out.

Damn!" he said through clenched teeth as he angrily cut off the playback. No sense in running through it again. There was little doubt left that this was an irrevocable decision on the part of the higher-ups. "Of all the stupid narrow-minded—"

He turned and saw the tery standing in the lock.

"Jon?"

"You live within the fear?" the tery said, a tone of awed wonder in his gruff voice.

"The fear?" He was thrown by the reference for an

instant, then realized that Jon was referring to the craft's ultra-sonic repeller that induced a flight response in the autonomic nervous system of any higher organism within range. "Oh, that! I use it to keep out curious creatures. But how'd you get in?"

"I thought Tlad was in trouble. But you are not really Tlad, are you?"

"No, I'm really Dalt. Steven Dalt." For all his beastial appearance, this tery had a quick mind. Dalt tried to match his quickness but could come up with no lie that would ring true enough to save his cover. He thought carefully before he spoke. The tery respected him, felt indebted to him—he had come through the fright field because he thought Tlad was in trouble. Why destroy that store of confidence with an obvious fabrication?

"But you are still my friend, are you not?" Jon asked with a pleading innocence and sincerity that Dalt found touching.

"Yes, Jon," he told him, "I'm still your friend. I'll always be your friend. I'm here to help you and the psi-folk, and I'll need your help most of all to do it." Dalt reached a hand toward the tery's right shoulder and removed a fine silver thread. "I planted this tracer on you before you went to Adriel's rescue. I've got them here and there among the psi-folk . . . helps me keep track of things."

He laid the thread on one of the consoles, then picked a small disk from a slot by the lock and placed it in the tery's hand.

"Hold onto this as we walk through the 'fear.' It will protect you from it. I've got one in my belt buckle."

Together they walked undisturbed through the shimmer that protected Dalt's craft visually and the neurostimulatory field that guarded it physically, and stopped in the shade of some neighboring trees.

Dalt sat cross-legged on the grass and motioned for the tery to join him. "Get comfortable and I'll tell you all about me. After I'm done, hopefully you'll know

enough to want to keep what you've just seen a secret."

He started first with a historical perspective—how
the mother world decided it could colonize the stars
and get rid of all its malcontents, dissidents, and
troublemakers in a single stroke: a promise of one-way
passage to an Earth-type planet to any group of sufficient size that wanted to set up the utopia of its choice.
It was the era of the splinter world and there was no
shortage of takers. Soon the habitable worlds in a
sphere around Earth were peopled with all sorts of
oddball societies, most of which collapsed within a few
years of landfall.

The teratologist colony was an exception. Its
pioneers were all well-grounded in science and technology and managed to build a viable society. Their
goal was a world of physically perfect human telepaths
and they were on their way when the Shaper clique
took over. That's when teries and other monstrosities
were formed; that's when the Hole was started; and
finally, that's when the Great Sickness was born.

A small group of the teratologists banded together
during the plague and gathered samples of all the
available technology of their time into one spot and
sealed it up. They then wrote a brief history of the
colony in five volumes and buried it for posterity. . . .
They saw their civilization coming apart and wanted
something preserved. Before they, too, succumbed to
the Great Sickness, they beamed the contents of the
volumes into space.

The message was received. This was in the days of
the outworld Imperium, which had little interest in
rescuing diseased teratologists. So the message was du-
tifully recorded and forgotten. It was only after the
LaNague Federation rose from the ruins of the Imperium, and the Cultural Survey teams were started in an
attempt to bring surviving splinter worlds back into
the mainstream of humanity, that the transcript of the
five-volume transmission was found.

Steven Dalt, fresh from his infiltration of the feudal splinter culture on Bendelema, was given the job.

"Are you following me so far?" Dalt asked.

The tery neither shook his head nor nodded. "What is a planet?" he asked.

"What's a pla—?" Dalt then realized that for all its native intelligence, Jon's mind was primitively unsophisticated in its ability to grasp cosmological concepts. The stars were points of light, the planet on which they stood was "the world" and the primary it circled, "the sun." His talk about the LaNague Federation and splinter worlds and interstellar colonization and been totally incomprehensible to the tery—like discussing the big bang theory with someone who still believed in a geocentric universe. Yet he had listened patiently and with interest, whether through personal regard for Dalt or through a desire to have someone—anyone—address him as a fellow rational being, Dalt could not say.

"Let's put off that explanation for some other time, Jon, and just accept the fact that I was sent from a faraway land to see how things were going here."

Things were not going well at all, as he soon discovered after landing and camouflaging his craft. A preliminary survey had located the population centers, made language recordings, and returned to Fed Central. Dalt absorbed the language—a pidgin version of Old Earth Anglic—via encephalo-augmentation and was ready to talk to the natives and assess their suitability to handle modern technology. Since they favored hard consonants in their names, he turned his own around. And since he did not want too close contact with the locals, he posed as a reclusive potter deep in the forests.

His advent coincided with Mekk's order for extermination of the Talents and he found himself acting as potter and confidant to a unique group of telepaths. Here was something every Cultural Survey operative dreamed of finding: A group of humans split off from the mainstream of the race, developing a separate and distinct life style. This was the very purpose for which the CSS was formed.

But on this planet they were marked for extinction.

So Dalt had sent an urgent request by subspace laser for an intervention by the Federation Defense Force to protect these psis and let them follow their course. And had been turned down.

"So now it's up to you and me," he told Jon the tery. "I'll get no help from my friends back in my homeland"—*and I can't even use a blaster, though I'll be damned if I won't carry one with me when we go to the Hole*—"so we're going to have to carry the show."

The Talents removed their camp deeper into the forest, putting more distance between themselves and Mekk's fortress. Then the archers moved forward and ringed the fortress in small groups.

The war began. They became the perfect guerrilla force, striking then disappearing like fish in the sea. When Mekk's generals sent a hundred men out to search the surrounding trees, they found nothing. When they sent ten men out to investigate a minor disturbance, none came back.

The net result of all this activity was a gradual withdrawal of the patrol lines around the fortress, a tightening of perimeters that gave Dalt, Rab and the tery a chance to seek out and finally uncover the old entry port to the corridor that ran parallel to the Hole. They moved rocks and dirt until there was an opening just big enough for the tery to slip through. Dalt nodded to Rab, who was to wait by the entrance and use his Talent to summon help if necessary, then followed—and entered Hell.

Dalt had been expecting the worst, but nothing hinted at in his transcript of the teratologist history had prepared him for the sight that greeted him.

The forgotten corridor stretched before them with a gentle curve to the left. The left wall was composed of a thick transparent substance that jutted out into the Hole at a forty-five degree angle. Its outer surface was smeared with a mixture of dried blood, excrement, and dirt, undoubtedly left there by generations of Hole inhabitants trying to claw their way out.

But there was no way out. The rock that made up the floor, sides, and ceiling of the Hole had been treated by the Shapers to make it impervious to any digging or tunneling attempts. The only access to the outside world was through the vertical shafts leading to the ventilation grates, and these were lined with the same impenetrable glassy substance that now separated Dalt and Jon from the Hole. The porous rock that remained within had been treated in another way: It glowed. All corners of the Hole were dimly lit by an eerie blue-green phosphorescence. The light arose from all sides, totally eliminating shadow and adding to the surreal, dreamlike quality of the hellish panorama before them.

For food, the Shapers had developed a rapidly growing fungus that hung from the ceiling of the Hole in stalagtitic abundance. For water there were a number of underground springs that fed into a large pool at the center of the cavern. The temperature was a damp, cool, subterranean constant. For those who required shelter, a hidey-hole could be dug into the porous rock that had not been treated against it. There was no wood, there was no fire, there were no tools of any sort.

None of the Shaper mistakes would ever escape, none would ever starve, none would ever die of thirst, none would ever freeze.

And none would ever know a moment's peace.

There was no social order in the Hole. The strongest, the fiercest, the ones that best hunted in packs—these ruled the Hole. The weak, the timid, the sick, the lame became either food or slaves. The sense of entrapment, the foul living conditions, compounded by generations of inbreeding, had reduced the inhabitants of the Hole to a horde of savage, imbecilic monstrosities.

As Dalt and Jon walked along the corridor, they watched scenes of nightmarish barbarism that were a part of day-to-day existence in the Hole. A creature with an amorphous body, six tentacles, and a humanoid head shuffled along, picking up morsels of fungus and stuffing them into its mouth. Without warning, another creature, reptilian in body with horny plates projecting from its back—and again, the humanoid head, always a humanoid head—launched itself from a burrow about a meter off the floor and landed on the tentacled creature's back. With sharp fangs it tore into the flesh of its victim's neck until blood spouted over both of them. The victim rolled onto its side, however, and managed to wrap one of its longer tentacles around the attacker's throat.

The two outsiders did not wait to see whether one's oxygen supply could outlast the other's blood supply, but left the combatants writhing on the other side of the window as Dalt led on.

"There's a door somewhere along here," he told Jon. "The Shapers made one entry from the corridor into the Hole. I just hope we can open it when we find it."

The tery said nothing and Dalt glanced at his companion, wondering if he could hold his own in there. Jon would have two advantages—his intelligence and his hunting club. Dalt had wanted to give him a blaster, but the tery had been too frightened of its power. He felt more comfortable with the weapon that had protected him and helped feed him for most of his life. So a club it was.

I wouldn't go in there with two *blasters,* Dalt thought, glancing into the Hole again. He estimated from the difference in light levels between the cavern and the corridor that the monsters on the other side of the window probably didn't even know the corridor existed. The light from the phosphorescent stone would reflect off the filth smeared on the window making it look like an unusually smooth section of the wall. The Shapers had probably wanted it that way so they could watch without being seen.

Jon stopped and pointed to something on the window. "What is that, Tlad?"

Dalt saw a round, dark splotch about the length of a man's arm in diameter edging its way down the Hole side of the window. He tried to get a peek at what it looked like on the reverse but it must have been flat and disk-shaped, for he could make out no protrusions from the other side.

A movement to the right caught his eye. Down a narrow path came five dark shapes, low to the ground, scuttling. The disk must have had an eye on the other side and it, too, must have seen the approaching shapes, for it reversed direction.

Then the shapes were close enough for Dalt to make out details: They had normal human heads and torsos, but all resemblance to humanity as Dalt knew it ended there. Each had a dark skin and eight legs—four to a side—which were articulated spider-style. But it was the naked hunger-fury in their blank, idiotic faces as they swarmed up to the window and attacked the disk that made Dalt leap backwards and slam against the far wall of the corridor. He knew he was safe. The movement was involuntary.

Then came a further horror. After the spider gang had peeled the disk from the wall and was carrying it away to wherever it was they lived, Dalt saw its other side. There were only a few details, but even in the dim light a fleeting glance showed beyond a doubt the features of a human face.

Jon's eyes snapped to him. He had seen it, too.

"This is how they must live?" he asked Dalt. "Why was this done to them? Why must this be?"

Dalt arched himself away from the wall and came over to the tery. He had developed a genuine affection for this innocent in beast's clothing. Jon could not comprehend the corruption of spirit that could occur when one human found he had absolute control over the existence of another. But then, neither could Dalt.

"Jon, my friend," he said, putting his hand on the tery's shoulder as they began walking again, "none of this *must* be. All this is a construction, a product of the worst in us. It doesn't *have* to be, but it is. Nothing that can happen to us by chance is anywhere near as awful as what we somehow manage to do to each other by design."

"We?" Jon said. "What is we? I would never do this!"

"I was speaking of all humanity in general—and that includes you, my friend, like it or not."

"But I am not a 'we' for this," Jon rumbled in his deep voice. "I would like to be a 'we' with you and Rab and Komak and Adriel, but no . . . I am not a 'we' in this. Never!"

The note of finality in Jon's voice made Dalt decide not to pursue the matter any further. They walked on in silence, watching an endless variety of depraved forms that skulked, leaped, crawled, shuttled, scuttled, and ran through the small area of the Hole that was visible to them.

The door was unmistakable when they came upon it. The windowed wall of the corridor had been one long, uninterrupted, seamless transparency. After following the curving passage along an arc of approximately forty degrees, they saw the window end at what appeared to be a huge steel column, perhaps three meters across and reaching from floor to ceiling. The window continued its course on the far side of the column.

"This has to be it," Dalt said as he inspected the smooth metallic surface. Finding a recess large enough to admit four fingers, he inserted them and pulled. Nothing. He scanned the door again and found three small disks at eye level. "The code—I forgot!"

He reached into his tunic and pulled out a slip of paper. The combination was *Clear, 1–3–1–3–2–3–1–2.*

"Clear? How do you clear?" The transcript had never said. It gave the combination sequence, but never explained how to clear the circuit.

Playing a hunch, Dalt pressed all three disks at once, then tapped in the sequence. When he put his fingers into the notch and pulled this time, a panel swung out on silent hinges, revealing a small chamber. The ceiling began to glow as they stepped inside.

Before them was another door, a narrow one, secured by four steel bars as thick around as a man's thigh. Dalt noticed a wheel on the wall to his left and began to turn it. The bars moved. The first and third bars began to withdraw to the right, the second and fourth to the left.

Dalt stopped turning when the bars had moved half their distance.

"All right. We know we can get in. Do we want to?"

Jon cocked his head questioningly.

"I mean," Dalt said, "can you make it? Is there really a decent chance of your getting to the cache and back again through that . . . that nightmare?"

He was not merely trying to give the tery an easy out; he was seriously concerned with the feasibility of this entire mission. No one had thought it would be easy, but the Hole was proving to be a more awesome obstacle than he had imagined. And for all Jon's strength and cunning, he seriously doubted he could last for very long in there.

"I must go."

"No, you mustn't anything!" He paused briefly, then: "I don't want you to die, Jon." He meant it. There was something in this misshapen young man that he wanted to preserve and keep nearby. He didn't know whether to label it innocence or nobility or a combination of both. But it was good and it was there and he didn't want to see it torn to pieces in the Hole.

Jon tried to smile—it was a practiced grimace that did not come naturally to his face. "I will not die."

"You may. You may very well die. So think hard before deciding."

"There is nothing to decide, Tlad. I am the only one who can go. A human—that is, one who looks like a human—cannot go. Only a tery. So I must."

"No! We can find another way. The Talents can hide and grow and maybe wait this out. You don't have to die for them!"

"I will not die. I will save them, and then they will have to recognize me as a man. They will have to accord me the honor of thinking of me as a man."

So that was it, Dalt thought. This was the tery's trial by combat into the human race.

"That's not necessary, Jon. You—"

"I am going, Tlad." Again that note of finality. "Tell me what to find."

"*If you go at all, you're going to have to go twice!*" Dalt shouted, then waited for the expected effect.

Jon remained impassive. "Then I shall go twice. But tell me why. I was to find the cache and bring back sufficient weapons for the Talents to—"

"There will be no weapons for the Talents," Dalt said. "I fear they will harm the psi-folk as well as help them. The weapons in the cache will give them too much power and may even lead to the rise of another type of Mekk . . . one with the Talent. The cache must be destroyed."

Jon made no comment, but locked his eyes with Dalt.

"Do you trust me?" Dalt asked finally.

"I'd be dead if not for you."

"That doesn't mean I'm right and that doesn't mean you should trust me. It only means I—"

"*I trust you!*" Jon roared and his voice was deafening in the tiny chamber.

"Good," Dalt said in a low voice. "Because I trust you, too."

In the dust on the floor of the chamber he drew a picture of the explosive device he wanted Jon to procure from the cache. It was ovoid in shape, small enough to fit comfortably in the tery's hand, and powerful enough to set off a chain reaction among the other weapons stored there. From the inventory described in Dalt's transcript, there was enough explosive power available in the cache to make a shambles of Mekk's fortress above, permanently ending his petty empire of fear.

The device had a timer that could only be set by hand—detonation by remote control was impossible, unfortunately. That was why the tery would have to make two trips: the first to bring it back to Dalt for the time-setting; the second to return it to the cache.

"And the Hole dwellers? What happens to them?" Jon asked.

"This entire cavern will collapse. Their misery will be over."

The tery considered this in silence.

"I think that's for the best," Dalt said. "Don't you?"

"I trust you, Tlad." That seemed to be enough.

Dalt then showed him how to work the combination studs, and drilled him until he had the sequence firmly committed to memory.

"That's all I can do for you," Dalt said after a final run-through of the description of the device and the combination. "A door identical to this outer one here is imbedded in a wall of rock adjacent to the central pool. Head straight out from here and you should find it. And keep moving!"

He turned the wheel until the bars on the inner door were fully retracted, then ran out to the window to make sure all was clear. Returning to the chamber, he grasped Jon's huge right hand in his own.

"Good luck, brother."

Jon growled something unintelligible, then together they pulled the door open. Dank, sour, fetid air poured over them as the tery leaped through and began to run. Dalt pushed the door closed and turned the wheel until the bars just overlapped the edge of the door—just enough to keep some Hole dweller from lumbering through by accident, but not enough to cause any significant delay when Jon returned.

Then he went to the window and watched. And waited.

XIII

The stench.

It struck him like a blow. The odors of rotting flesh, stale urine, and fresh feces assaulted his acutely perceptive olfactory senses as soon as the door opened. But above all was the unmistakable scent of kill-or-be-killed tension. It saturated the air, permeated the walls.

He moved straight out from the door and entered a winding passage that curved left then right. The palm of his right hand was sweaty where it gripped his hunting club. Jon was frightened. He had disguised his fear when talking to Tlad—had almost hidden it from himself, then—but now it came screaming to the surface. He was trembling, ready to strike out at or jump away from anything that moved or came near him.

This was not the forest. The rules here were all different, as unique as they were deadly. The softly glowing rock walls on either side of him were pocked from floor to ceiling with burrows and recesses. Any mad, frenzied creature of any shape imaginable or otherwise could be lurking within, ready to pounce.

He maintained his pace at a wary trot, first upright, then bent, using his left arm as an extra leg, eyes continually moving left, right, above, and behind. So far, no sign of Hole dwellers. There were dark things pulled back tight into the burrows around him, he knew—things that might rush and leap upon him were he smaller and less sure-footed.

The passage widened ahead and forked left and right. His innate sense of direction led him to the right, but as he started down the new path, there came a cacophony of scraping feet, growls of rage and grunts of pain from around the bend not far ahead of him. And it was moving closer.

Looking up, he spotted a ledge within reach above his head. He pulled himself up and lay flat on his belly with only his eyes and his forehead exposed. The noises grew louder, and then the source staggered around the bend in the passage.

It looked at first like a huge, dark, nodular creature with multiple human heads and uncountable black spindly arms waving frantically in all directions. But as it moved closer, Jon realized that it was a gang of the spiderlike teries he and Tlad had seen earlier— perhaps the same gang, perhaps a new one—attacking another larger creature en masse.

The lone victim suddenly reared up on its hind legs and threw off four or five of its attackers, but an equal number remained attached. Jon saw that this creature was vaguely human in form, although grotesquely out of proportion. Its round, bald head was affixed to its body without benefit of a neck; its shoulders were massive, as were its arms, which reached nearly to the ground when it raised itself erect. From the shoulders the body tapered sharply to a narrow pelvis and ludicrously short, stubby legs. Jon also saw what the spider gang was after: not the creature itself, but the three small wriggling children clinging to its underbelly. That and rudimentry breasts labeled it a female.

And a female to be reckoned with! Her hugely muscled arms swatted fiercely at the members of the spider gang, keeping them away from her young as she struggled to reach shelter. She was holding her own until two of the spider-men attached themselves to her back and started clawing at her eyes. This happened as the group passed beneath Jon and it would have been to

his advantage to let them all move on by. But something in that misshapen mother's defense of her
equally misshapen young touched him and he had to
intervene. Just this once.

He leaned over the edge of the ledge and swung his
club at the nearest spider-man on her back. The blow
cracked across the middle of the creature's spine and it
went spinning to the floor where it lay screeching in-
coherently and kicking—but only the two forward legs
were kicking. The second glared up at Jon with unfo-
cused fury in the imbecilic eyes of its human face, then
launched itself upward with a howl. There was no revenge motive in its action, only hunger at the sight of
what appeared to be a more vulnerable prey.

The howl caught the attention of the other gang
members and for an instant they withdrew from their
attack on the mother and her young. She did not hesi-
tate to take advantage of it: a huge arm lashed out
and grabbed one of the spider-men by two of his legs,
then lifted him and smashed him against the floor
again and again until the two limbs were torn free of
their sockets and the rest of the pulpy body skidded
across the floor to land against a wall and lay still.

Jon was not watching. The spider-man's leap had
brought him to the ledge and from there it lunged directly at Jon's face. He battered at it before it could
reach him. Four wild bone-breaking swings of his club
and the creature was knocked from the ledge. The rest
of the gang looked on its three fallen members and
fled back the way they had come.

The mother went over to the creature with the injured spine and halted its screeching with two crushing blows to the head. She then checked the body of
the one that had fallen from the ledge. Satisfied that
none would ever bother her again, she backed up to
where she could get a look at Jon. Standing erect, she
stared at him, her dull mind trying to comprehend
why he had helped her. The two legs she had ripped
from one of the spider-men were still clutched in her

hand. The three little monstrosities clinging to her abdomen began to wriggle and squeal. Without taking her eyes from Jon, she put the bloody end of one of the legs up to her wide mouth and nibbled off a piece of raw flesh. She chewed rapidly without swallowing, then took small bits of the masticated meat from her mouth and fed them to her young. With an abrupt motion, she walked over to the ledge and held up the untasted leg to Jon.

He leaped to the ground and fled down the passage, retching.

These were once human? he asked himself when his stomach had settled and he had slowed from a run to a jog. *Or are they still human despite what they've become? And where do I fit in?*

No answers came.

He arrived at the central pool, a stagnant body of water fed by a slow underground spring. It was dark in this region. Perhaps the excess moisture had a deteriorative effect on the phosphorescence. Whatever the cause, it made finding the door Tlad had described more difficult.

Jon began scouting the water's edge, looking for a rock wall with a door in it. He found it almost by accident—if he had not been dragging his left hand against the rock as he searched, he would have passed without noticing it. But his fingers felt a long vertical groove and he stopped to inspect. The notched handle was there. So were the three studs.

Water rippled behind him. He turned and saw nothing at first. Another ripple and he spotted something floating on . . . no, rising *from* the pool. He could not make out the shape and did not care to. Whatever it was, it did not wish him well.

Brushing off the studs, he quickly tapped in the code, 1–3–1–3–2–3–1–2, then grabbed for the notch. The door stayed firm. He tried the code again and still no result. A glance over his shoulder showed him that something monstrously large had risen from the pool and was looming over him. He tried the sequence again and beat frantically at the door when it did not open. Then Tlad's words came back to him: "Whatever you do, don't forget to clear."

Jon hit all three buttons at once and tapped in 1–3–1–3–2–3–1–2 and pulled. It moved! Dust, dirt, and pebbles powdered him as he dropped his club, thrust both hands into the notch, placed his left foot against the wall and pulled with desperate strength. He didn't have to look behind now—moist air from the formless behemoth's cold wet surface was wafting against him as it reared over him.

The door suddenly jerked open and he fell back against something cold and slimy, then he catapulted himself into the opening and pulled the door behind him. It closed only half way. Fallen debris was jamming it open. The creature outside, however, solved the problem for him by lumbering against the door and forcing it closed with its weight.

The room seemed to sense Jon's presence. Panels in the ceiling began to glow, adding to the luminescence in the walls, as he tried to gather his wits. The room was loaded with crates: they lined the walls and stood in long rows before him. Where to begin?

After a brief rest—this was the first time he felt safe enough to let down his guard since leaving Tlad—he started with the pile on his left and moved along the wall, tearing open the flimsy packing of the crates with his hands. Some held books, others drawings and pictures, but most of the contents were totally incomprehensible to him. More things he didn't understand! There were so many!

Tlad was one. Why did he trust that man? He had already lied to everyone a number of times . . . Tlad wasn't his real name . . . he did not come from the coast . . . he was not a potter. Why trust a liar? Tlad had spent days talking to Jon, trying to explain where he came from and why he was here. All Jon could glean from the monologues was that he came from far away and wanted to help the Talents and all other teries.

But he had *talked* to Jon, treated him as a man, thought of him as one. Because of that, he would do anything for Tlad . . . even aid him in deceiving Rab and the Talents by destroying the weapons instead of bringing them back. Tlad said it was for the best and Jon believed him.

He found the bombs eventually, crates of them, all neatly stacked against the wall. They were egg-shaped as Tlad had said, with a smooth, shiny surface. These could kill? These could destroy the Hole and Mekk's fortress as well? It did not seem possible. But he had trusted Tlad this far . . .

Only one was needed. He cupped this in the palm of his hand and returned to the door. Pressing his ear against its smooth metal surface, he listened for signs of activity outside. All was quiet. The door moved easily at his touch and he stepped back as it swung outward. Nothing but the narrow path and a smooth expanse of water awaited him. The inhabitant of the lake was gone.

The lights in the cache room dimmed slowly as he exited and were fully extinguished by the time the door clicked shut. He looked down and saw his club where he had dropped it. It was covered with slime— everything was covered with slime. Wiping the handle of the weapon clean against the fur on his leg, he followed the slime trail along the edge of the pool and noted that it wandered off into the passage he had planned on taking back to Tlad.

He changed his plans. Despite the fact that the path in question was the one that brought him here and was the only one he knew, and despite the fact that his greatest fear in the Hole was to become lost, he decided on an alternate route. He would trust his sense of direction on a strange path more than he would trust his club against that dark behemoth from the pool.

The new passage was not very much different from the other and he made good time, loping along on his hind legs with the bomb cradled in his left hand against his chest, and his club swinging back and forth in his right. Then trouble. Rounding a bend in the passage, he literally ran into a pack of nine or ten spider-men.

Without the slightest hesitation, they were on him with a howl. Jon backed up slowly, swinging his club sparingly but with telling effect, always keeping it menacingly before him. After the initial assault, the gang kept its distance, constantly trying to flank him, constantly trying to get behind him. But while Jon was keeping them in front of him, he was unknowingly allowing himself to be backed into a dead-end branch of the passage. When he realized his position, it was too late. They had him boxed in.

Now they attacked in earnest—a suicide charge on three levels with some leaping for his legs, others for his arms, and others for his head. Whirling and swinging his club, kicking when opportunity presented, he managed to hold them off until one of the spider-men landed on his back and started gouging at his eyes—this seemed to be a favorite tactic of theirs. He shook the creature off, but lost his balance in doing so and went down on one knee. The gang swarmed over him and Jon felt himself start to fall onto his back. He raised his left arm for balance and suddenly felt powerful fingers close about his wrist. With a force that threatened to pull his arm from its socket, he was lifted free of his attackers, hauled into the air and unceremoniously dumped into a cave beside the mother monster he had aided earlier.

She hissed and pushed him behind her, then returned her attention to the furious spider gang below. As they swarmed up the wall, she sat back and waited for them. As soon as one would poke his head inside the cave mouth, she would punch at it with one of her huge fists. She seemed to be enjoying herself.

Jon found that he had lost his club but still held the egg-shaped bomb. He looked around for something else to use against the spider men but found nothing. He did, however, find the corpse of one of the gang members slain earlier. The mother's young were clustered around it, nibbling. Noticing a light toward the rear of the cave, he stepped over the grisly feast and went to investigate. The tunnel curved sharply upward but the light ahead was an irresistible lure. He climbed swiftly.

There was a break slightly smaller than his head in the back wall of the cave. Light poured through it—not the sickly phosphorescent glow that permeated the Hole, but a brighter, cleaner, familiar light. Sunlight.

Jon put his face to the opening and peered through. He found he was looking into a large vertical shaft with sheer, smooth, unblemished walls. From above where the sunlight filtered down, a gong was clanging and a man began screaming. By leaning his shoulder against the wall, he found he could twist his neck and see to the top of the shaft. A heavy iron grate covered the opening. Above that was blue sky and humans.

The grate was lifted as a naked, struggling, terrified man was brought to the edge. His arms were tied behind his back, his screaming had stopped, reduced now to pitiful whimpering. A voice was speaking in measured tones, its words indistinct, perhaps praying, perhaps reading a sentence . . . something unsettlingly familiar about that voice . . .

It stopped and the man began screaming again. The two troopers holding him gave a powerful shove and he fell free with wildly flailing legs and a cry of utter despair and terror that followed him all the way down the shaft, ending abruptly in a chorus of growls and scuffles from the waiting Hole dwellers below. Jon could not see the floor of the shaft and did not want to.

He watched instead the faces of the troopers above him as they squinted into the dimness below in an effort to catch some of the more grisly details of their ex-prisoner's fate. Then a third face joined them in peering over the edge and Jon felt his hackles rise: it was Ghentren, the captain from Kitru's keep.

Suddenly, it was all back—the grief, the rage, the pain. Somehow his close association with Dalt had pushed it all to the back of his mind, layered it with scar tissue, and smoothed it over. But nothing had healed. It was all still there, fresh as ever, as the boiling heat in his chest told him. He wanted Captain Ghentren's blood as much as ever. The balance craved restoration . . .

. . . and would have it!

Jon pulled back from the opening and looked at the death egg in his hand. Here was the key. He would need Tlad's help in gaining access to Ghentren, and the bomb would assure Tlad's cooperation. He hefted it in his left hand and began to slide down the incline toward the mouth of the tunnel.

The mother creature awaited him with her brood clustered about her. The spider gang was gone—either driven off or finally and forcefully convinced of the futility of trying to gain entrance to the cave. She pressed back against the wall to let him pass and as he did so she hissed and bared her teeth at him. It was not a smile or even an attempt at one, but rather a warning that all was settled now and if she ran into him again it might well be his body that wound up providing nourishment for her young.

Leaping to the floor, Jon paused to get his bearings and noticed two dead spider gang members at the foot of the wall. His club lay between them, untouched— the hands of the spider-men were not built to wield such a weapon. He retrieved it, then made his way out of the cul-de-sac and back down the passage toward the doorway to the observation corridor and safety.

When he had almost reached his destination, Jon halted and searched the softly glowing dirt and rock that lined the walls on either side of him. A loose stone was located at eye level and pried out. After scraping out a small hollow, he placed the bomb within and pressed the stone back over it, then stepped back and surveyed his work. Satisfied with the job of concealment, he turned and ran the rest of the way back to Tlad.

XIV

Dalt's heart leaped when he saw Jon's familiar form break from a pile of stony rubble and race toward him. He jumped back from the window and dashed into the lock. Grabbing the wheel on the wall, he spun it until the locking bars slid free of the door, then pulled it open. Jon leaped through and helped him close it after him.

"Thank the Core! You made it!" he said. It was all he could do to keep from hugging his big, bearish companion. All the while Jon had been gone, Dalt had imagined a thousand gruesome deaths and had sworn never to forgive himself if anything happened to him in there.

But now it was over and the tery didn't look any worse for the wear—no, wait a minute—there was blood on his face, neck and back . . .

"You all right?"

"Yes, all right," Jon said in his growlly voice. He was breathing easily, evenly as he stood there. "Only hurt a little."

"Did you find the cache?"

"Yes. Found it. Found the bombs—many of them." There was an odd tenseness about him as he spoke.

"Well . . . where is it?"

An instant of hesitation. "Out there."

"You dropped it?"

"I hid it."

Dalt was baffled. "Explain, Jon."

The tery quickly recounted what and whom he had

seen in the air shaft. He concluded by telling Dalt that the captain had to die.

"Oh, he'll die all right," Dalt assured him. "Everyone up there—Mekk, the priests, the troopers—they'll all go when that one bomb sets off the others."

"No. You do not understand. He must not die without knowing. He must realize that his death restores a balance that was damaged when he killed my parents. He must know that before he dies."

"It's called vengeance, Jon," Dalt said slowly. "And you've certainly got some coming—generations' worth. But the bombs will provide it with interest."

"No," the tery repeated. "You do not understand. He must—"

"He must squirm and plead and beg before you kill him? Is that what you mean? Is that what you want? You want to sink to some of his tactics, is that it?"

Struck by the vehemence of Dalt's voice, Jon made no reply.

"You're better than that, Jon! Rab told me how you killed Dennel and Kitru, but that was different—that was when you were trapped in the middle of hostile territory. What you're talking about now is not like you. It's cold-blooded and not worthy of you." His voice softened. "You may not know it, Jon, but there's something noble and good and decent about you. People sense it. This Captain Ghentren is scum, no better and no worse than the others up there. Don't dirty your hands on him!"

"But the balance—"

"Blast the balance! The bombs will take care of that!"

"*No.*" The note of irrevocable finality in the tery's voice brought Dalt's arguments to an abrupt halt. "The bomb will not be replaced in the cache until I have seen the parent-slayer's blood on my hands!"

"And now blackmail," Dalt said in a low whisper. "You learn fast, don't you." He ached inside as he faced Jon. The poor fellow had been through so much in such a short time. His home, his security, his very identity had been shattered, and something within him clung desperately to the belief that all would be set right by the death of this Captain Ghentren.

"What do you want me to do?" Dalt asked, dully watching innocence crumble before him.

"Find Ghentren," the tery rasped. "It is still day and you can go above in the fortress and find out where he sleeps. I will visit him tonight and restore the balance. Then I will return and replace the death egg after you have done what you must do to it."

Dalt considered his options and found he had none. He was bound by the Cultural Survey Service regulations to work within the technological stratum of the society under observation, but that wasn't holding him back now. Only a full Defense Force combat rig would get him through the Hole, and there wasn't one of those available to him. If he decided to abort the entire mission, it was as good as handing all those weapons directly over to Mekk, for sooner or later the Overlord would find a way to get to them. And that would be the end of the Talents and anything else that dared to deviate from the norm on this world.

Damn the Fed and damn the CS Service! Why couldn't they establish a protectorate? He was getting tired of asking himself that question and receiving no answers . . . no answers he liked.

"Since I have no choice," he told Jon, "and since the future well-being of our friends, the Talents, depends on placing that bomb"—he looked to the tery but saw that he remained unmoved—"I'll do what I can. But I'll need your help to get to the surface."

Jon said nothing but stood quietly, waiting for Dalt to get started. Feeling at once saddened and exhausted, Dalt spun the wheel that locked the door into the Hole and turned away. The diagrams in his transcript of teratologist history had shown one or two air shafts leading up from the observation corridor, as they did from the Hole. These, however, were equipped with ladders. They found one further on down the passage. Dalt climbed up the rungs imbedded in the wall of the shaft and clung to the underside of the grate to see where he was.

The opening appeared to be situated in an alley. Shadows were lengthening and all seemed quiet. He sensed no one about. Moving his hand along the edge of the grate, he found what he wanted: a lever, rusty with disuse. After applying most of his weight to it, there came a creak of metal on metal and the lever moved, releasing the grate.

Moving that was another matter, however. The full force of the muscles in his back and legs was not enough to budge the heavy iron structure. The combination of ponderous weight and rusty hinges was proof against his strongest efforts.

But not against Jon's. The tery glided up the ladder and threw his shoulder against the grate. With an agonized whine of protest, it swung upward until there was enough of an opening for Dalt to squeeze through. The tery let it fall shut as soon as he was clear.

A quick glance around showed Dalt that his initial assessment had been correct: He was in a deserted alley, blind at one end. He peered down into the shaft and saw Jon's face hovering on the other side of the grate.

"Wait here," he told the terry. "Get ready to open this thing as soon as you see me. I don't know what I'm going to find up here and I may want to get back down there in a big hurry."

"I will wait," was Jon's only reply.

Dalt walked slowly to where the alley merged with a narrow thoroughfare and looked about. There was little traffic this time of day. The civilians from the village down the hill had sold their wares or done their assigned tasks and were gradually filtering out of the fortress and returning to their homes. They were all required to be out of the fortress by sunset anyway.

He watched two peasant-types pass by and fell in

behind them. All Cultural Survey operatives undergo in-depth training in human behavior and mannerisms, the rationale being that humans will behave like humans, no matter how long they have been separated from the rest of the race. There would always be exceptions, of course, but in general the CS theory had been proven correct on many a cut-off splinter world. Dalt had been taught to utilize an array of subtle non-specific behavioral cues to give him an aura of *belonging* in any milieu. Calling on that training now as he walked the streets of Overlord Mekk's fortress, he appeared to be a civilian who was used to traveling within these walls and who knew exactly where he was going.

Actually, he had no idea where he was going, but knew he did not want to go through the gate and down to the village, which was where the two men he was following were headed. He turned off at an intersection and went hunting for barracks or any other place where troops might be gathered at this time of day.

It was nearly sunset when he found a group of them clustered about the door to a tavern of sorts, sipping mugs of ale and laughing. They had no doubt just come off the day watch. Dalt approached and stood slightly off to one side, affecting an air of humble deference to their positions as defenders of the Overlord. Finally, one of them turned to him.

"What are you standing there for?" he asked in a surly tone. He was dark, middle-aged, with a big belly and no hint of kindness or mirth in his laughter. "Looking for a drink?" He casually flipped the dregs of his mug at Dalt who could have easily dodged the flying liquid, but chose instead to let it spatter across his jerkin.

He carefully brushed himself off while the troopers roared and slapped the fat one on the back. Adjusting his clothes, he checked on the position of the blaster tucked inside his belt—it was against all CS regulations to carry one but he knew Mekk's troops were selected for their brutality and he had no intention of letting some barbarian swine like this fellow stick a dirk between his ribs just for fun, regulations or no regulations.

"I'm searching for Captain Ghentren," he said when the laughter had quieted enough for him to be heard.

"You won't find him here," the fat one said, more kindly disposed now toward a man he had embarrassed and degraded.

"I bring some of his personal effects from Kitru's realm," Dalt said. "He is awaiting them."

"Well then you'd better rush off and find him, little man!" the fat one roared and went to refill his mug.

Dalt took a gamble. "I'll find him sooner or later, and I'm sure he'll be glad to learn of all the help I received in carrying out his errand."

This brought a sudden change in mood to the group of troopers. Their laughter died and the fat enlisted man turned and studied Dalt. The gamble had paid off—Ghentren was not known as one of the more easygoing officers.

"He's quartered in the red building over there," he said, pointing. "But he's out on patrol now. Should be back after sunset."

Dalt turned to see which building he meant, then walked the other way, leaving an uneasy knot of troopers behind him. He was drawing a mental map and picking out easy landmarks for Jon to follow in the darkness when a bell sounded from the direction of the gate. That would be the warning signal for all civilians to leave the fortress. He quickened his pace.

XV

Jon found waiting for Dalt an agonizing experience. If he were captured by the troopers for being inside the fortress without a pass, he would be dealt with harshly—perhaps lethally—and it would all be entirely the tery's fault. And it had all been a bluff. If Tlad had held firm and refused to go up into the fortress, Jon knew he would have had no choice but to place the bomb as he had originally promised. But his intransigent posture, augmented by his genuine craving for revenge, had fooled Tlad.

As he watched the sky darken through the grate, he became more and more apprehensive. He was about to promise himself that if Tlad returned unharmed he would abandon all plans to kill Ghentren, that he would give up restoring the balance in exchange for Tlad's well-being, when he heard footsteps approaching. A voice above him whispered.

"Open up! Quick!"

It was Tlad's voice. Straining, he pushed the grate upward until Tlad could slip under it, then let it down slowly. Both clung to the ladder rungs in silence for a few heartbeats, then descended to the floor.

"You found him?" Jon asked, his resolution of a moment before completely forgotten. Knowledge that the debt incurred by the slaughter of the two beings in the world he had loved most was soon to be settled vibrated through his body, blotting out all other considerations.

Dalt nodded in the dim glow that washed through

the transparent wall of the observation corridor. "Found him. But I'm warning you—don't do it. You won't be the same man when you come back."

"Tell me where he is." The tery's mind was on a single course now. With obvious reluctance, Dalt knelt and drew a map in the dust on the floor, showing Jon which way to best travel without being seen.

"He's in a red building here," he said, pointing. "Just where in that particular building he'll be, I don't know." He looked up and caught the tery's eyes. "It's too risky for you. Don't go."

"I won't take long," Jon said. He turned and glided smoothly up the ladder into the darkness above. There was a creak, followed by a clank, then nothing.

He felt consumed by a terrible urgency as he moved from shadow to shadow along the narrow, ill-lit streets. He felt as if everything would be put right when Captain Ghentren was dead—the sun would move more smoothly across the sky, the breeze would blow cleaner, the world would have brighter days. Ghentren had become a blot on all Creation, a defect that had to be removed. Only then . . . only then would everything again be as it should be. The end of Ghentren consumed him, obsessed him, inflamed him—

The red building lay ahead. Jon had to detour through three back alleys to avoid passing across a wide courtyard lined with off-duty troopers. Reaching the building, he stole from window to window, listening for a voice, looking for a face when he dared. He found the captain in a corner room. He was seated on his cot. A woman stood before him.

"Pay me first," she said, giggling. "That was our agreement."

"I could have you arrested for being within the walls after dark," Ghentren said with a playful smile as he reached into the coin pouch at his belt.

"I and others like me have been an exception to that rule, long before you ever came here."

A table with a lamp and a low wooden stool completed the furnishings of the room. The door to the left was closed and bolted.

Jon was through the window and standing in the middle of the tiny room before either of them noticed him. Ghentren shot to his feet as the girl began to scream but the tery was faster than either of them. With a single motion he shoved the girl back into the corner of the room where she huddled stunned and gasping for breath, then ripped the captain's reaching arm away from the hilt of his sword. Wrapping the fingers of his right hand around the man's throat, he lifted him clear of the floor and held him there.

"*Look at me*!" Jon said in a low growl, his face a hand's breadth from the captain's. He seemed to be surrounded by a bloody haze that narrowed the world's population to two individuals, he and the captain, forever locked in combat. Nothing else existed at this moment, nothing else mattered. He could feel within his body the arrows that had killed his father, feel across his throat the bite of the blade that had cut off his mother's life. He had hungered for this moment.

"Do you remember me?" he hissed into the captain's terrified face. The mouth worked but no words passed the lips. He shook his head: no, he absolutely did not remember the beast that held him by the throat.

"Remember the two teries you killed near a cave when you were working for Kitru?" Jon said. He wanted Ghentren to remember. He must know why he was dying. "Your archers killed the male and a swordsman nearly beheaded the female—remember?" Still no light of recognition in the eyes. "And the son, the young tery who charged you with a club—remember what you did to him? Remember how you and your men chased him and sliced his flesh until he could no longer stand? Remember how you left him for dead?"

Jon caught an impression of movement out of the corner of his right eye. The girl, still cringing in the corner, was rising slowly to her feet. He ignored her, and brought Ghentren's face closer to his own until their noses almost touched. *"He did not die!"*

Ghentren remembered. It showed in his eyes. Horror and mortal fear of a slow, agonizing death accentuated the terror already distorting his features. There was something else: a kind of irrational disbelief that this was really happening. Yet there was no denying the solidity of the form before him, nor the pressure on his windpipe.

More movement to Jon's right—the girl was edging along the wall toward the door. He was about to reach for her, to thrust her back into the corner, when the man in his grasp did something that took the tery completely by surprise. He began to cry. Tears rolled from his eyes as his body jerked with deep, pitiful sobs. Jon let him go and watched as he sank to his knees and begged in a choked voice for mercy. His pants were soaked with urine down both legs and he shook with unconcealed terror.

Feeling as if he had been suddenly doused with icy water, Jon took a step backward and regarded his nemesis. The red haze was gone, as was the rage. He was aware of the woman somewhere in the room behind him, bending toward the floor, but his mind was now completely filled with wonder at his own stupidity. Was this blubbering, groveling creature even worth slaying? Was this the man whose death was to restore the balance?

What a fool he had been! Risking Tlad's life and bartering with the lives of all the Talents just to come and personally put an end to the days of one man. Tlad had been right—Ghentren wasn't worth it. His right hand felt unclean now after touching him . . .

Turning to go, he caught a blur of movement behind him. Before he could react, the back of his head seemed to explode. His knees gave, and as he fell he saw the girl standing there with the wooden stool in her hand. He tried to rise but Ghentren was up and had grabbed the stool from the girl. Jon saw him raise it, saw it descend, then saw nothing . . .

. . . pain in his hands and in his feet . . . can't move them . . . the cool night air on his face . . . opening his eyes and looking down on a cheering, jostling crowd of troopers . . . and beyond them, others . . . all watching him . . . a loud gong echoing through the darkness . . .

. . . there's wood against his spine and against the backs of his outstretched arms . . . he looks right and left and sees spikes through his palms, nailing him to the wood . . . same with his feet . . . and there's rope around each of his arms to keep him from sagging too much and ripping free of the spikes . . .

. . . he hangs outside the fortress on a cross of wood . . .

. . . a voice below droning may this be a lesson to all not of True Shape who should dare to raise a hand against one of the guardians of the Overlord . . . a slow death instead of a quick one . . .

. . . there's kindling below, around the foot of the cross . . . the one in robes who was speaking puts a torch to it and steps back . . . light flickers off the faces of the men circled below . . . Ghentren the parent-slayer is among them, his face joyously hate-filled . . . the man he had spared stands safe now below and cheers the flames upward along with the others . . . men . . . humans . . . he had so wanted to be accepted as one of them . . .

. . . one of *them*? . . . why? . . . look at them . . . look at their glee in the face of another's agony . . . why had he wanted to be a man at all? . . . better to have stayed a tery forever . . .

. . . and then he remembers Tlad and Komak and Rab . . . and Adriel, of course . . . it was their acceptance he had craved . . . they were the humanity he had sought . . .

"I AM A MAN!" he shouts to those below as the

heat builds . . . suddenly there is silence . . . awed
. . . shaken. "I AM ONE OF YOU!"

. . . someone laughs, nervously . . . then another
. . . a stone flies out of the darkness and lands on his
right shoulder . . . then there is laughter and jeering
all around . . . and more stones . . .

. . . he has to close his eyes now . . . the heat is
too much . . . the fur on his legs is burning, but the
pain seems far away . . . the Talents . . . he failed
them . . . now Mekk will get the weapons and exterminate them once and for all . . . they counted on
him and he failed them . . . what can they do now?
. . . the pain comes nearer . . . each breath seems
to contain flame . . . thoughts run together . . . am
I dying as a man or as a beast? . . . does it matter?
. . . does anyone in the laughing darkness out there
know that a man is dying up here? . . . does anyone
care? . . . will anyone remember me? . . . does anyone who knows me know I'm dying . . . will the Talents curse me and hate me for failing them? . . . not
Adriel . . . please don't let her hate me . . . please
let someone remember me fondly after I'm gone . . .
please let someone say, just once, that there was a good
man . . .

All became pain and confusion, and soon the pain
passed beyond all comprehension . . .
. . . leaving only confusion.

XVI

Jon was late.

The sound of the gong made Dalt uneasy. There was something ominous in its tone and Jon was late. He could have been back and forth to Ghentren's quarters three times by now. Faintly heard laughter drifted in from the far end of the alley as Dalt waited under the grate. A passing voice shouted something about "a burning."

That did it. He was frightened now. Jon was in trouble—he was sure of it. He pressed up against the grate but still could not budge it. Leaving the latching lever in the open position, Dalt descended as rapidly as he knew how and hit the floor running. If he were wrong, Jon would be able to lift the grate and get down the airshaft on his own when he returned. If his suspicions were correct and Jon was in trouble . . . there had to be something he could do.

The ceaseless struggle for existence in the Hole went unnoticed through the viewing wall to his right as he ran down the corridor. He came to the opening where the rocks had been pulled away and climbed out into the fresh night air. Rab was supposed to be waiting but Dalt could find not a trace of him. There was no time to waste looking for him. It was perhaps two kilometers along a ravine and up a hill to the fortress. Dalt ran all the way.

He saw the flames as soon as he topped the bank of the ravine, but wouldn't allow himself to think that Jon might be in any way involved. They leaped high, those flames—six or seven meters into the air. The conflagration stood to the right of the gate, a short distance from the outer wall, and was surrounded by a knot of people. A trooper shouted to him as he ran up.

"Where have you been? All villagers are to report to the gate when they hear the gong. You should know that by now. Get up there and learn a lesson!"

Dalt made no reply as he hurried on. He noted that the civilians were keeping to the rear of the circle of spectators, most with averted eyes. The front ranks were completely taken up by troopers, cheering, laughing, and drinking as they watched the burning body affixed to the cross.

He suspended all emotion as he pushed his way to the front to confirm his worst fears. No facial features were left on that charred corpse. None were needed. The barrel chest, the shape of the head and legs . . . unmistakable.

Jon, the tery, the man, was dead.

There were voices around him and Dalt heard them as if from a great distance.

"—hear he could have killed the captain but didn't—"

"—and she says he had Ghentren up in the air by the throat and just let him go—"

"—'s like they say, these teries are stupid. Could have killed him clean and got out the same's he came in, however that was, and didn't do it. Deserve to die, all of 'em—"

"—oughtta burn them more often—"

"—better'n running them through—"

Dalt had feared that he might fly into an uncontrollable rage, that he might grab his blaster and start burning holes into these savages, but that was not to be the case. The blaster would remain hidden in his belt. An icy calm had slipped over him. He turned quietly away and strode toward the forest.

He felt dead inside. Everything had gone wrong on this accursed planet and this was the final blow. He had grown to love Jon and now he was dead, horribly dead. If only . . .

If only! There was a long string of *if-only*'s trailing through his mind, starting with the Shapers and their perversity, on through his CS superior's refusal to authorize a protectorate, up to and including his own attempts to discourage Jon from trying to settle his personal score with Ghentren. If only he had tried a little harder, maybe he could have convinced him not to go . . . if only he hadn't tried so hard, maybe Jon wouldn't have hesitated, maybe he'd have dispatched that captain and been back in a few minutes' time. Perhaps he would have hesitated anyway because of the innate nobility that made him Jon. Dalt didn't know.

One thing he did know, however, was that Jon would still be alive if a protectorate had been set up. The CS service was at fault there. Always hesitating, always stepping back, always mincing around . . . he was through with a hands-off policy as of this moment. Those scum back there liked fire, did they? Well, then fire they'll—

"You're to stay by the gate until you're dismissed!" said a trooper standing back from the crowd. He started to move forward to block Dalt's path, then retreated. Perhaps there was something in the way Dalt held himself, in the way he moved; perhaps the trooper caught a glimpse of Dalt's white, tight-lipped face. Whatever it was, the lone sentry decided to let this one pass without an argument.

Not too much further back, Dalt came upon Rab standing in the darkness, a staring, motionless figure, transfixed by the flames.

"Rab!" Dalt shook his shoulder roughly. "Rab, are you all right?"

Rab blinked twice, then staggered. For a heartbeat or two, he didn't seem to know where he was. Then he recognized Dalt.

"Tlad! I saw it all! It was horrible! They're all monsters in that fortress! What they did to Jon . . . I never dreamed anyone could—"

Dalt put a hand over his mouth to silence him. When he spoke, his voice was cold, flat, emotionless. "I know. We've got to tell the rest of the Talents."

"They already know. I acted as a conduit and transmitted everything I saw back to them. They know about Jon, now, and are all witnesses."

"Adriel?"

Rab glanced back at the dancing flames. "Komak will tell her. Tonight I was glad she was without the Talent. We've lost a good friend—another life Mekk will answer for some day. But for now, what do we do next?"

"We split up. You go to your people in the forest and stay there. No one is to venture near the fortress until morning. *No one!*"

Rab looked at him questioningly, but before he could speak, Dalt hurried on.

"Remember what I told you when you asked me how to fight a myth?"

Rab's brow furrowed momentarily, then he nodded. "Another myth—a bigger and better one."

"Right! And the new one starts here. Tonight. It will be about a creature everyone persecuted because he was called a tery, but he was really a man. And how one day he was captured and died horribly at the hands of his persecutors. You spread the word about that, Rab. And tell the world what happened to those who killed him."

There was no reply from Rab. He stared uncomprehendingly at the man he knew as Tlad.

"Don't worry, Rab. I'm not mad. Not yet, at least. But something is going to happen tonight, and I don't want it passed off as a natural catastrophe. I want people to remember tonight and know that it happened for a reason."

"What's going to happen?"

Dalt's face was a mask. "Something I'm going to have to live with the rest of my life."

Rab watched in silence as Tlad turned and trotted off into the trees, knowing with an unaccountable certainty that he would never see him again.

Dalt brought his ship to a silent hover over Mekk's fortress. Except for a few sputtering torches, all was dark below. Perhaps a few embers glowed around the base of the cross that held the tery's charred remains, but Dalt could not see them from where he was. The villagers had returned to their frightened hovels far down at the base of the hill. All was quiet.

He pointed up the nose of his slender craft and aimed his ion drive tubes at the fortress. He had to do this *now*. If he gave himself time to think, if he actually allowed himself to weigh the risks of firing an ion drive within a planet's atmosphere, he would abandon the whole idea. But Dalt was not thinking now. He was doing.

During the course of the rest of his very long life Dalt would analyze and reanalyze the reasons for what he was about to do. Eventually he would conclude that it all hinged upon the uniqueness of Jon the tery. If anyone else in his group of contacts on the planet had been immolated outside Mekk's fortress, he would have grieved, cursed, ground his teeth with the rest of them, and continued the mission. But Jon's death had temporarily unhinged Dalt. There had been something very special about that rough beast who was a man; something clean, free, and innocent; a certain incorruptible saneness that was singular and precious in his experience. And now it was gone—lost to Dalt and the rest of humanity forever. Gone . . .

. . . but he would see that it was not forgotten. Jon deserved better than to have his ashes scattered to the wind. He deserved a more permanent memorial, an enduring tombstone. And he would have it.

A long blast from the tubes that drove his craft through peristellar space would prove disastrous here in an oxygen-laden atmosphere; the Leason crystal lining would crack and Dalt and his craft would become a tiny, short-lived sun. But a short blast . . . a short blast would obviate the need for a protectorate; a short blast would also obviate the need for a CS operative below. It would have the same net effect as the bomb he had wanted Jon to plant in the cache: Mekk would be gone, his fortress would be gone, the cache of Shaper relics would be gone, and the Hole would be gone. All with one short blast, and far more dramatic.

As he reached for the lever that would activate the drive, Dalt steered his thoughts away from those things, just as he steered them away from the painful memories of Jon the tery.

He began composing his letter of resignation from the Cultural Survey Service.

". . . with the image of the immolation seared upon their minds, the Talents, led by the Apostle Rab, spread the word: that God had chosen to send his messenger in the form of what was then considered a lower life form. God did this to show us that teries were men, too, and that we are all brothers."

"Amazing!" Father Pirella said as he followed Mantha toward the place called God's-Touch. "Our 'messenger' did the same—he came as a member of a persecuted race."

"And was he killed like ours?" Mantha asked.

"Very much so."

"And did God show his wrath then?"

"Wrath? No. God showed his love by forgiving them all."

Mantha considered this briefly. "Hmmm. Perhaps God had less patience with Overlord Mekk. Perhaps he loved our messenger more."

He pushed aside a branch and suddenly all the foliage was gone. They were standing on a gentle rise. Before them lay God's-Touch—a kilometer-wide expanse of green glass. Whatever had once occupied this spot had been melted and fused by a blast of what must have been almost unimaginable heat.

"God left no doubt as to his feelings in this matter. He laid his finger upon Overlord Mekk's fortress and since that day no one has ever persecuted a tery."

AFTERWORD
by Gordon Eklund

For the past several years, I haven't read very much science fiction and, perhaps more disturbingly, a lot of the books I do start I never get around to finishing. I'll read a chapter or two or three and enjoy it well enough, but the next thing I know I'm reading something else, and I never get back to the sf book.

For a time, I took this phenomenon seriously and I worried over it. The natural impulse was to lay the brunt of the blame on the product involved, but, unfortunately, I'm pretty firmly convinced that as much good sf is being written now as in any previous year, and besides, as I said, I usually liked what I did read. Another easy assumption was to say, well, it must be the job. I was writing several pages of sf most days, and a plumber doesn't usually fix sinks on his days off. After some consideration, I was forced to decide that this wasn't an accurate solution either. Even if writing (and fixing sinks) qualifies as work, reading does not, and the two processes (writing and reading sf) don't have a great deal in common.

No. The real reason, I now think, it that, when I first started reading sf, the field appealed to me for very individual reasons that had more to do with who and what I was at the time than they did with general literary values, and because I've changed since then, the appeal has necessarily lessened, and it's a rare book these days that can still reach me in the old way. One such story that did was *The Tery* by F. Paul Wilson, and that's why I've elected this rather roundabout course toward discussing that fine novella.

When I talk about reading sf for special reasons, I am not referring to the fabled sense of wonder. A great deal of sf still reaches me on that level of appreciation, but so do very many non-sf books. If the scope of Smith's Lensmen series is pretty awe-inspiring, it's no more so than Moby Dick. No, what I'm actually talking about, the private appeal sf once had for me, has to do with the oddball orientation of much good sf, its fascination with freaks and underlings, its ability to place one inside the skins of such creatures, its humanism by way of the inhuman.

I was twelve years old when I read my first science fiction story. That story was "Desertion" by Clifford D. Simak, and once I'd finished that particular story, I knew I was hooked for life. "Desertion" and *The Tery* don't have a whole lot superficially in common, except that both are good stories, but I believe a link exists: I respond to both stories in similar ways for similar reasons. Both stories are about freaks—and both stories are about what it means to be human.

"Desertion," for those who may not have read it, is an outwardly simple short story about a future time when humanity wishes to colonize the great planet, Jupiter. Because of the obvious obstacles to human survival presented by the inhuman surface conditions prevalent on that planet, it proves necessary to transform humans physically into an entirely different species. By the time the story ends, the human colonists on Jupiter have become truly Jupiterian.

Why does *The Tery* remind me of that story? Because both stories deal with human beings who are no longer human and yet retain all the characteristics that make a human being truly human; both stories are about people who are different—and better.

At the age of twelve, I was, if you haven't already guessed, thoroughly convinced that I was different from everybody else—and better. I was an oddball, and thus the instant appeal of sf as soon as I was exposed to it.

Because of this, the character of the tery is very much my favorite thing about Wilson's story. When in the first chapter we first glimpse him, nameless and nearly dead, we assume him to be (at least I did) some alien form. Soon enough, we learn that this assumption is incorrect: the tery is an animal. A little later, this, too, is turned around: the tery is a mutant. And finally, gradually and movingly, we learn the truth of just how human the tery is.

The saddest thing about the story is that the tery is doomed to die. If there's one characteristic that binds nearly all the oddball protagonists in and out of sf, it's the necessity of their common fate. Wilson, in narrative terms, provides a sufficient explanation: the death of the tery is brought on by a private mission of rescue and revenge. Wilson is a careful plotter; he won't ignore story values just to make a point. Nonetheless, I still can't help thinking that all of this is quite beside the real matter: the tery dies not to save the Talents; he dies because he's too damned human to live.

And that's the Christ parallel, which the story makes plain enough in its opening and closing scenes. The story of Jesus is just another oddball tale, the archetype for the hundreds that followed, including this one. If it were written today, the Gospel According to Matthew would fit snugly into the mainstream of sf. Jesus was different from other men—and better. He was a god, but he might as easily have been a mutant, esper, alien, or freak. Every society needs its Jesus, the story seems to be telling us; a truly decent world cannot exist without at least one.

The whole story brims with characters who are at odds with those who surround them. If the tery is the most obvious oddball, he is hardly alone: Adriel, the girl, a freak because she's too nearly normal; Rab and the other Talents, threatened with extinction till saved

by the even odder tery; and even Tlad/Dalt, the
Earthman. As the one truly normal character in the
book, he stands out as the oddest, most truly alienated
of them all: the man forced to kill in order to prevent
murder.

Where *The Tery* at last transcends its theme is in
the story's most memorable scene: when Dalt and Jon
first view the creatures of the Hole. Here, the contin-
uum of freakism is extended into our worst night-
mares, probing a deep and mythical realm. And these
dreadful creatures remain very much human—Wilson
never allows us to neglect that—different but not better. They are human beings cut adrift without their
humanity, rank parodies of the way each of us lives.
The physical make-up of a being is irrelevant; it is
only the inner shining light that divides the human
and the inhuman.

Science fiction at its best is invariably optimistic. In
these ugly times, albeit no uglier than most that have
come before, there is a range of purity and innocence
in such an attitude. Human beings are worth preserving not because of what they inately are but rather
because of what they might possibly become. That is
the point of "Desertion" and that is the point of *The
Tery*.

Dell SF

THE FAR CALL

by Gordon Dickson

The people and politics behind a most daring
adventure—the manned exploration of Mars!

In the 1990s Jens Wylie, undersecretary
for space, and members of four other nations,
are planning the first manned Mars voyage.
But when disaster hits, it threatens the
lives of the Marsnauts and the destiny of the
whole human race and only Jens Wylie
knows what has to be done!

*A Quantum Science Fiction novel
from Dell $1.95*

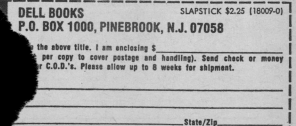